THE CRONE WARS
5

RISE OF THE CRONES

LYDIA M. HAWKE

**Published by Michem Publishing,
Canada**

RISE OF THE CRONES

April 9, 2024
Copyright © 2024 by Linda Poitevin

Cover design by Deranged Doctor Design
Interior design by AuthorTree

ISBN: 978-1-989457-18-4
MICHEM PUBLISHING

CHAPTER 1

I SAW THE CROW IN THE WINDOW OVER THE SINK AS SOON AS I entered the kitchen in Edie's house. We stared at one another through the dark glass, neither of us blinking.

I scowled.

The crow ruffled its feathers.

I considered taking the broom outside to chase it away, but even if I did, I knew without looking that there would only be more of them sitting in the shrubs and perched along the fence. It didn't matter that it was dark out, or that it was a bitterly cold winter night, because this was no ordinary crow, and neither were its companions. No, these were my personal harbingers. My messages from the Morrigan.

And what I'd come to view—in a justifiably jaundiced light, after what I'd been through—as my nemeses.

I turned my back on the crow and went to the fridge. It was empty, of course. We'd been here a week already, I'd fed the last of the freezer's contents to Gus and Harry this afternoon, and I was alone.

My entire being ached with grief and loss and exhaustion. The portal Harry had opened over Camlann had dumped all that remained of my life into Edie's frozen garden: Gus, Harry, a damaged and unconscious Lucan, and me. Me, with the powers of a goddess and the magick of the original Crone surging through my body, setting off random flares in my belly and along my skin. Powers that had come too late to save the others who had sacrificed their lives to get me through the door and into the god world. Powers that stubbornly refused to bend to my will—my *need*—to heal the shifter I'd torn from Morok's grasp.

I had no Jeanne to let herself in at the back door to bring

1

me another casserole or make scrambled eggs for me. No Jeanne, no Anne, no Maureen, no Nia, no Elysabeth, no Keven ... not even a highly irritating Bedivere. And no—

I closed the fridge on the last name and the pain it held. I leaned my forehead against the hard, cool appliance door. I didn't have to look to know that the wretched black bird still sat on the windowsill. I could feel its beady eyes on me, willing me to turn around. To let it in. But I didn't care two figs for what the goddess might want of me this time. I was done with her and her manipulations. Done with all of her kind.

Sparks danced along my arms, an uncontrollable manifestation of the anger seething in my core as I remembered Freya's fireside story in the Otherworld: a story that had begun with Morok and the Morrigan, Morok and a dalliance, and the Morrigan and Odin—a story of lust, jealousy, and spite that had ended in Morok coming to Earth. With cosmic repercussions.

Lies.

Deceit.

The loss of too many beautiful, powerful women to even begin counting.

A splintered world.

And this. Me, Lucan, Gus, Harry ... and an empty fridge.

I jolted back from said fridge as a crackle of power jumped from me to it, leaving a blackened, dime-sized spot on the white enamel.

"And that," my Edie-voice said dryly.

"Yes, that," I agreed out loud. I did that now ... again. Talked out loud to my memory of Edie. It didn't matter that it wasn't really her ghost anymore. After her voice had faded away altogether in the Otherworld, it was nice to have rediscovered her in her former house, even if only in this capacity. It was nice to have someone to talk to who answered back.

Relatively speaking.

A sneeze sounded behind me, and with a sigh, I moved to

snuff out the flames licking at an already-charred chair leg. The blue dragon curled up beneath the kitchen table grinned toothily at me and rumbled in the back of his throat, his version of a purr, learned from the orange cat he'd adopted as his *muzzer* in the Otherworld.

Crouching, I patted out the last of the flames. Thank goodness Harry sneezed less now than he had when he was smaller, or he'd have burned the entire house down by now. I reached under the table and rubbed one of the small, pointy ears protruding from the side of the dragon's head. He'd grown in the week since we'd arrived. Most of his blue fluff had fallen off except for odd little patches here and there, and his skin had turned leathery like that of his parents. He was the same size as the Great Pyrenees dog that lived at the end of the block, and every time he went into or out of his hiding spot, the table moved a few inches with him. But it made him happy to be there, and goodness knew he deserved a little happiness.

Harry closed his eyes and extended his neck with a sigh of contentment—again mimicking his muzzer—and I scratched beneath his chin. I still wasn't sure it was wise to have adopted the ball of blue fluff Gus had saved in the Otherworld, let alone to have brought him back to Earth with me, but neither could I imagine life without him.

Especially since none of us would *have* a life if he hadn't created that vortex above Arthur's stone in Camlann. Not for the first time, I wondered if the little dragon's circular flight that day had been a reaction to grief at thinking he'd lost his Gus, blind panic at the disintegration of Camlann as the Between devoured it, or …

Or if it had been intentional.

I would probably never know, but whatever had triggered his focused circle of flight that day, I would never forget what I owed him. What we all owed him.

At least, those of us who remained.

3

My mood plummeted again, and I pushed hands against knees to stand straight, needing to escape my thoughts. My hips protested the change in position, but I ignored them. They protested every change these days, as did my knees and my back—and my wrists and elbows, too, if I thought about it. I preferred not to.

Part of it was inactivity, yes, but I suspected that my stiffness was due as much to the emotional as it was to the physical. A slowing down of mind, body, and soul in the aftermath of Camlann. I needed movement again—movement like the self-defense Lucan had taught me—but keeping myself, Lucan, and the animals alive was as much as I could manage.

My gaze strayed back to the empty fridge. Well. All I'd been able to manage up until now, anyway. Tendrils of panic curled through my chest as I tried—and failed—to think of options. There weren't many, and none of them were good.

A snort escaped my throat at the thought of wandering into the social services office to inquire about respite care for a wounded wolf-shifter, a cat who'd used up all his nine lives and then some, and a growing baby dragon who preferred to eat rats but would settle—grudgingly—for ground beef.

"At least you still have your sense of humor," observed my Edie-voice.

Fat lot of good that did me. I scowled. Securing food had become my all-consuming concern—no pun intended—

"*Ha!*" the Edie-voice said. I ignored it and continued my thoughts.

Even if I did leave the house and risk being seen, I had no idea how I was going to pay for anything, or get it back here, or if the house would still be standing when I did get back without anyone here to snuff out Harry's fires, or—

Or if Lucan would still be alive when I returned.

An image of him, curled up on his side in Edie's bed, flashed into my mind and took away my breath. Thin to the point of gauntness, his skin was gray, and his hair and overgrown beard were dull, and the lesions on his neck that remained from the collar I'd torn from his wolf hadn't healed. He slept almost around the clock, waking only for meals and the bathroom. His amber eyes, on the few occasions they'd opened, held an emptiness that reminded me of the Between itself, and he hadn't spoken a word since we'd returned.

Not one.

Whatever I'd brought back from Camlann—whatever I'd separated from Morok in that last, desperate battle—it wasn't the Lucan I'd once known. He'd responded to none of the healing I'd tried, not even when I'd climbed naked into bed with him the way I had before, when I'd found the house in ruins and Keven frozen in stone after Morok had taken the Crones. Back then, Lucan's fire had risen to meet my own, melding and meshing with it, creating the healing that he'd needed. But now ...

Now, it was as if he had no fire of his own at all.

A flash left my fingertips and set fire to a tea towel looped through a cupboard handle. Hastily, I knocked it to the floor and stamped out the puddle of flames on the black-and-white tiles. I was becoming as much of a hazard as Harry. I really needed to get a grip on these powers I'd brought back with me from Camlann—and on myself.

It would be so much easier if I could just get us to the Earth house, but even if I'd been able to find the ley line to take us there—I'd searched repeatedly, without finding a trace of one—there was no guarantee that the house still existed. If Lucan had been strong enough for me to leave him, maybe I could have walked to the woods to find out, but it was a big maybe. Especially in a cold that was sharp enough to freeze unprotected extremities in minutes.

I curled my fingers into my palms and closed my eyes as I took a deep, steadying breath, trying not to think about the life stretching before me if Lucan didn't recover. A life without family or friends. A life spent alone in Edie's house, without even her ghost to keep me company. Gus wouldn't live forever, Harry would outgrow the bounds of roof and walls—I didn't have the wherewithal to even contemplate what I was going to do with him at that point—and coward that I was, I couldn't bring myself to see my son or grandson after my role in Natalie's death.

I shuddered at the memory of the scene I'd left behind in the cavern when I'd passed through to the Otherworld. The rampaging Cernunnos, Jeanne throwing hex after futile hex at the god to draw him away from the Crones and midwitches, the horribly disfigured, unmoving form of Bedivere—and the stone ceiling collapsing onto all of them, my son's wife included.

No, I would not be seeking out Paul. I couldn't. Not for a long, long time. My own grief had all but swallowed me already, and I knew without doubt that I couldn't bear his as well. Not when it was wrapped up in layers upon layers of guilt.

The fingers I'd curled into fists at my side suddenly flexed wide, and two fireballs rolled from them and smashed into the cabinet by the sink. A startled Harry bolted, taking the table with him. He dived through the doorway into the hall, the table bounced off the doorframe hard enough to send it back to where it had begun, and the mug I'd left sitting on it smashed to the floor.

"For *fuck's sake*," I growled as flames enveloped the cabinet door itself this time. I considered and discarded the idea of attempting to summon Water and instead snatched up the scorched tea towel from the floor to beat out the fire. What was *with* this return to uncontrolled magickal outbursts? I had more power now than I'd ever had, and—

A sharp crack came from the window above the sink, and I looked up from my firefighting efforts to see a fracture line running across the pane of glass, dividing the crow on the other side into two halves. A frisson ran down my spine, and an unbidden, unwelcome thought flashed through my mind: *Something is coming*.

The back door crashed open behind me.

Blindly, instinctively, I whirled and threw a wall of protection across the kitchen between the door and all that remained in my life. In the same instant, I hurled a fireball at whatever had come *through* the door.

CHAPTER 2

FORTUNATELY FOR JEANNE, HER REFLEXES WERE ALMOST AS good as my newly acquired ones.

Almost.

"For the love of God, Claire, it's me!" she yelped, slapping at the sparkling blue flames dancing atop her head and ducking away from the ones she'd deflected into the wall beside her. "It's Jeanne!"

I caught back a second fireball before it left my fingertips, gaping at the apparition before me. Because that's what it had to be, right? An apparition, because Jeanne was—

"Jeanne?" I croaked. My outstretched hand trembled. So did the rest of me as my brain slogged its way through shock and disbelief and into a state of numbness. I had seen her die. I'd seen all of them die. Jeanne, the Crones, the midwitches, Natalie, Bedivere …

"But you didn't," my Edie-voice whispered deep inside the fog. *"Not really. You saw Cernunnos attacking them, and you assumed, but you didn't see them die."*

Common sense said it was impossible. The cavern had begun collapsing as I'd passed through the wall into the Otherworld, the Crones and midwitches had fallen to the stone floor, Bedivere's twisted form had been still and unmoving, Jeanne had faced Cernunnos on her own, and it had only been a matter of time before the Earth god had overwhelmed her, and …

And yet, here she was.

The last of the churning blue flames in my hand dissolved. Distantly, I felt their heat return to the Fire at my core. Jeanne. My Jeanne. Neighborhood friend, Daughter of Hestia and keeper of the Book of the Fifth Crone, and—

The protective wall between us dropped as, eyes misty behind her red-framed glasses, Jeanne held her arms wide. I didn't hesitate. Strong, capable arms wrapped around me and squeezed so tightly that I struggled to breathe, but I didn't care. Jeanne had survived. She'd survived, and she was here, and I wasn't alone.

I wasn't alone.

I pushed Jeanne away and clamped my hands over her shoulders as I stared into familiar—and oh, so blessedly alive! —eyes. "How?" I croaked. "How did you—the others— Cernunnos—*how*?"

Jeanne blinked back tears and wiped at the ones escaping beneath her glasses. "As soon as the door closed behind you, he just—vanished. Not a *poof* kind of vanish, more like he dissolved into the cave wall. Or maybe the wall absorbed him? I'm not sure how to describe—"

"What about the others? The Crones?" I interrupted, not giving two figs what had happened to the god. "The midwitches?"

"They're all fine. It took Yvain and Percival forever to dig everyone out and get us back to the house, but—"

"Yvain and Percival? They came to help?"

Jeanne nodded. "As naked as the day they were born," she said. "Apparently, they don't even own clothing anymore. Not that it matters, because they only stayed until Bedivere was healed enough to—"

"Bedivere?" My grip tightened on her shoulders. "Bedivere's alive?"

Another nod. "A little the worse for wear, but yes." Her gaze softened as her eyes teared up again. "And so is Natalie, Claire. Natalie's alive, too."

It took a moment for the words to sink in. Another before I reacted—before I *could* react. And then relief slammed into me, flooding my entire being and taking me down at the knees. Jeanne caught me as I sagged, her hold on me fierce as

9

I grappled with the hundred thoughts and emotions all trying to escape me at once.

I wasn't alone. The Crones and midwitches and Bedivere had survived. The mother of my grandson was alive. *I'd* survived. I'd made it back from Camlann and brought Gus and Harry and Lucan with me. I'd rescued Lucan from Morok and destroyed the dark god once and for all. The house still stood, and Keven with it, and the magick to heal Lucan was there, and—

And we'd done it.

We'd won the war.

It was over.

It—

"Claire," said a faint, hoarse voice behind me.

I pulled back from Jeanne so fast that we both staggered, whirling to find a sheet-draped Lucan doing a slow collapse in the kitchen doorway. For an instant, my brain refused to process what my eyes saw, and utter shock held me immobile.

Not Jeanne. She dived across the room in time to catch him before he hit the floor, breaking his fall, one hand protecting his head. By the time I reached her side, she was already running quick, professional nursing hands over his limbs, searching for injury.

Amber eyes, glazed with fatigue but *there—present*—met mine over her shoulder.

"Claire," Lucan whispered again. "Something is coming."

"It's okay." I stroked the back of my fingers along his cheek, his overgrown beard rough against my skin. My heart ached at the realization that, ill as he was, he'd still dragged himself out here in an attempt to protect me.

Oh, Lucan, I thought.

"It was just Jeanne," I replied reassuringly. "You remember Jeanne, don't you? She's a nurse. She'll—"

Lucan caught my hand in his, shaking his head. "No," he said. "The ley. Something is coming through the ley."

"It's okay," I reassured him. "I looked for the ley lines when we got here, and there are none. Nothing can get—"

"None?" Jeanne interrupted, her voice sharp. With the fingers of one hand still cradling Lucan's head, she seized my wrist with her other hand and stared at me over her glasses. "No ley lines at all?"

"Um," I said, blinking back. Belatedly—oh, so belatedly—it occurred to me how unnatural that was. The ley lines were everywhere. Keven had told me that in the beginning, and I'd seen them for myself once I'd been able to tap into them. Lines of energy that crisscrossed the Earth, that could be used for the transportation of magickal beings. Lines that *should* have been here, but I'd been so caught up in my own misery that—

"It's worse than we thought," Jeanne muttered.

"What is?"

She shook her head at the question. "Later," she said. "We need to get moving." She dropped my wrist and peered down at Lucan. "We'll have to move him like this. Do you have something we can—dear goddess, what in heaven's name is *that*?"

The question ended on a pitch an octave higher than it had begun, as she turned her head and came nose to nose with Harry. The startled dragon hissed like a cat in return, because he'd learned from the best. But this time, for the first time, a stream of sparks accompanied the hiss.

Jeanne shrieked and fell over backward onto her butt, her hair afire for the second time since her arrival. I dived to grab Lucan as she let go, but I was too late, and his head hit the floor with a *thunk* audible even over the racket that had erupted.

Harry exploded into the air, wings beating furiously as he tried to escape the kitchen. One flap took out the ceiling light fixture, another swept the countertops clear of toaster, coffee pot (not that I'd had coffee to make), the last remaining can of soup I'd brought up from the basement storeroom, and everything else that sat on them.

A third almost knocked my head from my shoulders.

"Harry!" I bellowed, my ears ringing from the blow. "Knock it off!"

The not-so-little-anymore dragon dropped from the air so suddenly that poor Gus, who'd chosen to investigate the commotion, narrowly escaped being squished. I ignored the cat and glared at the dragon.

"Table," I ordered, pointing. Blue leather tufted with fluff waddled in a circle and then slunk back into his makeshift cave. I turned back to Jeanne, who had put out the fire in her hair and was fussing over Lucan again.

She glared at me. "What in all of—" She broke off, pressed her lips together, and shook her head. "Never mind. We don't have—but seriously—a *dragon*? No, you can explain later. Right now we have to figure out how to get all of you—a *dragon*?—out of here without causing a panic. I can bring the car to the back gate, but I have no idea how we'll all fit—I can't believe you brought a *dragon* back with you!"

In between the *dragons* punctuating her words, Jeanne checked the back of Lucan's head—presumably for blood after its abrupt connection with the floor—sent several disbelieving glances in Harry's direction, shook her head in equal disbelief each time, and hoisted herself to her feet.

"A blanket," she announced. "We'll use it to carry him."

"I—" I began.

"*Now*, Claire, unless you want him to die right here on Edie's floor."

I bristled at Jeanne's sharp tone, but I swallowed my would-be retort. I might have saved Lucan from Camlann and Morok, but I was clearly losing him now, and objectionable tone aside, Jeanne was right. We had to get him to the others. To Keven and the house that still existed.

My questions would wait.

"Blanket," I repeated, stepping across Lucan's again-unconscious form in the doorway. "On it."

Arriving in Edie's room, I did a quick scan to see if there was anything else I might need. There wasn't. I'd lost everything either in the Otherworld or in the Camlann splinter—my staff, my rucksack, its scant contents. I'd even left my robe behind in the hut. We would leave Edie's house as empty handed as we'd arrived, except for the blanket we needed to move Lucan.

My fingers closed over the duvet Lucan had shoved to one side of the bed. They curled for an instant into the residual warmth clinging to the fabric, then I hauled the queen-sized cover into my arms. As I turned toward the door again, a movement at the dark window caught my eye.

The damned crow was following me.

CHAPTER 3

"EVERYTHING OKAY?" JEANNE ASKED, FROWNING AS I STOMPED back into the kitchen, narrowly missing Lucan's outstretched fingers.

"It's fine," I muttered. Evaded. Outright lied. Because nothing was fine. Nothing about any of this was fine. Not Lucan, not us landing back here in Edie's house, not bringing a dragon with me, and not having a damned harbinger peering at me through the window every time I turned around—

My gaze met Jeanne's, held it for an instant, skidded away, drifted back. *"Something is coming,"* whispered Lucan's voice in my memory. I hugged the duvet against myself.

"How did you know we were—" I began, but the peal of the doorbell swallowed the rest of my words. And my breath.

Jeanne and I stared at one another, neither of us moving. A little part of my brain detached itself from the rest and assessed our situation. I'd been careful to keep the street-facing side of the house dark, but we'd been here for a week, so I supposed someone might have noticed us by now. A neighbor? The police? The police called by a neighbor?

The doorbell rang again, then again and again, its sound growing more insistent. A pounding of fist against insulated metal followed. And then a bellow.

"I know you're in there, Jeanne! Your car is sitting right there!"

Gilbert. Of course it was Gilbert.

Beneath the table, Harry and Gus both growled.

Jeanne sighed. "I'll handle it," she said. "You get the duvet spread out." She didn't exactly roll up her sleeves as she shouldered past me, but she moved with such purpose, such determination, that she may as well have done.

I hesitated beside Lucan's still form, then dropped the duvet at his side and followed my friend. That Jeanne had changed enormously was obvious, but I doubted that her bully of a husband had done so, and I would not let her face him alone.

The one-sided argument was already in full swing by the time I got to the living room.

"—had enough of this," Gilbert huffed, his arms flailing at his sides on the porch as Jeanne blocked his entry. "I haven't had a decent meal or clean underwear in weeks, Jeanne. The house is falling apart! You need to get over whatever bee you have in your bonnet and come home where you—"

His gaze connected with mine over Jeanne's shoulder as I digested the no-clean-underwear-in-weeks idea, and his expression turned from belligerent to downright ugly.

"*You*," he spat. "I should have known *you* were behind all of this." He shoved his wife to one side and stalked toward me. "I've a good mind to—"

An invisible force lifted him from his feet and threw him against the wall beside the door, then held him there. I blinked at the hand that I hadn't consciously raised but that was still outstretched toward him. A hand that had gathered Air to it and blasted it in a targeted wind at the wide-eyed man whose feet were now dangling many inches above the floor.

Targeted and purposeful—but only just. Because magick crawled over my entire body like an itch that demanded I scratch it. An itch that would scratch itself if I didn't. The wind pushed harder against Gilbert, and his eyes widened. Ugliness gave way to the beginnings of fear.

"*Fuck*," whispered the Edie-voice.

Jeanne slammed the door shut. "That's enough, Claire," she said. "We need his help."

I heard, I thought, but did I care?

"Claire!" Jeanne grabbed my arm and pulled on it. "Enough!"

Her touch jolted through me, severing my hold on the magick—or perhaps the magick's hold on me. The wind holding Gilbert ended abruptly, dropping him to the floor with a suddenness that sent him sprawling face first across the hardwood.

He staggered upright, but Jeanne's attention was on me, not him. Her eyes narrowed with concern.

"Are you okay?" she asked. "That was—"

"Assault," Gilbert interjected, his voice shrill. "It was assault, is what it was. I don't know how you did that, Claire Emerson—"

The crawl of magick became sparks snapping outward from my fingertips, and Gilbert scurried backward until the wall brought him up short again.

Jeanne's hand, still on my outstretched arm, squeezed. "Enough," she said again. "We can use him."

Leaving me to get myself under control again, which demonstrated a level of confidence in me that I didn't share at that moment, she marched over to her husband and held out her hand.

"Keys," she said.

Gilbert gaped at her. Then gaped at me. Then gaped at her again. Then snapped his mouth shut and narrowed his eyes in suspicion. "Keys to what?"

"Well, given that I've left you, it certainly wouldn't be to the house now, would it?" she said. "The keys to your car, obviously."

"What do you want with my car?"

"Yes, what *do* we want with his car?" I asked, the idea distracting me from my sparking fingers—and the knowledge that Jeanne had moved out of their house.

She half turned to me, keeping her hand out for the keys she'd demanded. "With everyone—every*thing*—we have to take with us, we won't all fit in my little hatchback, and it wouldn't be wise to leave anything behind."

She had a point. But we wouldn't all fit in Gilbert's car, either.

Jeanne flapped a hand at me, reading my mind. "You can drive Gilbert's car, and—"

"No," said her husband, staring at the sparks dancing from my hand. "No way am I giving her my vehicle. I'm not giving her *anything*."

"Fine. Then Claire can drive my car, and I'll drive—"

"No." Gilbert stuck his own hands into his pockets. The keys hidden in the depths of one gave a little jangle, and he scowled and hunched his shoulders. "No one is driving my car but me."

Jeanne crossed her arms and turned her head to peer at me over her glasses. "You could make him, couldn't you?"

Her brazen question surprised me, and then I understood its purpose and shrugged. "Probably. But it might be messy."

Gilbert gave a muffled squawk.

"How messy?" Jeanne asked, and Gilbert squawked again.

I hesitated, because there had been more truth in my response than I cared to admit. The itch of magick had settled beneath my skin again, but it still felt ... well, if not wrong, then certainly not right.

"Too messy," I said. And despite my unease, which I saw reflected in a shadow of concern that crossed Jeanne's expression, a part of me rather enjoyed watching the color drain from her husband's face. A greater part of me, however, was becoming antsy. Twitchy. Lucan needed healing, and—

Something is coming, the shifter's voice whispered in my mind.

I dropped my tingling hand back to my side. "He can drive," I told Jeanne.

She wrinkled her nose in doubt. "Are you sure that's wise?"

"I'm sure we don't have much choice. Lucan needs—well. You can take him with you, in case he takes a turn for the worse, and I'll ride with Gilbert and"—I dropped my voice to an ominous whisper as I let a little ball of fire slide from my fingers and dance in the air before me—"the others."

Gilbert slumped to the floor.

BY THE TIME GILBERT CAME AROUND, JEANNE HAD TAKEN HIS keys from his pocket, moved his car to join hers on the street by Edie's back gate, and helped me roll an unconscious Lucan onto the duvet.

We considered ignoring Gilbert's objections in favor of Jeanne's plan that the two of us drive the cars, but we quickly abandoned the idea when we tried to move Lucan by ourselves. Even when Gilbert woke up to help and there were three of us, we still ended up dragging him more than carrying him out to Jeanne's little car. Thank the goddess—

I scowled. Maybe I should thank the Weaver instead of the goddess from now on, given that the Morrigan deserved no gratitude whatsoever. On the other hand, the habit was so deeply ingrained at this point that I'd likely never remember —and honestly, neither it nor the Morrigan were worth the effort.

I peered through the fog of my breath as we huffed and heaved our way along the unshoveled walkway to the gate. The quiet street was bright with Christmas lights and inflatable decorations dotted most of the snow-covered lawns, but no one stirred outside except us. Regardless of what deity I thanked, I was still grateful for the cold that kept the neighbors in their homes, because it would have been damned difficult to explain to anyone what we were up to.

"Are you sure he wouldn't be more comfortable in

Gilbert's back seat?" Jeanne wheezed as we caught our breath before trying to load Lucan into the rear hatch of her car.

I had no doubt he would, but given the nasty looks her husband kept slanting his way, I knew that Gilbert recognized him from the Switzerland incident, when Lucan had transported the other man to a remote town there and abandoned him. So I also had no doubt that Gilbert would take the first chance he got to push the shifter out of a moving vehicle.

"No." I shifted my feet in the snow, trying to ease the pinching of Edie's too-small boots around my baby toes. "But he's better off with you in case something happens. And besides, the others don't know you very well. They might be … skittish."

Jeanne pursed her lips. "Good point. All right, let's load him."

It took three attempts, mostly because Gilbert dropped his end twice, but we eventually got Lucan into the vehicle and as comfortable as we could make him in a space four sizes smaller than he was. With fingers that had gone numb from the unseasonably cold December weather—I hadn't been able to find any gloves or mittens in Edie's closet—I tucked the duvet under his chin and leaned down to brush my lips against his forehead.

"Hang in there," I whispered, "we're almost home."

Home. At the sound of the word, every fiber of me suddenly yearned for the house and its occupants. Goddess, but it would be good to be there. Good to see the others, to feel the house's magick seep into my pores, to—

"We should go." Jeanne touched my elbow. "The sooner we get him to Keven …"

I straightened and closed the hatch. "I'll get the others," I said. "Gilbert, wait in your car, and do yourself a favor—don't look at what I bring out."

He drew himself up haughtily. "Don't you tell me what to

do," he snapped. "I'm doing you a favor here, remember, and—"

I flexed my fingers and took a slow, deep breath. Gilbert snapped his mouth shut. He skittered sideways, almost fell into the snowbank, recovered, and beat a hasty retreat toward his vehicle.

Jeanne sighed beside me. "Please tell me he wasn't always this bad?" Then, when I didn't answer, she sighed again. "That's what I was afraid of. Oh well, I'm rid of him now. Go get your cat and"—she shuddered—"that dragon-thing. I'm not sure how much longer we have before she tracks me here."

My hand on the icy back gate latch, I paused. "She who?"

"Baba Yaga, of course. The others were supposed to keep her distracted, but she was set on coming to get you herself, and—"

"Baba Yaga?" I echoed. "*The* Baba Yaga?"

"I told you." Jeanne blinked. "Didn't I? About her and—" She stopped and waved a hand. "I must've gotten distracted, but we don't have time for questions. We've escaped notice so far, but if Baba Yaga turns up, the whole neighborhood will know about it. Hell, the whole town will." She pushed me through the gate. "Hurry."

I stumbled through the snow toward the back door, too astonished to protest, because Baba Yaga? And what had Jeanne meant by *and*? And what? Or who?

I stomped inside the back porch to clean the snow off my boots, which did nothing for my pinched toes, then reached for the kitchen doorknob. And had she just used *hell* as a profanity? Jeanne?

"Miracles do happen," my Edie-voice said dryly.

I smiled, briefly wondering if Edie's voice would follow once I left her house. Then I pushed open the door.

A large, leathery bundle of pure joy danced around my legs, almost knocking them out from under me. It took several tries, but at last I got a grip on the wriggling dragon long enough to heave him into my arms. He snuggled against me, a welcome warmth against my chest. I'd been able to get Edie's winter jacket on but zipping it up had been a no-go.

I cuddled the dragon closer and turned to leave, then hesitated, looking back at the kitchen. A shiver ran down my spine. I might be returning to the Earth house—*my* house—and to the people who waited there for me, but …

My gaze trailed over the familiar cupboards, the black-and-white tile floor, the curtains tied back from the window. Countless times I'd taken refuge here, both when Edie was alive and after she was gone. I breathed in the familiar scent, one that somehow still held the faint, lingering essence of Edie. Oh, how I missed that woman. I thought about the times I'd left here without a backward glance, taking the house and the friend for granted, expecting that they would continue to be here for me when I came back. When I needed them.

But Edie was already gone, and something about leaving the house this time—

A movement outside the window drew my eye, and I stared at the dark glass that reflected the room back to me, and on the other side of the reflection …

The harbinger was back.

Something is coming.

Harry sneezed. I shifted him to one arm and patted out the patch of fire on the doorframe with my other hand, then switched off the kitchen light and stepped into the enclosed back porch along with Gus. I closed both doors and locked them—the one between house and porch, and the one from porch to outdoors—and then tucked the key into its hiding place above the window to the left, just in case.

Because this time, Baba Yaga was here, Lucan had woken long enough to give a warning, the crows were back, Jeanne had used *hell* as an epithet, and I would take nothing for granted.

With Gus trotting in my wake, I carried the dragon across

the dark backyard and through the gate. Jeanne stood beside her vehicle and Gilbert sat in his. My friend came around to open the back passenger door of her husband's car, and I shoved the dragon inside with a hushed but stern warning to behave and not move.

Whether because of the implied threat of the fingers I'd flexed at him or because he tried hard to pretend he didn't care about my presence, Gilbert stared straight ahead, making no effort to see what I'd brought out of the house. I hoped it stayed that way.

I stepped back so that Gus could jump in with the dragon, then slammed the car door shut. Jeanne was already at the driver's door of her own vehicle.

"I'll see you there," she said. "The others will meet us to help, and we'll be safer once we're in the house."

I cast a last look over my shoulder at Edie's house, sitting dark and empty, then opened the passenger door and got in beside a sullen Gilbert. Only as I did up my seat belt did Jeanne's words fully register.

Safer, she had said. Not *safe*, but *safer*. As if the Earth house itself was in jeopardy from whatever threat was looming. I flinched as the crows lining the fence along the sidewalk suddenly took to the air and flew over the car—an entire murder of them.

Then Harry sneezed in the seat behind me, and with a sigh, I reached out to slap the flames from a screeching Gilbert's comb-over.

CHAPTER 4

IT WAS A WONDER WE ARRIVED AT 13 THE MORRIGAN'S WAY without getting pulled over by the police. Or even in one piece.

"Slow down!" I snapped repeatedly at Gilbert. "Watch where you're going!"

This as he kept twisting around in his seat to see what was behind him, the threats I'd made forgotten. I reached back with one arm to pin Harry down, deep in the shadows where he couldn't be seen. Unless he sneezed again, of course.

With my other arm, I alternated between clinging to the door handle and grabbing for the steering wheel to keep us off the sidewalk and then out of the ditch. It was, to put it mildly, the wildest ride of my life. The wildest non-magickal ride, anyway. And we *did* arrive in one piece.

Jeanne was already waiting at the edge of the dark road. She stood at the rear of her car, its hatch open and the interior light illuminating the bundle that was Lucan in the back. Gilbert pulled a U-turn at the end of the road and drew up a few feet behind her vehicle. He switched off the engine, and our own interior light came on. In the continuing glow from his headlights, one of Jeanne's eyebrows rose.

Arms crossed over her parka and hands tucked into her armpits against the cold, she walked around to Gilbert's side and leaned down to peer through the window that he'd opened. Her gaze darted between the scorched comb-over and me and back again, then her lips twitched.

"It's not funny," snapped Gilbert. "I was on *fire*, for chrissake. What kind of monster sets fire to someone's *hair*? I should report you to the police, is what I should do. The whole lot of you."

His glare swiveled to me and then toward the back seat, but I caught his chin in my hand and forced his head away. He yelped at my touch and shrank against the door.

"Did you see that?" he demanded of his wife. "She hit me! That was assault."

"Oh, for the love of—" Jeanne exhaled a long sigh, rolled her eyes, and shook her head. Then, seeming to decide argument wasn't worth the effort, she straightened and reached with a mittened hand—she was the only one of us wearing remotely appropriate winter gear—to open the back door.

Harry and Gus tumbled out, and Gilbert reached for his door handle to follow suit. Swiftly, Jeanne planted a hip against the driver's door.

"We've got it from here," she told her husband, keeping her stout body between him and the dragon as I bailed out on my side, hissed to get Harry's attention, and pointed into the woods after the disappearing shadow that was Gus.

Reluctantly—and somewhat sulkily, I thought, though I didn't blame him—the little dragon shuffled after his muzzer into the brush.

"That's it?" Gilbert grumped. "That's all I get after being volun-*told* to drive *her*"—I couldn't see him, but I could well imagine the thumb-jab that accompanied the emphasized word—"and whatever else that was into the middle of nowhere in the middle of the night?"

"Thank you for your help," Jeanne said, and then repeated, "We've got it from here."

Gilbert's irritated tone turned into a whine. "Damn it, Jeanne, I don't even know who you are anymore. I haven't seen you since before Christmas—"

I'd reached Jeanne's car and was trying to figure out how she and I would manage to get Lucan out on our own, but Gilbert's words made my head whip around. I stared at his petulant face through the windshield. Since before—wait, it was *after* Christmas? As in *January*? No wonder it was so cold—and dear goddess, just how long had I spent in the Otherworld and Camlann?

Gilbert's litany of complaints continued. I tucked my numb fingers into my own armpits beneath Edie's jacket to warm them.

"—and the house is a disaster," he said. "And how long do you expect me to live on cold cereal and canned soup, for God's sake?"

"I made it clear when I left that I wasn't coming back, Gilbert," Jeanne said, her voice so quiet that I had to strain—unashamedly, I might add—to hear it. "So again, I suggest you either hire someone or learn to do things for yourself. Now go home."

She stepped back from his door and crossed her arms again as she stared down at him. In the light from the car's interior—Gilbert's headlights had shut themselves off by now—I saw neither regret nor guilt in her expression. There was no emotion, really, unless determination counted.

As Gilbert half opened his door and put one foot on the ground, I tensed, wondering what Jeanne would do if he got out. Wondering what I would do. With no Lucan able to whisk him off to Switzerland again, Edie's suggestion of turning him into a toad ranked rather high on the list of possibilities, and the fingers of my right hand twitched at the idea. I glanced at them and frowned as I shook off the sparks that gathered there. Sparks that, once again, I hadn't called.

Damn it.

Fortunately for Gilbert—and for me—he thought better of further confrontation and the car door slammed shut again. He started the vehicle, put it into gear, and stepped on the gas as he yanked at the steering wheel. Tires bit into ice and gravel, and the rear fender slewed dangerously—intentionally?—near me and Jeanne's car.

With the same lightning reflexes that I'd discovered in myself when Jeanne had barged into Edie's kitchen, I threw my hand out and gusted Air in his direction. The vehicle shifted sideways and surged past Jeanne's car. Then it slid to a stop again, and Gilbert's head poked out the window.

"I blame you for this, Claire Emerson," he bellowed. "I hope you burn in hell!"

With that, he floored the gas pedal again, bouncing the vehicle from one side of the narrow road to the other before slamming on the brakes at the intersection and fishtailing around the corner. As the sound of his motor faded and silence descended, Jeanne's shoulders sagged.

"Well," she said, making no attempt to meet my gaze. "Well."

"Jeanne," I began, but even as my voice trailed off— because what in the goddess's name could I say that would even begin to make better what I'd just witnessed?—iron clanged against stone in the trees behind us, and my heart leapt as I recognized the sound of the gate opening. And then a familiar voice came from the same direction, like gravel sliding over stone.

"Did you find her?" Keven asked.

The invisible weight I'd been carrying since Camlann lifted from my shoulders. I blinked away a sudden welling of tears and shored up sagging knees. I'd done it. I was home. *We* were home. We'd made it. And now Lucan would get the help he—

"What in the name of all the gods and goddesses did you do to him?" snarled another voice in the shadows, as familiar to me as Keven's was.

But maybe not as reassuring.

THE KNEES THAT HAD SAGGED BENEATH ME A MOMENT BEFORE went rigid, along with the rest of me. Bedivere stood so near to me that I could feel the heat of his breath on my frozen cheeks. So close that only from the corner of my eye could I see the arm extended to point at the unmoving form in Jeanne's hatchback.

"Enough, Bedivere," Keven rumbled from the other side of the gate that magick wouldn't allow her to pass. "See to your brother."

But the burly shifter ignored the gargoyle and took another step toward me, his chest pressing against mine. "I will know what you did," he said. "*Now.*"

Unbidden Fire flared in me, and I tamped it down hastily, remembering the last time I'd accidentally tried setting fire to Lucan's brother. It had not gone well. I opened my mouth to reassure him, but Jeanne beat me to it—her tone nowhere near the conciliatory one I'd planned on.

"Back off, Bedivere," she said. "I've had my fill of bullies for one day."

Bedivere's eyebrows shot up, and he turned his glower. "You dare—"

"Oh, stop," she said. "I saved your ass, remember? You don't scare me, and I won't let you try and intimidate Claire, either. Now, can you take Lucan by yourself, or do you need help?"

In utter astonishment, I watched Bedivere step back from me and, in apparent and very out-of-character obedience, turn to haul his brother's limp body out of the vehicle. He hoisted Lucan over his shoulder, shot me a look that said he wasn't done with me, and strode through the frozen brambles toward a path just visible beneath the half-moon.

I watched him go, a dozen thoughts vying for supremacy in my brain. Jeanne had saved Bedivere? Wait—she thought I was scared of him? That I needed protection? Had she not seen what I was capable of? Or maybe that was what she was trying to protect me from. Had she sensed my lack of—

My friend's mittened hand settled on my shoulder. "Come on," she said. "Let's get you inside before you freeze solid."

I pulled my gaze from Bedivere's retreating back and the precious cargo draped over it. I couldn't read Jeanne's expression, but her tone had been—

Guarded? suggested my Edie-voice.

Yes. But because of me, or something—

And then another voice joined us: female, autocratic, and shockingly out of place.

"Why," it demanded, "are you standing around here, woman? You assured me that you would come straight back to the house. It's been hours since you left."

My brain froze, refusing to believe what my ears told it they'd heard. Because no. That could not possibly be—but Jeanne had said that Baba Yaga was here, so maybe—but no. Because how?

"As for you," the voice continued, "you have a world of explaining to do."

Slowly, I faced the woods and the woman standing in the cold moonlight at the path's entrance. The armor- and leather-clad woman with pale hair twisted into a braid over one shoulder. The woman whose eyes I couldn't see but still knew to be blue. Ice blue.

My jaw sagged. "*Freya?*"

The Norse goddess who didn't belong in my world strode forward and seized my arm. "We'll talk at the house," she said —or perhaps it was a threat.

I pulled against her, trying to get my bearings. Freya? Here? But how? And why? "Wait. I—"

"Not *now*," she said, as if addressing an errant child. "We're too exposed here. Now get moving, or I'll carry you, too."

Jeanne's hand pushed between my shoulder blades. "Freya

is right. We need to get to the house before something—well. We'll explain everything there."

Between being pushed by one and towed by the other, we were at the gate before I dug my heels in enough to slow my momentum. I grabbed at the iron gate for good measure but let go again with a hiss of pain as frozen metal iced my palm.

"Harry," I said to Jeanne, cradling my hand. "Gus."

"They'll find their own way."

Jeanne pushed harder, and Freya growled her impatience.

I grabbed for the gate again, ice-burned palm be damned.

"And if they don't?" I asked. "You really want Harry running around the countryside on his own? Or finding his way into town instead of the house?"

The shove between my shoulder blades eased as my friend hesitated. "You don't know the danger," she began. Then she sighed and stopped pushing before I could ask whose fault that was.

"Fine," she said. "But be quick."

I pulled free of Freya's grip and backtracked toward the road, my anxious gaze searching the trees for signs of life. Despite the cloudless night and the half-moon shining above, the woods were as black as—well. I wrapped my arms around myself as the bitter cold seeped deeper into my core.

"Gus!" I hissed. "Here, kitty-kitty!"

A hand nudged again between my shoulder blades, and I glanced around to find that Jeanne had followed me.

"Quicker than that, or she really will carry you," she said, nodding back at the gate.

I followed her gaze to the armored goddess waiting by the stone gatepost, impatience etched in every shadowed line. For an instant, I hesitated, distracted by the whole Freya-on-Earth thing. There was so much going on here, so much that I didn't understand ...

But Jeanne nudged again, and I capitulated. I would get

my answers, but first, I really did need to find Harry before he—

The sound of a sneeze came out of the dark a dozen feet to the left, a small, leafless bush burst into flames, and an orange cat bolted past me. With a groan, I stepped off the path into knee-deep snow that filled my too-small boots.

Found him.

CHAPTER 5

CHAOS.

That was the only way to describe the state of the Earth house.

Complete, utter, unadulterated chaos.

I stood reeling in the midst of it in the great hall, which the house had fully restored in my absence—including the suits of armor that flanked the staircase. My fellow Crones surrounded me, all talking at once and asking questions one after the other, so fast that I couldn't have replied if I'd tried. They were surrounded in turn by a dozen or so women, some but not all of whom I recognized as the midwitches from the cavern.

Through them waded Bedivere with Lucan still slung across his shoulder, snarling at those who stood between him and the stairs. A scowling, silent Keven followed, with my cat riding atop her shoulders and a struggling dragon pinned beneath one arm.

Poor Harry.

I'd been relieved of him as soon as I'd carried him to the gate, where Keven and Bedivere had returned to wait with Freya. The gargoyle had told me in no uncertain terms that he would *not* be coming into the house, and I had told her in equally uncertain terms that he would be.

"His name," I'd told Keven, putting my hand on her granite forearm to stop her in mid-turn from me, "is Harry. He is one of us, and he will be in the house for as long as I say."

I still wasn't sure who had been more taken aback by my response, she or I. The gargoyle had gone still, as if returned to the stone from which she'd been carved. She had stared at

31

me for long seconds. Perhaps she had been as surprised by my sudden air of authority as I had; perhaps she had waited for me to back down and withdraw my words.

I had not, and in silence, she'd stood back to let me and Jeanne pass. Then she had brought up the rear of our little company with Harry tucked against her and Gus returned to his rightful place atop her shoulder. Bedivere had slanted narrow, assessing looks at me over his shoulder as he'd followed Freya—who seemed not to have noticed my exchange with the gargoyle—toward the house.

And the chaos.

I swayed on my feet. Maureen, nearest to me after having pushed her way between Nia and Elysabeth, stopped in mid-sentence and clapped her hands together above her head to gain the others' attention.

"Enough!" she called over the voices. "Claire needs to sit down before she falls down. Myriam"—she pointed to a frizzy-haired woman nearest the corridor to the kitchen— "you make some tea. Valerian, I think, with some skullcap. Anne, you and Elysabeth can make up her room, and Nia and I will—"

"You lived!" a new voice boomed, drowning out Maureen's words. Beefy fingers seized my arms and tugged me around, and I face-planted into the softness of an ample bosom. One hand pinned me there, and another patted me on the back hard enough to make my brain rattle. "You lived," the voice repeated happily.

Just as my lungs started to panic over their lack of air, the hands seized my arms again and pushed me away so that a beaming Baba Yaga could look me over, twisting and turning me this way and that.

"Is good," she pronounced. "I make soup."

Poised to follow Bedivere up the stairs, Keven changed direction and thrust Harry at an unprepared midwitch, who almost collapsed beneath the little dragon's weight—which, I thought somewhat bemusedly, probably meant Harry wasn't really that little anymore.

But I digressed.

And unexpected drama unfolded before me.

"*I* will make soup," Keven corrected Baba Yaga, reaching the kitchen corridor a step before the witch did and using her formidable bulk to block the witch's way.

Baba Yaga flapped both hands at the gargoyle. "*Pah*," she said. "Your soup no flavor. My soup better for witch."

"*My* soup," Keven growled back, "doesn't have unidentifiable bits floating in it. I will not allow you to poison Lady—"

"Desist!" Freya's voice cut like a whip across the bickering duo.

The entire room dropped into silence, and halfway up the stairs with his burden of Lucan, even Bedivere halted. He half turned, and in the light from the sconces lining the wall, I saw for the first time the damage that had been inflicted on him in the cavern. A jagged scar ran down one side of his face from his forehead to beneath his beard, one eye drooped, and his hand ...

Oh dear goddess, his hand.

My breath snagged in my chest at the sight of the twisted remains, three fingers short of what it should have had. That the shifter had regained the hand at all after losing it in his encounter with Cernunnos was a miracle—not to mention healing magick of the highest order—but ...

I closed my eyes. But I couldn't think about that now, because Freya. I'd forgotten about her for a moment—and really, really wished I could continue to do so, because I didn't think I was up for this right now. Not any of it—not the questions, not the answers, and sure as hell not Freya herself. Not when I was so tired and cold that I could no longer feel my toes or my fingers or any other part of me, for that matter, except ...

I sensed someone staring at me and opened my eyes again.

Keven's furious gaze met mine. The unspoken accusation behind her expression reminded me that this was *my* house now, that she was *my* gargoyle—insomuch as she could belong to anyone—and that Freya should not be issuing the orders.

What was the goddess even doing here, anyway? Or Baba Yaga?

Bedivere returned to climbing the wide stone staircase. I hesitated, torn between following him to see to Lucan or staying to sort things out down here. Bedivere gained the top of the stairs and disappeared into the corridor leading to the bedchambers. I sighed.

Seeming to take the sound as a sign of my continued weakness and/or incompetence, Freya shouldered her way through the gathered women to point at Keven. "Baba Yaga will make the soup," she said, her tone brooking no argument, "and you—"

"No," I said, stepping into my responsibility, my decision made. "Keven will tend to Lucan and make whatever she thinks he needs. I will eat with him. Baba Yaga, will you please feed everyone else?"

I felt Freya bristle beside me, but before she could object, Baba Yaga inclined her head.

"*Da,*" she agreed cheerfully. "I cook for uzzers."

"But not in *my* kitchen," Keven growled.

"*Pah!*" Baba Yaga responded.

Freya drew the sword at her side halfway from its sheath. The company surrounding her drew back a hasty but coordinated few steps, suggesting this wasn't the first time the goddess had threatened violence. I put a hand to my temple and massaged at the ache forming there. Just what in freaking hell had happened in my absence, anyway?

"Well?" the Norse goddess demanded, catching my eye. She stared down her nose at me in challenge. "You want to handle things? Then handle them."

The words *fuck you* hovered on my lips, but I bit them back

34

as a cooler, more rational part of me suggested that I should probably try to get more information before I started pissing off armed deities.

"The cooler, more rational part of you," my Edie-voice informed me, *"is a spoilsport."*

"Well?" Freya barked again.

Irritation surged in me. Without stopping to think it through, I swept one hand through the air and gathered the house's magick to me, then slammed a still-booted foot onto the stone floor and sent the magick coursing back down into the foundation—along with a healthy dose of my own.

I'd forgotten how much of the latter there was, now that I had Morgana's, too.

The poor house.

The vibration beneath my feet started off small enough, but its intensity escalated quickly. Before I could shout a warning, the floor heaved and bucked beneath us, throwing half the women to the floor in a tangle of limbs and the remainder against the wall. Freya herself fell against me, her mouth open in surprise. From down the hall, in the direction of the kitchen, came the hollow boom of …

Well … to be honest, I wasn't sure. Splitting rock? Expanding wood? I didn't know quite how I had achieved my end-goal, but I was sure I had. Reasonably sure, anyway.

Amid a shower of dust and grit that drifted down from the ceiling, Harry sneezed and set fire to the bottom post of the stair rail. I set Freya upright and away from me, patted out the flames, and turned to Keven.

"There may be a few things missing," I said, "but the kitchen is big enough now for the two of you. I'm going up to Lucan. He will need tea. I tried, but I had almost nothing I could give him, and he—"

My voice caught. I broke off and swallowed, blinking back the sting of threatening tears. "He's not doing well," I said. "At all."

A strong, gentle hand settled onto my forearm and squeezed. "We'll come with you," Nia said. Their gaze encompassed the other Crones and included Jeanne but skipped over Freya. "All of us," they added.

Their tone was firm and their message clear: I'd returned, and their allegiance was to me.

Which begged the question, I thought as my right foot settled onto the first stair and my hand onto the smooth, worn railing, of where my own loyalties lay.

CHAPTER 6

"TEA," ANNE MURMURED, PRESSING A MUG INTO MY HANDS. "Keven insisted."

I gagged at the thought of drinking anything, but the mug's weight and warmth were comforting, and so I nodded my thanks and curled my fingers around it. My gaze remained locked on the bed and its occupant.

"No change?" the former Water Crone asked of the room in general.

She and the three others—Maureen, Nia, and Elysabeth —had remained with me in Lucan's room, drawing up chairs on the other side of the bed and settling in to keep me company. Jeanne had followed shortly after and the four had chatted, asking no questions of me, although I knew they had many.

They had simply watched and waited ... and held space.

Bits and pieces of their murmured conversation had pierced my fitful dozing through the night, and my brain had tried to guess the context. Freya's name punctuated the whispers often, but I wasn't ready to deal with that yet—or with her—and so I'd carefully disengaged each time and slipped back beneath sleep's surface.

I was awake now, however, and there were questions. So very many questions.

"None," Maureen answered the one Anne had asked as the latter took her seat between Elysabeth and Jeanne. "But at least he's no worse."

I seized on her words. No worse was a good thing, right? Or at least, good enough for now? I watched the shallow rise and fall of the duvet covering Lucan's chest, willing it to continue.

Pale morning light filtered around the curtains at the window, which meant that it was sometime past seven, which meant that he'd survived the night, which meant that there was still hope. Hope that he might recover, might wake up, might open his eyes and turn that warm amber gaze my way again …

Hope that I might yet reach him and bring him back.

That, I knew, was the real issue.

Whatever Morok had done to him in Camlann, whatever Lucan had endured, he hadn't come back from it. Hadn't, or hadn't wanted to, or …

I swallowed hard and tightened my grip on the ceramic in my hands.

Or perhaps he hadn't been able to, because I hadn't brought *enough* of him back. Perhaps, in my desperate effort to rescue him, I had instead failed him—leaving a part of him there, or worse, still attached to Morok. Either way, whatever part I'd left behind had been destroyed, and the Lucan in the bed, the Lucan here and now—

"Claire?"

Anne's concerned voice broke into my dark thoughts, and I realized I had tears running down my cheeks. I swiped them away with the back of one hand and summoned a watery smile.

"I'm fine," I said. "Really. Just … "

"Exhausted?" Nia suggested.

"Worried?" Elysabeth added.

I nodded. "Yes to both. And …"

"Overwhelmed," Jeanne said. It was a statement rather than a question, and it was the most accurate of all because it encompassed it all. Camlann, Morok, the Between, coming back to Edie's house, Lucan—

A woman's bellow floated up from the kitchen below us, demanding even through the floor, and I flinched.

Freya.

Something is coming.

Overwhelmed or not, it was time. But first …

I lifted my gaze away from the shifter—the man—in the bed.

"Thank you," I said, looking to each of the women across from me in turn. "Thank you all. What you did for me in that cavern—what you all went through—"

Almost as one, five heads shook. A shadow by the window moved, drawing my attention. Bedivere. I couldn't see his eyes, but I included him in my gratitude. He, too, had sacrificed much.

"We did what we needed to do," Elysabeth said. "All of us."

"Yes," agreed Nia, reaching for Jeanne's hand beside them and squeezing it. "All of us. Because that's what we do."

The immensity of the strength underlying the declaration was outweighed only by its truth. Because it *was* what we did. It was what we'd always done, we women. Whether it was for family or friends or the entire world—and no matter how tired or empty or reluctant we might be—we always, somehow, found more in ourselves for the ones who needed it. And we would do it again.

I took a swig of the tea Anne had given me. Its heavy sweetness curled around my tongue and then slid down my throat, trailing warmth in its wake. I recognized notes of linden, lemon balm, skullcap, and nettle, heavily laced with honey, and my mind began unwinding in sheer anticipation of their effects. Keven was very, very good at what she did with herbs. I was glad I'd stood up for her against Freya. And rather proud of myself, too. Speaking of whom …

I shifted my butt back on the seat of the chair so that I was sitting straighter.

"Freya and Baba Yaga," I said. "When—how—?"

"On the doorstep," Bedivere growled from the window, stepping abruptly into the conversation, "claiming sanctuary."

I almost choked on another sip of tea. "Excuse me? Sanctuary from what?"

Maureen rolled her eyes at the wolf-shifter and heaved a sigh. "Freya wouldn't say—or let Baba Yaga say, either. Only that they'd followed you here and needed to see you. We tried to tell them you hadn't returned, but Freya insisted on waiting. It's … difficult to say no to the Norse goddess of battle and death, especially when she's armed."

Freya was, of course, also a goddess of love and fertility, but I suspected the others already knew that—and that the *armed* part rather negated those qualities.

"And Baba Yaga?"

A small smile quirked at the corner of Nia's mouth. "She may have come from the Otherworld," they said, "but she's still a witch. She's one of us."

"And she's Baba Yaga," added Elysabeth, as if that explained everything. Which it kind of did.

I took another sip of tea and returned my attention to the bed and its occupant. A heaviness had worked its way into my core. It felt warm and comfortable, undoubtedly the work of Keven's tea. My breathing began to slow, and the questions in my mind with it. Perhaps that was enough information for one sitting, I thought, as sleep tugged at my edges. I was here and safe, Lucan was in the best care possible, and I could figure out the rest later, after—

A throat cleared on the other side of the room, and when I followed the sound, determined brown eyes behind red-framed glasses met mine.

"It's your turn, now," Jeanne said. Her voice was gentle, but her expression brooked no argument. "If we're going to help Lucan, we need to know what happened."

And just like that, the effects of Keven's tea dissipated. I hadn't let myself relive the events of Camlann since landing in Edie's house. I hadn't dared. I'd kept them locked away in the darkest, furthest corner of my psyche that I could push them into, making myself stay focused on what needed to be done rather than what had already happened. I'd been afraid to do otherwise because—

The goliath.

Tea sloshed from the cup onto my lap.

Morgana.

I gritted my teeth and clenched the cup tighter, trying to keep it steady.

A wolf literally possessed.

Everything—all of it—returned in vivid Technicolor. The castle bailey and the fallen people there. The stench of a battlefield eternally soaked in blood. Bile rose in my chest and burned in my throat, and I closed my eyes. My every fiber balked at the thought of relating the horrors out loud, but I knew Jeanne was right. I'd already proved that I couldn't heal Lucan alone, and my friends couldn't help without knowing the full story. Without knowing that I may not have brought all of him home.

Or even enough.

Afraid I might shatter the mug in my rigid grip, I set it down on the night table by Lucan's head. His beautiful, unreachable head.

"Morok," I said quietly. "Morok happened."

In as few words as I could—and the most I could manage—I related my tale. I skipped the parts about my journey through the Otherworld, because none of that had bearing on the matter at hand, and began with finding Lucan in Camlann, bound by chains and Morok's magick. I described how I'd used my own power to separate him from the collar that had been fused to him, how I'd nursed him as best I could, how I'd waited and hoped ... and how I'd realized that the damage to him had been too great for me to heal even then. Even when I hadn't yet realized how much more there was.

I told them going after Morok on my own, about following the goliath to the stone and finding the inscription there, *"Whoso pulleth out this sword from this stone, is right wise King born of all England,"* and realizing who the goliath had once been. I told them how Lucan had followed me there, and how I'd thought the goliath—Arthur—was trying to kill him on Morok's behalf.

I paused, and a long silence fell over the room while I grappled with the memories. With the awful realization that had settled over me—the knowledge that Lucan had been Lucan no more.

I reached for my shifter's hand lying on the bed and threaded my fingers with his—my hand warm, his cold. Too cold. No one spoke. Not even Bedivere.

Then, in a voice devoid of expression, I continued our story. The goliath's breaking of the stone, how Morok-Lucan had seized the orb and smashed it, Morgana's appearance, and the transfer of her power to me. I left out the part about the Morrigan's power for the moment, not ready yet to share the enormity of what I carried in my core, what I still grappled to come to terms with myself.

What I grappled with, period.

And then I told of the battle I'd been forced to fight with the man I loved.

"I couldn't do it," I murmured, extending my other hand to cover our intertwined fingers, mine and Lucan's. Mine and my protector's. My story became disjointed, phrases and words strung together with no thought to grammar or coherence, just needing to be spoken. "Not even when he told me to. I couldn't bring myself to kill him. At the last second, I managed to separate them. I knew I couldn't save Lucan entirely, but I couldn't let him die as Morok. He deserved more than that. Better. And I still thought I could save him. Save us. So I trapped Morok—and then the Between came and the portal—"

"You foolish, *stupid* mortal!" Freya's voice spat from the bedchamber doorway.

I hadn't heard her come into the room. Under other circumstances, I might have jumped at her sudden intrusion, but these weren't other circumstances. These were *these* circumstances, when I was so focused on the hand I held— gripping it like the lifeline it might be for Lucan—that jumping at anything was just too damned much effort. I couldn't even be bothered to turn and look at her.

"It was *your* doing," she continued, and footsteps heralded her approach. "*Your* magick that ripped open the divide. Have you *any* idea what you've done?"

A rough hand seized my shoulder and would have spun me around in my seat, but the twisted remains of another hand closed over hers and a familiar, deep-chested growl sounded a warning. I looked up at Bedivere, surprised by his intervention.

"It's all right," I said. "She can't hurt me."

Not *won't*, because I wouldn't put it past her to try, but *can't*, because that *was* true. At least, not in any way that mattered. Bedivere's hand remained where it was for a few seconds more before he withdrew it from the goddess's shoulder. He didn't, however, step away from her.

Freya scowled at him, then at me. "*Do* you know what you've done?"

"I have no idea," I said with a sigh, "but I'm sure you're about to tell me. *Us.*" My gaze swept over the others in the room, including them in the conversation and whatever revelation the Norse goddess was about to make. As one, the four Crones and Jeanne all inclined their heads, acknowledging our solidarity. Prematurely, as it happened, because—

"You tore the very fabric of existence itself, you selfish

bitch." Despite the choice of vocabulary, Freya's voice held no real animosity, only a weary resignation that did more to drive home her words than anger would have done.

The room went still. So did my breathing. I stared at the goddess.

"I—what?"

"You split Morok from the body he inhabited," she said quietly. "That shouldn't have been possible. You had to have tapped into a power outside yourself to do it—a very great power. I'm not sure what it was, but it wasn't anything that any one of us is capable of. *That's* what tore open the divide holding back the Between."

"You don't know that," Maureen said, rallying to my defense even as my own head shook in denial. "Not for certain."

Freya's gaze flashed to her. "The coincidence is too great to be anything else. By her own admission, she"—an accusatory finger pointed at me—"split Morok from her lover at the same time that the creatures—the dark ones—began to flood the Otherworld in numbers greater than any we've seen before. We didn't have enough warning to mount a defense, and so we had no choice."

I tried to wrap my mind around the idea. The immensity of it. I wanted to deny it, but I remembered how Camlann had begun to crumble into the Between, into the dark of the nothing, the instant Lucan had separated from Morok. I had been there. I had seen it, felt it. Fled from it. I couldn't deny that, and so I had to face the possibility. My part in it. My responsibility.

Across the bed, a universe away, Anne spoke up. "You had no choice but to what?" she asked.

Freya's glittering blue gaze held mine as she answered. "Flee," she said. "The gods are fleeing to Earth, and *you* are to blame."

In the utter silence that followed the goddess's bombshell,

a thud sounded from out in the corridor—no, farther than that. The great hall below us. As if something had fallen or a door had—

"Honey, I'm home!" boomed a deep voice.

Another familiar and most unwelcome one.

CHAPTER 7

IF MY RETURN TO THE HOUSE HAD CAUSED CHAOS, ODIN'S invasion created sheer pandemonium.

He'd ridden his enormous black horse right through the front door and into the great hall, which felt significantly less great with a beast of that size dominating the space. Champing at the bit in its mouth, the horse pawed at the floor, striking sparks as iron shoes struck stone. Odin remained astride, looking down at the gathered company from his superior height—a calculated move on his part, I was sure.

On either side of him stood the two servants I'd met at his lodge, the Viking butler and the stout Thyra, both seeming unbothered by the enormous packs they carried on their backs.

And the pandemonium part? That came from a half dozen of Odin's Valkyries tossing furniture around the sitting room, the dozen midwitches and Crones attempting to stop them, Keven storming down the hall from the kitchen, Bedivere's wolf snarling as it blocked the foot of the stairs beside me, and Freya shrieking at her husband.

I stared at the animated tableau before me in a kind of numb shock. Only a few hours before, I'd thought myself alone in the world, and I'd wanted nothing more than to have my friends back. My fellow Crones, Keven, the midwitches and my house. Even Bedivere. But now …

Now I was reminded that one should be careful what one wished for. Or at least be more specific about it.

I ducked as a small side table from the sitting room sailed past my ear and splintered against Keven's granite bulk. A streak of blue went past me as Harry fled for the safety of the kitchen. A smaller streak of orange in the form of Gus followed. Freya's voice gained volume, and I tried to block out her words so that I could gather my wits and figure out what to do. Because *one* god on Earth had been too many. All of them?

That would be a fucking disaster.

"Enough!" I called out, but my voice was swallowed by the bedlam churning around me. I tried again with the same result. I would never be heard over this amount of noise. I rubbed a hand over a throbbing temple. How—

"Maman?" a single voice reached through the noise to seize my attention. My eyes darted to the still-open doorway, where a figure had appeared behind horse and rider. Horror filled me as, in what felt like slow motion, I saw Thyra draw a sword I hadn't noticed she wore. She turned and lunged for the newcomer, and instinct took over.

In a single space between heartbeats, I summoned Air to me. With one hand, I pushed it past horse and rider toward the stout woman whose blade aimed for my daughter-in-law's chest; with the other, I sent it swirling through the great hall and into the sitting room.

The first gust of wind hit the broad-backed woman like a sledgehammer, knocking her to the floor with a grunt audible even over the melee. The second left Crones and midwitches untouched as it threaded between them and whipped around the Valkyries, throwing the latter against the fireplace wall. The female warriors screeched in fury, but struggle as they might, Air kept them pinned there as slow silence descended over the rest of the gathering.

The sheer effortlessness of my actions left me breathless.

Or maybe it was the narrow gaze that Odin turned on me that knocked the air from my lungs. I swallowed against a suddenly dry mouth as Freya's gaze narrowed likewise. A shiver of unease slid down my spine. At least I had their attention.

Which meant that now would be a good time to say something. Ignoring my daughter-in-law for the moment, I opened my mouth to speak, but Odin beat me to it.

"I claim sanctuary," he announced. "I would live here."

I was pretty sure my jaw would have hit the floor if it hadn't been physically attached. I gaped at the god on the horse that pawed again at the stone beneath it. Freya launched into a new tirade. It was in Norse, but even if it hadn't been, I wouldn't have understood a word of it because I was too gobsmacked to process much of anything.

Seizing his advantage, Odin cut across his wife's voice as if she wasn't even there. "You promised me a favor," he reminded me. "I am collecting on that promise."

Freya gaped at him, her mouth continuing to flap soundlessly. Then she turned her fury on me. "You promised a favor?" She was back to shrieking. "After I told you—*specifically*—to do no such thing?"

My brain made a valiant effort to rally itself, which, under the circumstances, was pretty impressive, I thought. Needing a hand to wave placatingly at the goddess, I let go of the wind holding Thyra to the floor. The Valkyries, however, I kept pinned. Part of me was astonished at—and rather pleased with—the control I finally seemed to have gained over my magick; another, greater part couldn't help but worry about the other power seething under my skin … something I hadn't called on.

But I couldn't focus on both it and the Odin problem, and the Odin problem felt far more threatening at the moment. Assuming I could keep the power problem under wraps, anyway.

"It's a long story," I told Freya. "Suffice it to say I had no choice."

"I *gave* you a choice," she spat.

"Long story," I said again. "But I'm sure we can work things—"

She rounded on Odin. "*I* claimed sanctuary first," she growled at him. "You will leave."

Ignoring his wife as thoroughly as she ignored me, Odin held my gaze calmly. Coldly. "I am collecting," he repeated, "on that promise."

A ripple shuddered through the foundation of the house, telling me it was as unhappy with the idea as I was.

"*Fuck,*" said my Edie-voice.

There was no way that I could have both god and goddess living under my roof. Hell, I didn't even want Freya here, but at least she'd shown a willingness—sort of—to recognize me as being in charge. Odin, however, would be another story altogether.

An idea glimmered to life.

"Sanctuary," I said. "That's the favor you want."

"It is."

"All right." I nodded agreement. "I grant you sanctuary" —I held up a hand again as Freya took a breath in preparation for another diatribe—"but not in the house."

Odin's mount abruptly shifted sideways as the god's hands tightened on the reins. "That's not—"

"Your requested favor was sanctuary," I said, cutting him off. "You didn't specify where." I curled my free hand into a fist within the folds of my robe and lifted my chin. I had no idea where I was finding the courage to stand up to him this way, but I was tired of being talked over in my own house, damn it. Besides, fake it till you make it, right?

I met the hard gaze boring into me and held it without flinching—without daring to flinch—and continued, "You may set up camp in the woods, out of sight of the house. You're not to set foot anywhere in the clearing surrounding us, in the house itself, or anywhere outside the woods until I say otherwise. Those are my conditions, otherwise my promise is null and void."

The silence that followed my words made me think I wasn't the only one in the hall or sitting room who held my breath. Even Odin's mount stood stock still, as if it sensed the tension. The god of war stared at me for a long moment, his lips thin. A brief something—dark and ugly—flashed deep in his eyes, but it disappeared before I could identify it. Then, to my shock—and Freya's, judging by how her head snapped back—he inclined his head.

"I accept your terms," he said. "You have my ... gratitude ... for your generosity."

No sarcasm there, I thought a trifle hysterically as the air hissed from my lungs. Little rustles sounded throughout the hall as movement returned—probably other shoulders and backbones relaxing. I remembered I still held the Valkyries against the fireplace wall and abruptly recalled Air to me, uncaring that I dropped them too fast, and they landed in a tangled heap of limbs and bodies.

Uncaring because I'd also become aware of the Fire I held in my other palm. Fire which startled me with its pulsating, white-hot presence. Shocked me with its intensity. Sobered me with the certainty that I hadn't knowingly called on it.

Soon, I would need to address that and figure out what it meant—and how to handle it.

Soon, but not now.

Now, I needed to get back to Lucan—and to find out what had brought Natalie to my door again. But first, I needed to hug that woman.

CHAPTER 8

IF NATALIE HADN'T BEEN THERE, I WOULD HAVE SIMPLY returned to Lucan and left the others to deal with the aftermath of Odin. To be perfectly honest, I pretty much did the latter part anyway. The midwitches set about restoring order to the sitting room that the Valkyries had torn apart, a reluctant Bedivere agreed to accompany Freya on her self-appointed mission to settle our unwanted guests far enough from the house to satisfy my terms, and Keven went back to the kitchen where she'd left Baba Yaga unsupervised—testimony to her loyalty to me.

In short order, it was just me, Jeanne, and the four Crones left in the great hall with my daughter-in-law. Then, as if by unspoken agreement, Jeanne and the Crones quietly filed upstairs. Poor Natalie didn't stand a chance.

I folded my daughter-in-law into my arms so fiercely that I heard the breath hiss from her. And then I held on with all my strength.

"You really are okay," I whispered when I finally loosened my hold in response to her squirming. I gripped her shoulders and rested my forehead against hers. "I can't believe you're really okay. I thought—"

My throat closed against uttering what I'd thought. I blinked back tears—damn, but I seemed to be shedding a lot of those lately—and pulled back to stare into the dear, familiar face.

Tiny lines fanned out from the corners of brown eyes that had seen more than any of us should have seen—or known about—and my protective instincts heaped more guilt on top of that which I already carried. I braced my shoulders beneath the weight. Something else to deal with later.

"Paul?" I croaked. "And Braden?"

"Maman." Natalie patted my cheek with a gentle hand. "We're all fine. You can breathe, I promise."

I fought the urge to hug her again and nodded. "Good," I said. "That's good." Then I frowned. "But wait, if everyone is fine, why are you here? Did someone tell you I'd returned?"

Gentleness disappeared. "No," she responded tartly, "but someone *should* have. Such as *you*, maybe? Even if you didn't think I'd made it out, you still had Paul and Braden."

"I—" My throat tightened again. I didn't know how to explain the enormity of the loss and guilt I'd felt when I'd landed in Edie's house with Lucan and Gus and Harry. I couldn't find the words to describe my sheer, overwhelming inability to face my son after leaving his wife to die at the hand of Cernunnos in that cavern.

I'd taken the coward's way out by not contacting Paul in what I'd believed to be his own grief. Natalie and I both knew it. And I would have to live with it.

Natalie shook her head, then brushed back a lock of dark hair that had escaped the hairband she wore. "None of that matters right now, Maman. We have bigger problems."

"We do?"

"My job has been to keep an eye on the news and report back to the others. Everything seemed pretty quiet until today. Until this." She thrust a folded-up newspaper at me. "I think it's the gods, Maman. There are more of them, and they're turning up everywhere."

NATALIE'S USE OF *EVERYWHERE* MIGHT HAVE BEEN AN exaggeration, but not by much. The Crones had joined us in the kitchen, and the front page of the highly regarded newspaper spread before us on the kitchen table made it clear that we had a bigger problem than Freya and Odin's feud on our hands.

Much bigger.

Persons claiming to be deities had surfaced around the globe, with mixed—and sometimes jaw-dropping—responses to their presence. In Taiwan, the appearance of the sea goddess Mazu had led first to widespread celebration—and then to a crippling of the economy, as workers took to the streets and businesses ground to a halt. Lakshmi's emergence in Delhi had had roughly the same effect, with the added bonus of riots and the trampling of hundreds of citizens. In Greece, a man claiming to be Hades had been arrested and was being held pending psychiatric evaluation; similar incidents had been reported in Egypt with the arrest of Isis, in Japan where the goddess Amaterasu had claimed ownership of the Grand Shrine of Ise, and in more locales than could be counted where men of every age and description were claiming to be Jesus.

Not all of the latter were real, of course—perhaps none were—but the chaos they had created was.

"Well," said Maureen, when Anne's voice died away after the third reading-aloud of the article.

"Well," agreed Nia.

"How do they not believe them?" demanded Freya, who had returned to the house in the middle of the first reading. Still wearing her boots—because goddesses didn't appear to care much about decorum—she paced the newly expanded kitchen from Keven's woodstove to Baba Yaga's and back again. She underlined her words with waving arms, and the stomp of a boot heel punctuated each turnabout. "They are gods! They are more than human! They have powers! They cannot be denied this way."

She stopped abruptly on the other side of the table from me and slammed her hands down on the newspaper. "You will do something, Claire Emerson. *You* brought this on us. It is because of *you* that we had no choice but to return to this world."

My elbows resting on the table and hands cradling my forehead, I stared at the newspaper, trying—valiantly, in my opinion—to wrap my head around these new events. Not for the first time since learning that I was Crone, I would have liked nothing more than to turn my back on the whole damned mess and walk away. To go back to being just Claire Emerson, grandmother, slightly clingy mother, somewhat bitter ex-wife, bored with my life and lacking purpose and blissfully unaware of the machinations of gods and goddesses and the fragility of our entire world as the Between hovered at its edges.

Also not for the first time, I knew I would do nothing of the sort.

Even if by some miracle it turned out that I hadn't—as Freya believed—been the cause of the forced exodus of gods from the Otherworld, I could hardly stand by and do nothing.

I placed my hands flat on the newspaper-covered table and stood. "I'll go back to the Otherworld," I said. "I'll repair the divide."

"Maman, no!" Natalie, seated on my left, clutched at my arm.

A murmur of dissent rippled through the room, passed from Crone to midwitch and back again. I caught fragments of low whispers—*"can't … not again … we almost died …"* My heart ached at having to ask these amazing women to step up with me once again—and at the thought of asking even more of Nia, Elysabeth, Maureen, and Anne.

Even Crones had their limits.

But we weren't there, yet. I still had Freya to deal with first.

"You." The Norse goddess stared down her nose at me. "You think *you* can do what *we* could not?"

"Not alone, no," I said, gently disengaging myself from Natalie's grip. "But with help, maybe. And you told me you hadn't had time to muster your defenses, so you haven't really tried, have you?"

Her scowl deepened. "And what if your attempt makes matters worse?"

Not *our* attempt. *Your* attempt. No pressure there, right?

"You can't stay on Earth, Freya," I said, trying to reason with her. "First, humans aren't the same now as they were when you left. We've changed. Grown. We're not as accepting of things like magick and claims to godhood. Read the headlines! How do we know that Jesus himself—the real Jesus—isn't one of the ones they've arrested?"

Freya snorted. "Doubtful. He's a total recluse, that one. And even if he is, he'll escape. He's been through this before, remember? He proved his powers then, and he'll do it again. We all will."

It was like trying to reason with a brick wall. I scrunched the newspaper into my fist and waved it under her supercilious nose. Goddess, but she was as bad as the Morrigan.

"Or you'll *all* end up being sedated and put through every test imaginable while the powers-that-be-here try to figure out how to replicate you for their own use," I snapped. "Because —and I repeat—we're not the same as when you left. You don't have a place here anymore."

Blue eyes glittered a challenge at me. "Then we will *take* our place."

I let the crumpled paper drop back onto the table, curled my hands into fists, and wrapped my arms around myself to keep from throwing them wide in impatience. And to hide the sparks I could feel dancing across my palms.

For a moment, the only sound in the kitchen was the rhythmic *chop chop chop* of Baba Yaga's knife as she sliced her way through a mound of carrots. Everyone else, Keven included, stood still, waiting for my response.

"You could try," I agreed, "and you might even succeed, although again, I think you seriously underestimate how far humans have progressed. And even if you do"—I held up a hand as she opened her mouth to speak, then repeated— "even if you do, how long do you think you'll have before this place is gone, too? Do you really think the Between will stop at the Otherworld?"

Baba Yaga's knife stilled. The Norse goddess glowered at me, slow understanding clashing with denial in her eyes. One hand curled into a fist at her side. The other went to the hilt of her sword.

The magick beneath my skin stretched and pushed, calling without my consent to the Fire at my core, Earth at my feet. I gritted my teeth against it and counted my blessings that the others were too focused on the drama playing out before them to notice the wisps of smoke curling up from beneath my fingers.

"Control yourself," my Edie-voice warned. *"You don't know what will happen if—"*

I'm trying, I snapped back at it. My feet shifted beneath me, widening my stance. I tried to move them back together, but they wouldn't obey. Freaking hell, I thought. Freaking, freaking hell.

Then, just when I thought I might lose my internal battle, Freya spun on her heel and stalked toward the garden door. I sagged in relief as she tore it open and disappeared into the frigid afternoon. The door swung on a single hinge for a moment, and then it crashed to the floor—and so did something in the room above us.

Lucan's room.

CHAPTER 9

I HIKED MY ROBE UP PAST MY KNEES AND TOOK THE NARROW back stairs two at a time, my heart lodged in my throat and panic fueling my feet. Every footfall brought fresh self-recrimination. *I should never have left him. How could I let myself be distracted? How could I forget about him? Where in hell are my priorities?*

And on it went until I burst through the door of his bedchamber. At first glance, the bed was empty, the room equally so. I skidded to a halt, scanning the room from window to fireplace to wardrobe and back, but Lucan wasn't there—and neither was the midwitch who'd been keeping watch over him. There was no one. Nothing. No sign—

Across the room, a woman's head popped into sight over the edge of the rumpled bed. "Thank goddess!" she exclaimed. "One minute he was asleep, and the next he was vaulting out of bed. I tried to catch him before he fell, but he was too heavy. He was calling for you, milady. He kept saying—"

The midwitch broke off, climbing to her feet as Keven brushed me aside with the sweep of a granite paw and lumbered across to join her. The gargoyle squatted beside the fallen shifter while I tried to reconnect my brain and my feet —a difficult task, with sheer terror in the way—and then she grunted and stood straight again.

Before I'd made it halfway to her, she'd picked up the limp form, set it back onto the bed, and pulled the duvet over it. I changed course in favor of the nearer side of the bed.

"Is he ..." I couldn't finish.

"Alive," Keven said. Then she looked across at me. "For now."

I shouldn't have left him, I thought again, even though my presence had made zero difference to his condition over the past week. The midwitch who'd been attending to him twisted her hands together. Bev, I thought. Or maybe her name was Sandy? Freaking hell, I needed to make more of an effort to get names straight.

"I'm so sorry, milady. I tried. I really—"

"It's all right," I said, gritting my teeth against her use of the title. Would I ever get used to it? I forced a reassuring smile. "If anyone is to blame, it's me. I should have come back sooner. You said he kept saying something?"

"Just your name, milady," Sandy-Bev replied, and I cringed internally.

Nope. Never getting used to it.

Others had arrived to join us: the four Crones and Jeanne, a half-dozen other midwitches and Natalie, and Bedivere. The latter shouldered between me and the bed to stare down at his brother for a moment, his expression giving no hint at his thoughts. Unlike the sideways look he gave me as he pushed past me again on his way to take up a post by the window.

There was no mistaking the thoughts behind that.

I pressed my lips together and curled my hands around fistfuls of my robe. I understood the blame that Bedivere directed at me. Hell, I shared it. I gazed down at the familiar, haggard face framed by a tangle of long hair splayed out on the pillow, remembering him as he'd been before Camlann. Remembering how he'd been when I'd found him there.

I was afraid—so afraid—that I had saved him for myself, for my own sake, rather than his. That I had done him the greatest disservice I could have done by not letting him die in Camlann. That deep inside him right now, he remembered what Morok had made him into—what the god had made him do—and he couldn't get past that.

Or perhaps didn't want to get past it.

"Maman?" Natalie's gentle voice intruded on my memories.

I sucked in a quick, shallow breath and made a concerted effort to tuck away my guilt. A guilt I would carry with me for a lifetime, because even dead, Morok had managed to maintain a hold over me—over the world itself—that I wasn't sure I could break.

I met Natalie's concern and forced what I hoped was a reassuring smile to my lips. "I'm okay," I said. Doubt flickered in the brown eyes, and I uncurled one of my hands to give hers a squeeze. "Really."

She studied me for another second before deciding to trust me and nodding acceptance. Lying had never been a life skill I'd aspired to, but I seemed to have mastered it.

I glanced at the window. The light around the edges of the curtains was fading. "It's getting late," I said. "You should get home to Paul and Braden."

"But—"

"Natalie." I took my daughter-in-law's face in both my hands. "I don't even know what we're going to do yet. Or when or how. Go home. Be with your family."

Be with my *family. Please.*

She wavered. "You'll let me know when you've decided? Because I'll help, of course. To open the door, I mean."

"Of course," I agreed, pulling her in for a hug. Oh yes, I'd mastered lying, all right. There was no way I was letting Natalie anywhere near that cavern again, and I didn't care how many lies and reneged-upon promises it took.

Beyond Natalie's shoulder, Nia raised an eyebrow at me. I shook my head at them, an almost imperceptible movement that I hoped Natalie wouldn't feel. She didn't. She simply pulled back and, with a kiss on each of my cheeks in her French-Canadian way, she left.

The midwitches accompanied her from the room, and before I could even ask, Bedivere followed.

"I will see her through the woods," he said.

"And I," said Keven, "will finish that healing potion."

I followed them all as far as the door. Bedivere and Natalie went down the corridor toward the great hall; Keven followed the midwitches toward the back stairs and kitchen. I listened to the many feet descending, then waited. At last, the front door opened and then closed, and I uncurled my fingers from the wooden doorframe, shut the bedroom door, too, and turned back to the room.

My fellow Crones—Jeanne included—stood before the fireplace, their arms crossed and their expressions uniformly severe. I held up a hand against the protests, the arguments, the concerns ... all of it. I may as well not have bothered.

"You can't go back," Elysabeth said. "Even if we could open the door again—and it's a big if, Claire, because dear goddess ... *Cernunnos?*"

"I know, but—" I began.

"You barely survived the first time," Anne interrupted. "And that was when the Otherworld was still intact."

"But it—"

"There must be another way," Maureen said. "Something we're missing."

Five mouths opened as all of them prepared to talk at once. I held up both my hands against an onslaught of words that would change nothing. That *could* change nothing.

"Stop," I said. "Please. Just stop."

Five mouths closed again, and five pairs of eyes stared at me.

I let out a long, slow breath. Now came the tricky part.

"There is no other way," I said. "There is only this way. If Freya is right about the damage I did to the divide, the Between won't stop. It will come, and it will unmake everything, not just in the Otherworld, but in ours, too. Because that is what it does. That's the sole purpose of its existence.

Am I sure I can repair the divide? No. Not even a little. But I have to try."

None of the other women spoke. From the kitchen below came the muffled sounds of pots and pans being moved, dishes being rattled, the boom of Keven's gravelly voice, Baba Yaga's somewhat less gravelly reply. And then—

"Claire."

I dived for Lucan as he lurched from the bed. I couldn't stop his fall any more than the midwitch had been able to, but I did manage to cushion him this time. We fell together in a tangle of limbs and duvet, robe and ... magick.

Power crawled over my skin. Beneath it. Through it. Hell, it felt like it was *becoming* my skin. Becoming me.

Fire seethed at my core, Air whispered over my arms, Water trickled through my veins, Earth reached up from the floor to wrap around me—and then all of them reached for Lucan. Reached, met nothing, reached further. As if they'd taken on a life of their own, the elements pushed against him, seeking, demanding—

Lucan seized my face in his hands and stared down at me as I lay beneath him, his amber eyes wild and the muscles of his throat working beneath his unkempt beard. Then, as suddenly as he'd come to life and dived from the bed, he lost consciousness again and slumped across me.

The magick in me swirled faster. The elements tangled with one another, fighting for dominance. I grew hotter, then colder, then Lucan's weight lifted from me, and hands slid beneath my shoulders and levered me up from the floor.

Before I could utter a warning, sparks snapped along my skin, and Nia's voice yelped. They dropped me again, and my shoulder blades bounced against the floorboards. I closed my eyes and seized on the pain, holding onto it with every ounce of focus I could muster.

Slowly, grudgingly, the elements receded beneath my surface. I waited another moment to be sure I was back in control—although the very idea made me want to laugh in a decidedly not-in-control way—and then opened my eyes again and pushed myself upright until I was sitting with my arms supporting me.

Lucan was back in the bed, Nia cradled their hand against their chest, and all five women stared at me again, this time in consternation and a hint of—well. It wasn't quite fear, but it was close enough to send a stab of remorse through my heart.

Anne was the first to speak.

"I don't suppose there's an explanation for"—she gestured at Nia, then at me, then at Lucan—"that?"

It took everything I had not to close my eyes again, because where did I even begin? How could I tell them that the goddess they served was now—at least mostly—me? Or that I was her. Or whatever the hell it was that had happened in Camlann.

On the other hand, how could I not tell them? I needed their help, they needed to save their world, and—

And dear goddess, Lucan wasn't done yet.

"*Run!*" he shouted from the bed. I scrambled to my feet as Jeanne threw herself across his body to keep him in the bed. Anne did the same across his legs, but not even their combined weight could hold him still. Nia and Elysabeth joined them—Nia between the two other women, and Elysabeth grappling with his feet from the end of the bed. With no more room to help on their side and Lucan continuing to buck like a man possessed, Maureen scuttled around to my side.

Already on the bed beside Lucan, I waved her off. "Get Keven!" I yelled over Lucan's roars.

Maureen changed direction and dived for the bell rope at the bedside. She yanked it furiously, swearing with equal vigor, and then joined the efforts to hold Lucan down. His head thrashed from side to side, and I couldn't get a grip without hurting him, and—

"Lucan!" I bellowed. "Enough!"

And just like that, he went still. Utterly and completely. For a moment, the only sound in the room was the panting of the four women holding him down, and then Lucan's head turned toward me. His amber eyes met mine and recognition glinted in their depths.

"Claire," he said. And then his gaunt face took on an expression of sadness so profound that it pierced my heart. "I cannot protect you, milady," he whispered. "*Run.*"

CHAPTER 10

IT WAS KEVEN'S IDEA TO RESTRAIN LUCAN. THE OTHERS HAD sided with her—even Bedivere, who had returned from seeing Natalie to her vehicle and now scowled at the proceedings from his preferred window post. I hated the idea with every fiber of my being, but I couldn't fault their reasoning. We couldn't leave him unattended the way he was, and there weren't enough of us to keep watch over him around the clock. Especially when it had taken five of us to hold him in the bed this time.

I stood near the fire with Keven as I watched Jeanne supervise the tying of my once again unconscious shifter's hands and feet to the four bedposts. I hadn't been able to bring myself to help, unable to get the image of Lucan's shackled wolf out of my head. I hugged myself across the hollowness that resided behind my breastbone.

"It's just a matter of time, right?" I asked the gargoyle at my side. "Until he recovers, I mean. Like he was before?"

Keven looked down and sideways at me. "I assume you've tried everything you did before."

I nodded. "Everything," I said, remembering the time that the Morrigan had shrieked at me to hold him skin-to-skin, the time that the magick in me had meshed with the magick in Lucan and brought him back from what I had been certain was the brink of death. But that time had been different. This time, for five straight nights I had held his naked form in my arms, and there had been nothing. Not so much as a hint of magick in him rising to meet mine.

Nothing.

Keven's gaze narrowed on me. "There was more that happened in Camlann," she said. It wasn't a question.

I closed my eyes. "Yes."

"I cannot help him if you don't tell me, milady."

I hesitated. A part of me knew she was right, but another part—

I became aware that the others had finished securing Lucan's limbs to the bed and returned their attention to me—and that they'd heard Keven's words. I tightened my arms around myself, bile rising in my throat at the thought of telling them about the full extent of Lucan's starvation. About his wife and child and the missing fingers. He wouldn't want them to know. I was certain of that.

I was equally certain, in the depths of my soul, that this was what held him back from healing.

I stared at the crossroads before me. Share a story that wasn't mine to tell, or allow this beautiful, magickal man to die? I exhaled a long, shuddering breath.

"I don't know if he'll remember, so you must never say anything to him," I said, my gaze traveling over those present, including them all in my ferocity. "Promise me."

"Milady," Keven began.

"*Promise*."

"Very well. You have my word."

I looked to the others again, and they each nodded in turn. Anne, Nia, Elysabeth, Maureen, Jeanne ... Bedivere, who glowered ferociously as he did.

I gritted my teeth and clenched my hands into fists. There was no way to phrase this delicately, and no reason to try.

"He was chained up in his own hut," I said, my voice flat, "with no food or water and the bodies of his wife and child within reach."

My stark words dropped like boulders into water, sending ripples outward that I couldn't stop, couldn't call back. Ripples of confusion, then slow understanding, and then dawning horror mixed with revulsion. One of the Crones—I couldn't tell which—gasped, and I squeezed my eyes shut, wincing at the sound.

Footsteps sounded. I opened my eyes in time to see a wordless Bedivere stalk out of the room—and then I felt the agony rolling outward from Keven. It slammed into me with all the force of the stone gargoyle herself, although she hadn't moved at all, and the magick that perpetually roved beneath my skin flared in response.

Too late, I remembered Keven's role in the deaths of Lucan's wife and son. Remembered that she'd taken the son's name as her own in memory of him—and of what she'd done. Shit. Well done, Claire. Well done.

I scowled at the tendrils of Earth reaching up through the floor to wind through me, the Fire uncoiling in my core. With more determination than control—I really was going to have to work on that part—I shoved the rogue magick back beneath my surface. I did *not* have the patience for that shit right now, and none of us had the time. Distantly, I registered the slam of the front door and surmised that Bedivere had left the house. I rested a hand on Keven's thickly muscled stone arm.

"Don't." I shook my head at her. "This wasn't on you, Keven."

The gargoyle shifted from one foot to the other, then back again, her great body swaying with her pain. Grief was etched in her every line as she shook her head. "The woman and child died at my hand, milady. It is very much on me."

My voice turned fierce. I would *not* let her blame herself. "It was a war, Keven, with Morok at its heart. *He* is the one to blame. For that, for this"—I waved my free hand at Lucan and then at the world in general—"for *all* of this. Him, not you, not me. *Him.*"

The truth of my own words jolted through me. In a flash, I saw how ready I'd been to take on blame myself. Blame for Lucan, for the mass exodus of the gods to our world, for

Freya's accusation … for all of it. I blinked at the insight—and then scowled at my own willingness to have accepted the responsibility.

Because taking responsibility was what I did. It was what I'd always done. What *we* had always done, I suspected, as I looked around at the group by Lucan's bed, because we'd been told our entire lives that we *were* responsible for just about anything that happened to or around us.

"Lies," my Edie-voice whispered. *"Deceit."*

The flash of insight turned blinding. Fucking Morok again.

I shook Keven's arm as well as one could shake a stone almost as large as oneself. It was enough to get her attention. "Lies," I told her, repeating my Edie-voice's words and willing her to understand them. "Deceit."

I tried not to think about the ways in which the words applied to all that I still held back from her. That was a problem for later, I told myself, because one crisis of faith at a time.

The gargoyle stared at me. For a moment, I was afraid that she wouldn't be able—or willing—to hear the truth, but the agony of self-recrimination in her gaze slowly faded, giving way to understanding. She heaved a great, shuddering sigh and lowered her head in a single nod of acceptance.

"Thank you, milady," she said quietly.

I nodded back, but my brain had already skipped several steps ahead. Because I might not be to blame for what had already happened, but I was still entirely responsible for what happened next. And I was still going to need help.

I half turned, so that my gaze could encompass the other women as well as Keven. "Freya is wrong," I said. "I'm not to blame for the tear in the divide, but I do have to try to fix it. And I need to try to fix him, too." I pointed at the bed. "Now that you know everything that happened to him, we can do that. We can—"

"Milady." Keven's voice cut me off.

It was a single word, but the ring of truth behind it was unequivocal. Irrefutable. In the space of one heavy, awful heartbeat, the very core of my being went still. I closed my eyes.

"You can't heal him," I said flatly. The magick crawled beneath my skin, over my body, through it, wanted to become it.

"I cannot heal what is not physical. No one can. He is lost inside himself right now, and only he can find his way back."

I wondered what would happen if the magick *did* become me. If I didn't contain it anymore. Would *it* be enough to make Lucan come back to me? I curled my hands into fists against the power that flared at the thought of release, against the ache of wanting.

"Don't," warned my Edie-voice.

As if she, too, sensed my rising magick and knew my thoughts, Keven added quietly, "He must *want* to return, milady."

"I can no longer protect you," Lucan's voice whispered. In my mind's eye, I saw again the profound sadness of his expression. I thought it had been regret, but what if it had been something more? Something else entirely?

What if it had been his farewell?

Out in the winter night, the mournful howl of a wolf rose and fell, rose again.

CHAPTER 11

MORNING BROUGHT A CONTINUING RUCKUS FROM ODIN'S CAMP (did they *ever* sleep?), a still-unconscious Lucan, the discovery that Harry had joined us in the bed and now snored against my side, and a headache from having cried myself to sleep.

After the others had left, I'd crept under the duvet and curled into Lucan's side to rest my head on his too-thin shoulder. Then, finally, I'd let fall the tears I hadn't wanted the others to see. Tears of loss and exhaustion—and of utter doubt.

Because beyond how I would manage without my shifter, another worry loomed: I wasn't sure I had another fight in me.

Fortunately—or unfortunately, depending on how I looked at it—the tears had ended and the damned, dogged resilience that had plagued my entire life had surfaced sometime during the night. I would have preferred it hadn't.

I lay on my back, one arm across my throbbing forehead and the other rubbing between Harry's ears as the dragon rumbled his approval. It was early enough to still be dark out, and beside me, Lucan's breathing was shallow and irregular. He hadn't moved during the night. Hadn't tried to turn over, hadn't tugged at his restraints, hadn't been aware of my presence at his side.

My grief at the thought of leaving him had given way to a small, quiet terror in the back of my mind. Would he still be here when I got back? Would I even *come* back?

I squeezed my eyes shut tighter. I didn't want to do this—any of it. I didn't want to leave Lucan or my family or Keven or Gus or Harry. I didn't want to face Cernunnos again so that I could battle my way into an increasingly hostile Otherworld. And I sure as shit didn't want to have to figure out how to repair a divide I hadn't even known existed until yesterday —or to face a formless, mindless Between and the horrifying monsters that I would prefer didn't exist at all.

This whole excursion was, in all likelihood, a fool's errand of epic proportions. Me, on my own, against all of that? The very idea was absurd.

But, as my damned dogged resilience had reminded me during the night, so had been my first foray into the Other-world. And my rescue of Lucan. And my destruction of Morok. And all of the other impossibilities that I had managed to overcome since learning I was Crone.

Footsteps passed by in the corridor, and the low murmur of voices reached me through the door. It was time to tell the Crones—tell my friends—the rest of my story and hope they would be able to find merit in the impossible. Giving Harry's ears a final rub, I rolled away from Lucan and reached for the bell cord to summon Keven.

KEVEN BROUGHT COFFEE FOR ME AND TEA FOR LUCAN, ALONG with the news that the ley lines had reappeared sometime during the night.

Lucan remained unconscious, but I untied his hands and, with the gargoyle's help, lifted him enough to trickle a little of the tea into his mouth. Once he'd swallowed, we settled him back onto the pillows. It wasn't much, but it would provide a little of the hydration that Jeanne had urged. I hadn't both-ered to remind her that he was a magickal creature in his own right and might not respond to standard nursing. First, because I didn't know that for sure; second, because it wouldn't hurt; and third, because I understood my friend's need to feel that she might still be in control of some small part of her life.

Emphasis on small, because the rest of this? So out of control.

Restraints in hand, I hesitated as I looked down on the shifter in the bed. Maybe—

"It is for his own protection, milady," Keven said gruffly. She took one of the strips of cloth that Anne had torn from a sheet from me and went around the bed to loop it around Lucan's right wrist.

Jaw tight, I wrapped the second strip around his left one. In silence, we secured both to the bedposts, and then Keven picked up the tray with Lucan's still mostly full cup.

"Will you come down for breakfast?" she asked.

"I'd rather eat here, if it's not too much trouble." I'd have preferred not to eat at all, but the damned, dogged resilience didn't think that was an option—and Keven wouldn't either, if I'd been brave enough to suggest it.

I wasn't.

"I will let the others know," she said, "and I'll bring a tray up shortly."

After she left, I took my mug of coffee with me to the window and sipped at it as I watched the light snow falling outside. The weather seemed to have had no dampening effect on Odin or his cohort, and I wondered how long it would be before someone from the outside world heard and came to investigate.

I shuddered at the thought. And at the repercussions that would surely follow, just as they had followed the other gods' and goddess' presence in the world, which was a whole other problem. It would have been nice if my subconscious could have solved that one for me while I was sleeping, too.

I took another sip of coffee. It was surprisingly good, which meant that someone other than Keven had likely taken over making it. Try as I might, I'd never been able to convince the gargoyle not to boil the stuff.

A tap sounded at the open door of the bedchamber, and I looked over my shoulder to find Jeanne and the Crones gathered there.

"Keven said you were up," Jeanne said. "May we?"

She gestured into the room, and I nodded. "Of course."

The five women filed in, each of them glancing toward the shifter in the bed as they passed, each of their gazes lingering on the restraints before turning to me, heavy with questions.

"No change?" Anne asked.

"No. He hasn't woken up at all."

"And you?" Elysabeth's voice was gentle. "Are you okay?"

I considered the many possible answers to the question, decided I didn't particularly like any of them, and instead waved at the chairs they'd occupied the evening before. "We need to talk," I said, by way of response. "I have something I need to tell—"

The slam of the front hall door cut me off and sent a tremble through the house—not a vibration, but an actual tremble. Right down to the structure's foundations rooted in the magick of Earth itself. The power in me snarled in return, and I steadied my grip on it.

Freya was back. And judging by the thud of boots, she was in a mood—and coming upstairs.

Fucking hell. I wasn't ready for her. I mean, I wasn't sure one could ever be ready for a force like Freya, but I was especially unprepared right now. I'd wanted a chance to talk to the Crones and Jeanne first. To tell them the rest of what had happened to me in Camlann and hope it was enough to convince them and myself that it might—*might*—mean I had a snowball's chance in hell of—

The bedchamber door slammed open with only slightly less force than the front door had and bounced off the stone wall beside it. The house cringed again. I forced down shoulders that had climbed up to my ears and made myself meet the ice-blue gaze with all the calm I could muster.

"Good mor—" I began.

"How?" the Norse goddess snapped without preamble. She crossed her arms across her armored chest. "How will you fix the divide?"

"Honestly? I have no idea."

"And yet you demand that I leave here and go with you."

"I ask that you fight for your own world with me, yes. If I really did tap into some other power as you said, then maybe I can do it again. Maybe *we* can."

Freya scowled. "You don't even know what you did in the first place. How can you possibly hope to do it again? To hold back what we as gods and goddesses could not? You, a mere mortal, alone and—"

"If you and the others are with me, I won't *be* alone."

"And what about *them*?" She pointed at the semicircle of women watching our debate. "Who will remain here to protect them from these Mages they so fear?"

"Are you saying that *you* would do so if you stayed?" I raised a skeptical eyebrow. She snorted, and I waved away whatever words might have followed. "It doesn't matter, because they won't need protection. I can teach them what they need to know. Enough to fight the Mages until I can repair the divide and return to help them."

Five sets of eyebrows as skeptical as my own shot up, and the Crones and Jeanne exchanged a flurry of glances.

Freya regarded me for a moment, then strolled across the room, sauntering between Elysabeth and Maureen to circle me slowly. I would have liked to have said that I held myself still through sheer force of will, but the truth was that Earth had seized my ankles and wound up through my legs to hold me immobile, and I couldn't make it release its grip.

My calm demeanor was becoming more challenging with every passing second.

"You're different," Freya said at last.

My Edie-voice snorted. *"She has no idea."*

I frowned, momentarily distracted from the goddess. Was it just my imagination, or was that voice sounding more and more like actual Edie every time it spoke?

"Not your imagination," the voice said, and I rolled my eyes at it. Because obviously I wasn't going to trust the voice to tell me that it was—

Freya stopped in front of me, studying me as she would something she'd scraped off her boot. The voice and I would have to finish our discussion later.

"Something happened in Camlann," the Norse goddess said. "Something more than the powers of the witch Morgana. What have you not told us?"

I wondered what my odds of success would be if I tried to send her away until after I'd spoken to the others. Then I decided not to waste my breath. I'd only have to tell her the story as well, at some point, so I might as well get it over with.

I would not, however, tell it alone.

I tugged again at Earth. It released me this time, and I walked carefully around the bed and set my coffee mug on the nightstand. Then, taking a seat in the chair beside Lucan, I reached for the hand tied to the post nearest me. There was no response from him, but the simple act of touching him, of feeling his skin against mine, anchored me. Reminded me that I was still the Claire he had believed in.

"You're right," I said. "There was more in Camlann than I'd expected." I turned my attention from Freya to the Crones, because this part of the story belonged to them. "The pendants the Morrigan gave us here held only a fraction of her powers. The rest of her magick was divided in that first splinter, just as Morok's were, and half of them remained there."

"Half …?" Anne breathed the word, her eyes wide with shock. "But how? And how do you know?"

"She hid them," I said. "In—"

The crash of metal and pottery hitting stone cut me off, and I jerked my head around to find Keven in the doorway, Gus curled around her neck as if he'd never been away from her. An empty tray dangled from one granite hand, its contents splattered across the floor at her feet amid utensils and bowl shards. A dozen emotions shifted across her expression. She hadn't yet asked if I had found Morgana's form—*her* form—in Camlann, and I hadn't yet told her, because I hadn't known how to explain leaving her behind there, and now it was too late to find a way. Too late to be gentle.

Now she knew.

"Me," she said, her voice rougher than usual. "She hid them in me. I remember now. And you found me."

"You found *me*," I corrected. Tears stung the backs of my eyes, and my throat ached with grief for her—both for the gargoyle she had become and the woman she remembered. "You were wonderful and brave and knew just what to do, and —and I'm sorry, Keven, but I couldn't bring her back to you. I had Lucan and … "

And I made a choice, said the silence into which my words trailed off. *I chose Lucan over you.*

"I'm sorry," I whispered again, my grip tightening on the hand of the broken man I'd brought home with me instead of the whole woman who might have been. My choice was both something I would make again and something that would forever haunt me, and words did not exist to explain that to the former Crone who had sacrificed so much.

For a long moment, Keven stood with head bowed, staring at the mess on the floor at her feet. No one in the room moved or spoke. Even Freya had the grace to remain quiet and give the gargoyle space to process the revelation into which she'd walked. At last, a gravelly sigh gusted from the hulking figure.

"You did the right thing, milady," the gargoyle said, her voice devoid of inflection of any kind. "It is best this way. I'll fetch rags and clean this up. And more soup." She turned to go.

"Keven."

She looked back at me, and I cringed from the vastness of the loss behind the stone eyes. The grief.

"Your magick," I said. "Maybe we can try to——"

The ponderous head shook. "No. It belongs to you now, milady. I trust you will use it wisely."

She shuffled down the corridor, her steps slower than I'd ever heard them, and her words lingering in the air. In my mind. In my guilt-ridden heart.

I trust you.

I had no time to wallow in them, however, because with the gargoyle gone, Freya rounded on me in the fury she had harbored for millennia for the goddess who had bedded her husband. Rounded on me, drew her sword, and lunged.

"The *Morrigan*," she hissed. "You're the *Morrigan*."

CHAPTER 12

FOR THE SECOND TIME IN THE SPACE OF MINUTES, A CRASH reverberated through the room. This time, it was accompanied by the sound of glass falling onto the stone floor—and by the rush of wings as a murder of crows exploded through the window and swirled around Freya.

The Norse goddess changed target mid-swing, and the sword hissed past my ear to swing in an arc above her head. But the crows flapped out of reach and then coalesced into a solid black cloud between us. The cloud shifted, took form, and became—

"*You!*" Freya spat.

"Oh, give it a rest, Freya," the Morrigan said wearily, waving long, slender fingers tipped with black nails at her. "I was hardly his first dalliance, now, was I?"

"Dalliance! *Dalliance?*" Freya's sword sliced through the air and came to a stop at the side of the Morrigan's long white neck, its blade quivering with the fury that radiated from its wielder.

The Morrigan didn't flinch. Freya didn't pull back. I wondered if one goddess really could kill another.

"*One wonders if it would be a loss if they did,*" muttered my Edie-voice that sounded like actual Edie. But it couldn't be, because Edie had crossed the veil before I'd even gone to the Otherworld. Could she really have come back? But how? And why?

"*First of all, duh,*" said the voice. "*Second, it's called magick for a reason, and third, because it's also called friendship for a reason.*"

There are moments in life where sheer gratitude seems to fill a heart so full that it feels like it might actually burst. Realizing that I had my friend back—relatively speaking—was one of those moments. Immediately getting yanked back into the goddess-war without time to savor the leap of pure joy that I felt … was not.

"… not just a dalliance, you feathered freak," Freya was snarling, "and you know it. If it hadn't been for you—"

"If it hadn't been for me, you'd still be excusing his seductions and pretending you didn't care, and for what? A place in his shadow?" the Morrigan mocked. "You're better than that, Freya. Or you could be, if you'd get out of your own way."

The Norse goddess's face turned an interesting shade of purple, and I decided it was time to intervene before my death question was answered. I released my grip on Lucan's hand, levered myself up from the chair to stand between the women, and pushed Freya's blade away from the Morrigan's neck.

"Enough," I said wearily. "Just … enough. For goddess's sake."

I almost laughed at my use of that phrase under the circumstances but decided that any humor in this situation was a figment of my exhaustion. I shook off both as best I could, because nothing about the situation was funny, and I had no time for tiredness. I focused on Freya.

"Whatever I've done, I'm going to try to undo. If I have to do it alone—"

"You won't," said Anne from the other side of the bed. "We'll do everything we can to help, and I'm sure the midwitches will, too. You'll need us to open the portal, remember?"

And to go up against Cernunnos again, but she didn't say that. She didn't need to. The grim expressions on Jeanne's and the other Crones' faces left no doubt that they remembered. Despite having to face the horned god again, however, they all still nodded agreement with Anne … and then regarded the two goddesses with varying degrees of sadness.

No, I thought. Not sadness. Disillusionment. It was a hard blow, discovering that those you'd held in such high esteem—worshiped, even—had feet of clay. I understood it well, after learning about the origin of gods from Freya in the Other-world. Her words were imprinted on my memory forever: *"Did you not hear what I told you? About how we began? We were as human as any of you, Claire Emerson.* You're *the ones who insisted on placing us on pedestals. We've always fought amongst ourselves—for reasons of love, lust, revenge, greed, power."*

I would share that story with the Crones later, too, but for now, I returned to the goddess problem at hand.

"If *we* have to do it alone," I told Freya and the Morrigan, even though it would be only me doing the actual crossing into the Otherworld, "then we will. But given that *we* are not the ones who started this entire mess, we could use your help."

I caught back the *please* that hovered on my lips, because I was damned if I would beg. The goddesses might still be more powerful than I was—well, Freya might be, I thought, remembering that I now possessed the bulk of the Morrigan's powers, even if I couldn't control them—but they had lost most, if not all, of the awe I'd once held for them. Not to mention any modicum of respect.

Freya's nostrils flared and her head drew back, as if she knew what I was thinking and hadn't ruled out decapitating me on the spot. I raised my own chin in response and met her glare for glare, remembering who—and what—she really was and trying not to let the slither of magick beneath my skin find its way out.

This time, it was the Morrigan who intervened in *our* standoff. Or at least distracted us from it.

"Agreed," she said. "I will accompany you."

"As you should," Freya growled, "because this whole mess is on you. I, on the other hand—" She stopped as the strains of the unending, raucous, drunken party in the woods suddenly increased in volume, with Odin's voice rising above the others. Her gaze swiveled to the Morrigan, and for an instant, her expression darkened with renewed wrath.

I sensed the gathering of power in her and put myself between her and the bed. Fire roiled at my core, ready to shield Lucan and the others from her temper. The Morrigan allowed her gown to become a fluttering of crows again, as if preparing for a quick exit. I braced for the worst but got the completely unexpected.

Freya snarled what sounded like it might be the Norse equivalent of *fucking hell* and slid her sword back into its scabbard at her hip.

"Fine," she snapped. "I will help. But only if it means *he* is the first to be returned to the Otherworld once we secure it, because I know damned well he won't join us voluntarily."

"Agreed," I said, and the entire room—occupants and house included—breathed a sigh of relief.

Then came more questions.

THERE WERE DOZENS OF THEM, RANGING FROM HOW TO WHY to what I thought we should do first. In the aftermath of the face-off with Freya and the Morrigan, their weight—and the weight of the expectations behind them—pressed in on me from every side. For a moment, panic held my brain immobile. I might have the powers of a goddess, but I was still human and this—all of this—was hardly within the purview of a grandmother who would, quite frankly, rather be baking cookies right now.

I raised both hands to my temples to massage the headache that had returned—surprise, surprise—and tried to tune out the words beating against me. A part of me yearned to crawl back into bed beside Lucan; another part of me recoiled from the idea. Now that I'd made the decision to move forward without him—

I looked around at a touch on my arm and grimaced at Jeanne. It was supposed to have been a smile, but ...

"You okay?" she asked.

I snorted. "Is there such a thing anymore?"

"It's"—her gaze went past me to the Crones and goddesses who had shifted, mercifully, to a heated discussion amongst themselves—"a lot."

"That it is, my friend," I agreed. "That it is."

"How can I help?"

"There's nothing ..."

I trailed off. I'd started to say that there was nothing she could do, that it was my problem, but ... was it? I regarded the woman who had asked. Who had never wanted to be a part of any of this, who had actively turned her back on both it and me after delivering the Book of the Fifth Crone to me, only to return when she was most needed. She'd taken on Cernunnos himself in the cavern, saved the Crones and midwitches there, found a way to bring me and Lucan—and Gus and Harry—back to the house and these amazing, determined women, and—

And fucking hell. I blinked as the proverbial light bulb went on in my brain, illuminating Jeanne and the Crones in a whole new way. I'd seriously thought of myself as being alone in this? When these women had all had my back the entire time? Dear goddess, I needed to give my head a shake. But later, because right now? Right now, Jeanne was right. I needed help.

"I don't know," I told her instead. "Because I don't know where to begin. There's so much—"

"Triage," she said.

"What?"

"Triage. It's what we do in the ER when we have multiple injuries come in and we can't look after everyone at once." She peered over the rims of her glasses at me, then looked pointedly at the others. "You have multiple injuries. Which one is the most critical that you can do something about right now?"

Conversation stopped as her words registered with the Crones and goddesses as well as with me. The question kicked my brain into gear, and I started making a mental list of issues that needed to be dealt with. Teaching the Crones how to access elemental magick without the aid of the Morrigan's pendants was one of the biggest, of course, but that would take time. Telling them the full extent of what had happened to me in Camlann, but that could wait a little longer—and not just because I was avoiding it. Learning how to control my own powers was pretty high on the list, but—

"The other gods," said Freya. "The ones who have already come through. We'll need them to come back with us to the Otherworld, too. Someone needs to bring them here." Her gaze turned to the Morrigan. Mine followed.

The suggestion made sense—and so did the idea of sending the Morrigan.

The black-gowned goddess stared down her nose at me. "I hope you're not suggesting that *I* be your messenger. Send *her*."

"I will stay to teach the Crones," Freya said.

"*I* will teach—"

The Norse goddess snorted, not very helpfully. "You cannot teach what you can barely access yourself anymore."

I intervened before things devolved back to the sword-blade-at-someone's-neck stage. "It's a good idea," I said. "And it would be the most helpful one. The ley lines have returned —you can still travel them, can't you?"

The Morrigan was unswayed by my attempt at stroking her ego. "That's beside the point."

"It's exactly the point, because the only other ones here who can do that are me and him." I pointed to Bedivere, who had at some point come unnoticed into the room and taken up his usual post beside the window—which, I noticed with a start of surprise, the house had already repaired. A testament to its growing skills, or to the amount of practice I kept inadvertently throwing at it?

"The gods won't listen to me," I told the Morrigan. "And I doubt they'll give a wolf-shifter the time of day, either. No offense, Bedivere."

The wolf-shifter in question grunted.

"They're not likely to heed me, either," the Morrigan pointed out. "I am hardly well regarded by my peers."

I refrained from asking whose fault that was, held up a finger to ward off the questions I sensed forming among the Crones who had once served the goddess, and then shrugged. "That may be, but you're still the best chance we've got."

Freya would actually be the best chance, but even if I had a hope in hell of convincing her to take on the task, the Norse goddess was right about her being the better teacher for the Crones. And if she could do that, maybe I could start working on my control issues.

"The magickal control ones, anyway," said the Edie-voice that —oh yes, with that kind of snark—was really, truly Edie. I mentally rolled my eyes at her.

"Would it not be better that I remain here, to help teach the magick to your Crones?" The Morrigan was still frowning, but less fiercely.

"I can do that. Perhaps not as well as you might," I lied for the sake of her ego, "but well enough, and I can't do the other at all. The gods will listen to you."

The Morrigan's already-thin lips pressed together until they almost disappeared as she weighed my arguments. I played my final ego card.

"Please," I said.

"*Fine*," the Morrigan snarled, and with a grumble I couldn't make out and a toss of her long black hair, she dissolved into a murder, spiraled above our heads, and swept out the window that Bedivere threw open for her.

My shoulders sagged in relief, and the rest of me followed suit.

CHAPTER 13

IN THE RELATIVE CALM FOLLOWING THE MORRIGAN'S departure—relative, because Odin's party continued unabated, but at least we no longer had two goddesses sniping at one another—Jeanne frog-marched me toward my chair beside Lucan's bed.

"You need to sit before you fall down," she said, unceremoniously pushing me into the seat and tucking a blanket over my lap. "You can have some of the tea Keven made for Lucan, and then you can take a nap."

"I'm fine," I said. "And we need to—"

"*We* need to be at our best if we're going to do what you suggest," my friend said tartly, "and *you* are most assuredly not anywhere near that. Keven and Freya can get us started, and tomorrow, if you're feeling up to it—"

"I—"

"*If* you're feeling up to it," she repeated, hands on ample hips, "we can work on a plan. Together."

I wanted to argue with her—and I did *not* want to leave Freya unsupervised—but with the way the chair held me in place and the blanket's warmth spread over me and the others nodded agreement and my entire body wanted to curl into a fetal position ...

Perhaps Jeanne had a point.

"*Ya think?*" asked Edie.

"Fine," I told them both, "but only a short one. We don't have time for more."

Every inch her ER nurse persona, Jeanne ignored me and ushered the others out of the room, including the Norse goddess, whose lack of objection would have surprised me if I'd had the energy to be surprised. Now that I'd succumbed to the rest idea, however, fatigue had sunk merciless claws into me, and it was all I could do not to fall out of the chair. Who knew managing unruly deities could be so exhausting?

And you've only just begun, the voice observed.

Nope. Didn't have the energy for that train of thought, either.

My gaze went to the bed and the man tied to it. A shell of the protector I'd once had and the companion I had come to love. Lost, Keven had called him. Somewhere inside himself where none of us could reach. Where not even my magick could find him.

Digging deep, I scraped together enough remnants of fading stamina to lean forward and lift Lucan's hand from the pillow it rested on. I cradled it between my own as I rested elbows on knees, letting my awareness shrink to just him. Just us.

"Where have you gone?" I murmured. "Did you come back with me at all, or …"

I trailed off, unable to finish, to give voice to the fear that Keven might be wrong. That he wasn't lost inside himself but not there at all. That I'd left some vital part of him behind— his very essence, perhaps—to be devoured by the Between along with the rest of Camlann.

But no. I let out a shuddering breath. If that had happened, he wouldn't have known me at all. Wouldn't have been able to tell me that something was coming or tell me to run. No, he was in there somewhere, and he just needed to—

A cup of tea appeared in front of my nose, and I blinked at it, then at the stone hand holding it. I lifted my gaze to the hand's owner. The tears that had prickled before spilled over my lashes.

"I'm sorry," I whispered to my gargoyle. "I'm so, so sorry."

Keven's mouth curved into a grimace, the closest thing to a smile that granite would allow, and for a moment, the same memories I'd seen in Morgana's eyes in Camlann reflected back at me in hers. Memories of wisdom and sacrifice and love, memories of the woman she had been and the gargoyle she had become ... memories of not one but two lifetimes.

"You did the right thing," she told me again, and this time her rough voice carried the ring of conviction. "Now drink, and then sleep. Jeanne is right. You need rest before anything else."

"It's not working," Maureen's voice grumbled from somewhere outside the cocoon of the duvet wrapped around me, "because it *can't* work. We have some magick, yes, but we're not Crone anymore. We have no hope of achieving what Claire has."

"You may not have what Lady Claire has, but make no mistake: You *are* Crones," replied Keven's gravelly tones. "A crone, by definition, is a woman of wisdom and power. That is you. That is all of you."

You tell them, Keven, I thought.

Someone sighed.

Duvet, my mind belatedly registered. I was in bed. I didn't remember getting here myself, so Keven must have ... and that labored breathing beside me was ...

I turned my head to the right, and my heart contracted sharply at the sight of what remained of Lucan.

It was obvious at a glance that he'd slipped further away from me than ever. His mouth had fallen open behind his beard, his gaunt cheeks billowed in and out with each breath, and his gray-tinged skin had drawn taut over the bones of his skull. I was losing him. With every shallow, ragged inhale and exhale, I was losing him.

The murmur of voices intruded again.

"—you mean well, Keven," Anne was saying, "but we've been over this a dozen times. The fact remains that just because we're old doesn't mean we're any more powerful than your average midwitch, and no midwitch is equipped to go up against the Mages. We simply can't do it."

Part of me—that damnably resilient part—prodded at me to sit up and tell the Crones what Freya had told me in Camlann but had obviously failed to share with them ... about the gods and goddesses once having been human themselves, separated from us by little more than our own human superstitions about the magick they wielded.

It was the same magick we all had access to, that made the Crones absolutely more powerful than the midwitches they called themselves. The midwitches were likewise more powerful, but we didn't have time to train them as well, right now.

Another part of me wanted to remain silent, cocooned in the warmth of the duvet that I shared with Lucan and pretending that I was still sleeping. Just for a little while longer. While I could, because—

Nia's voice tore open the cocoon. "If Freya is right about Claire being distracted by Lucan, maybe she'll be more focused once we bring him back. Maybe she won't need us to—"

I flailed my way upright in the bed. "We can bring him back?" I demanded.

All five women jumped, and Maureen clapped both hands over her heart. "Dear goddess, woman, you damn near gave me heart failure, popping up like that!"

I ignored her, trying to untangle my feet from the duvet so that I could stand. "How?" I asked. "How can we bring him back?"

Anne cleared her throat. "We don't know for—"

"*How?*"

Five silent faces regarded me. Six, if I counted Keven. I did.

I stopped fighting with the duvet and turned my glare on her, hope warring with a dozen different emotions in my chest —uppermost of which were anger at having been told there *was* no hope and fear of having that hope taken away again. No, not fear. Terror. Heartsick terror.

"You said we couldn't heal him," I accused.

The gargoyle sighed and came around the bed to the nightstand on my side. "*We* can't," she said, taking a mug from the little table and handing it to me. "But *you* may be able to reach him and lead him back."

My glare turned to a gape, and I took the mug from her automatically. "I can do that? With my magick? But why didn't you tell me before?"

"It was not something I considered ... possible."

"And now?"

"Freya has convinced me otherwise. And she has offered her help."

I narrowed my eyes, suspicion rearing up in me. "Freya," I repeated. "Freya *offered* help? Why?"

"Because I'm not as heartless as you apparently think I am," came the grumpy retort as the goddess in question stomped into the room. She rounded the bed and slammed a bowl onto the nightstand beside Lucan. Some of the contents —soup, it looked like—sloshed over the edge and onto the wood, and the goddess crossed her arms and glared at me, as if daring me to comment.

I did, but not about the soup. "I'm just surprised," I said. "You haven't exactly been the biggest fan of my ideas so far—"

"Because they're not good ideas."

I refrained—just—from rolling my eyes and sipped at the tea Keven had given me. "They might be, if you'd give them a chance."

"I spent three hours giving them a chance. It's useless.

What you want from *them*"—she waved her fingers disdainfully at the Crones and Jeanne—"cannot be done."

I really wanted to return to the topic of bringing Lucan back from wherever he was, but I couldn't let her words pass unchallenged. "Because you didn't tell them the most important part, damn it. They don't know—"

"I can, however, help bring *him* back to you."

Or maybe we could focus on that first. I clenched my fingers around the mug, wrestling with my conscience.

"She's trying to distract you," my Edie-voice muttered. *"I don't trust her."*

I know, I thought back, *and I don't either, but* ...

But Lucan.

I hesitated some more. Would it hurt to have the Crones wait a little longer to find out how the whole god/goddess thing really worked? Or at least to find out what Freya was talking about?

"How?" I asked, but because I'd told my Edie-voice the truth about not trusting the goddess, I directed the query to the Crones rather than her.

All four of them tried to answer at once. I managed to pick out a handful of words from the jumble—*bond, magick, joining, powerful*—before the Norse goddess bellowed over them.

"Enough! It is my idea, and *I* will tell her."

Now *that* sounded more like Freya. I drew my knees up under the duvet and rested the mug of tea on them. "Fine," I said. "Then tell me."

The goddess drew herself up, smiled with what I could only term smugness, and delivered her triumphant announcement as I sipped from the mug again.

"Sex magic," she said.

I sprayed my mouthful of tea across the bed.

CHAPTER 14

"SEX MAGICK?" I SPUTTERED, WHEN JEANNE STOPPED
pounding me on the back and I stopped coughing.

I was suddenly aware of the man beside me as I never had
been before—okay fine, as I'd at least tried to avoid thinking
of him … most of the time. I scrambled from the bed, forgetting that the duvet was still wrapped around my legs, and the
mug and its contents sailed across the room and splattered
against the wall. Keven's hand caught me before I joined
them.

I clung to her as I gaped at the Norse goddess, then each
of the Crones and Jeanne in turn. They weren't serious, were
they? They couldn't be serious. I waited for someone to laugh.
Smile. Look away. None of them did.

I blinked at them. "You *are* serious. That's—that's an
actual *thing*?"

"Thing?" Freya echoed.

I released Keven's arm and flapped a hand. "Real," I
croaked. "It's real?"

The goddess scowled. "Of course it's real. Why in the
world would I make it up?"

I looked to the Crones for confirmation. Only Jeanne—
unsurprisingly, given her conservative religious roots—avoided
my gaze. The others met and held it, each in turn, each
nodding affirmation. I turned my gape back to Freya.

"But—how?" I asked.

One blond eyebrow shot up. "You must be joking. You've
borne a child, have you not?"

Heat that had nothing to do with Fire flooded my limbs
and scorched my cheeks. "Of course I know *how*," I muttered.
"But … *how*?" I waved at the unconscious man tied to the bed.

The unconscious man that Nia and Elysabeth were currently *un*tying.

I swallowed hard. "I can't very well just—you know."

"Actually, you could," the goddess corrected, "but magick without mutual consent is corrupt. Dark." She shuddered at the idea—or perhaps at a memory—and nodded at the nightstand she'd set the bowl on. "We'll need to wake him first. That's what the soup is for. I had the witch make it for him."

By *the witch*, she meant Baba Yaga, and I winced on Keven's behalf, knowing how she felt about the other's presence in her kitchen. But the gargoyle grunted as she met my concern.

"The witch is skilled in ways I am not," she said. "And the goddess is right. This may be the only way to heal the mutt."

The gruffness behind her voice belied her seemingly harsh choice of words. The very fact that she had referred to Lucan as *the mutt* again showed how much she cared about the shifter —and how hard she tried to distance herself from that caring.

Nia and Elysabeth went to work on the ties at Lucan's feet, while Anne and Jeanne propped extra pillows beneath his head and shoulders, and I tried to wrap my head around the situation. The whole, entire, bizarre—

The complicity of the others suddenly registered, and my gaze traveled the group again. "You were all in on this? You all knew? You discussed me and Lucan and—and—"

My embarrassment knew no bounds, and I couldn't say the words again. I just couldn't. I'd made no effort to hide my feelings for Lucan, but neither had I gone out of my way to advertise them, and the idea that I—that he—that we had been talked about in the manner Keven suggested ...

The weight of mortification spread through my limbs. I wasn't sure I could look the gargoyle in the eye ever again. Fuck that. I was never looking *anyone* in the eye again. And I sure as hell wasn't—

"No," I said. Shaking my head, I retreated to the fireplace

and its warm, crackling comfort. "I just—no. We're not— Lucan and I aren't—"

Jeanne sighed, breaking into my jumble of thoughts. Forgetting my just-made vow, I lifted my gaze to hers.

"Yes," she said, her voice both prim and firm at the same time. "You are. We've all seen how you feel about him, Claire. As for how he feels about you, I could see that the first time I met him. Remember? On your front porch? You care for him, and he cares for you, and this is how you get him back."

Something about hearing it from Jeanne, of all people— and in such a matter-of-fact way—made it more real. Gave it more weight. Made it begin to settle into my core. Heat stirred in me again, but this time, it wasn't entirely born of embarrassment.

Freya cleared her throat, and I turned to her.

"The bond between you and the shifter is powerful," she said. "It may be enough."

"And if it's not?"

"If it's not, we hasten the inevitable." The goddess shrugged. "Either way, it is for the best. He is a distraction to you as he is, and we—they"—she nodded at the Crones— "need your focus."

Her words were akin to an accusation. They sliced through me, leaving a jagged gash in my heart. I wanted to deny them, but I could not. Harsh though they might be, they were also justified, because had I not just lain in bed and tried to pretend that I was still sleeping so that I could spend a few more minutes beside Lucan? Had I not just chosen the possibility of saving him over the necessity of saving the rest of the world?

Surprisingly—astonishingly—Freya's blue eyes, normally as cold as the ice they reminded me of, softened. "I am more than just a goddess of war, Claire Emerson. I would not suggest this if I did not think it would work. The bond you have with your shifter *is* strong. There is magick not only in you, but in that. You must at least try."

The reminder that she was the goddess of love and fertility didn't have more impact than her other words, but they helped to mitigate them. Because while the fertility part didn't apply to me at this stage of life, the love part ...

I dropped my gaze to the man in the bed, taking in the long hair splayed against the pillow. The beard that seemed never to grow longer or shorter. The thick lashes fanned against too-prominent cheekbones.

I remembered the glint of humor in the warm amber eyes, the deep rumble of his voice, the strength of the arms that had held me and kept me from falling apart. Yes, there had been a rush of long-dormant hormones when I'd first met him, but there had been more, too. There had always been more. Something greater. Something ...

"Magick," I murmured.

"Yes," said Freya, and from the corner of my eye, I saw her motion to Keven.

The gargoyle lumbered around the bed to the bowl of soup on the nightstand. She held a granite hand out over the bowl, the way I'd seen her do when she concocted her healing salves. But there were no sparks or fizzles this time, only a nod of satisfaction on her part as she gave silent approval to what Baba Yaga and Freya had done. Then, taking the bowl in her right hand, she slid her other arm under Lucan's shoulders and cradled him against her as she brought the soup to his lips.

"Drink," she ordered gruffly.

There was no response, and my heart shuddered. Were we too late? Was he too far gone even for—

Lucan's lips parted a fraction of an inch, and Keven tipped a little of the liquid into his mouth. Seconds slid past, and then the entire room—including the house, I thought—

breathed a sigh of relief as the muscles in his throat moved in a swallow.

A barely discernible vibration started in my belly. Did he know what Freya had suggested? Had he understood the intent? The vibration became a tingle, spreading through my veins, my limbs. The fact that he cooperated with Keven, that he drank the potion, did it mean he …?

Lucan's eyelashes fluttered, and then, for the first time since before Camlann, his eyes stared into mine with the warmth I remembered. The warmth I had craved. The warmth I hadn't known until now how very much I had needed to see again.

The air in my lungs went as still as the rest of me, frozen in the moment. Held captive by the recognition that reached out to me from the amber depths. A tremor of pure, utter joy traveled through my belly and along my limbs. The man I had once known was still there, still in him—and might yet come back to me.

Drawing her granite arm out from under his shoulders, Keven let Lucan settle back onto the pillows. She shambled toward the door, bowl in hand, and closed it as she stepped out into the hallway. The others, including Freya, had already gone, although I had neither heard nor seen their departure. A new silence settled over the bedchamber, with only the crackle of the fire to break it.

"Claire."

My name was hoarse on his lips but music to my ears. I drew a shuddering breath, wrestling with the threatening tears, the tightness that wanted to deny my voice, the tentative, fragile hope that had sprung to life in my chest.

"I don't want to lose you," I said. "Please—"

My throat closed against the plea I'd been about to make, and a tear slid down my cheek, leaving a cool path in its wake. I watched the war taking place in the depths of the familiar, beloved amber eyes, saw the horror that lived inside him at what he had done to his wife. It didn't matter that his actions had been driven by Morok's possession of him. It would never matter, because Lucan would have to live with the knowledge of the atrocity and the memories that would never, ever leave him.

Lucan alone had to decide whether he could do that. Whether he wanted to return to me. To stay with me. Not because he felt he had to, but because he wanted to. I could do nothing more than make the offer.

Of their own accord, my arms crossed over my belly and my hands grasped the folds of my robe and pulled it over my head. For a split second, the gaze I shared with Lucan was broken, and I faltered as I emerged from the fabric.

I clutched the robe's fading warmth to my naked chest and shivered as a lifetime of insecurities bubbled to the surface of my mind. A lifetime of doubts underscored by ... well, a lifetime. I'd never had the body I thought I should have had to begin with, and childbearing and several decades hadn't improved it. And while Lucan might be centuries old, he was still physically younger than I was by twenty or more years. Even after his ordeal, he was fit. Muscled. Beautiful. Whereas I ... I was not.

I was soft. My belly and breasts and arms and thighs sagged under the toll of age and gravity, and—dear goddess, what was I thinking, standing here like this? What could I possibly offer this man? Why in all the world would he—

Stop, whispered a voice deep inside my brain. It wasn't Edie's voice. It wasn't *a* voice at all. It was more like many voices, the ones that belonged to the ancestors—to all the women who had come before me, who had borne similar doubts and similar fears and judged themselves as I did. As every woman I'd ever known did.

Stop, they said again, and I listened, and in the quiet that followed, clarity descended, bringing calm and strength with it.

Oh goddess, the strength.

It came with an understanding that surpassed any I'd ever known. An understanding—a *knowing*—that this, what Lucan and I were about to share, was about more than desire and far, far more than my body or his. It was about completion. It was about Lucan and me, coming together in a rite as ancient as the Earth itself. It was magick. It was power.

It was *us*.

In the bed, Lucan lifted aside the duvet with a shaking hand, but his eyes had drifted closed again, and my breath snagged in my throat. His strength was failing. If we were going to do this, it was now or …

My robe fell to the floor, taking the last of my inhibitions with it, and I slid beneath the duvet and reached for him.

CHAPTER 15

I woke to sun streaming through the window, Keven pulling back the drapes, and an unfamiliar weight across my torso. I frowned, and then confusion gave way to memory, and memory to a flush of warmth, and then both to awkward discomfort as the gargoyle turned toward the bed. I hadn't faced a morning after in decades, and I'd never faced one where a third party was present.

"Um ..." I said. I peeked sideways at the figure tangled in the duvet with me. More accurately, half-tangled, as most of his torso was bared, along with a goodly part of one hip and a lean, muscled thigh. The memories surfaced again, warm and heavy and—

"The others are waiting for you in the sitting room. There is coffee there." Keven said, as if finding me naked in bed with Lucan was an everyday occurrence. She stooped to pick up my robe from the floor on the shifter's side of the bed and dropped it beside me on her way to the door.

My frown returned. No, she wasn't behaving as if this was an everyday occurrence ... it was more like she was doing her best to pretend it hadn't happened at all. Like she was avoiding the very idea, not to mention my gaze. Sudden misgiving gripped me, twisting my belly into a knot.

It hadn't worked. The magick hadn't worked. Lucan was—

"Wait," I said as Keven opened the door, because she couldn't seriously be leaving me alone with—

"Keven, wait!" I called out again, my voice strangled in my own ears.

But she didn't wait, and she did leave. The door closed

behind her, shutting me in the room—in the bed—along with a gut-punch of despair and the body of—

"Claire."

As fast as misgiving and despair had set in, relief was blessedly faster. And far, far more welcome. It washed through me, surfacing as tears in my eyes that I blinked away as I turned my head on the pillow to face the man beside me. I drank in the angles and planes of the familiar face and stared into the amber eyes I hadn't been able to look into for far, far too long. Joy bubbled up in my core and did a little dance along my veins. Dear goddess, it was good to see him.

I smiled through my tears. "You're alive," I whispered.

But there was no return smile, and the expression in his eyes wasn't one of warmth as much as it was ... horror? The dance of joy in my veins slowed, then stopped. Foreboding landed with a sickening thud in my belly.

"Lucan? What's wrong?"

"What are you doing here?" he asked.

My mouth flapped as I struggled for words, for an explanation ... for a reason *why* I needed an explanation. Lucan pulled his arm away, leaving my body as cold on the outside as it had turned on the inside.

"Claire," he gritted, "why are you in my bed?"

He doesn't know? My heart lurched. *He doesn't remember? Shit!*

"Fuck," Edie agreed.

He didn't remember, and he very obviously didn't want me here.

Because of course he didn't.

Because dear goddess, what had I been thinking?

Mortification held me immobile under a gaze that could only be termed accusatory—and then galvanized me into action. I stumbled out of the bed, hyperaware of my nakedness, the sags and wrinkles and softness that I had brushed aside the night before. All my insecurities returned, multiplied by a thousandfold, and I wanted to crawl out of my own skin … skin under which my magick had begun crawling again.

"*Shit,*" Edie said.

"Fuck," I agreed as Fire gathered in my core, seemingly fed by the waves of shame washing over my body, my mind, my very soul.

If I hadn't chanced to meet Lucan's gaze again, if I hadn't glimpsed a heat of his own banked in the amber depths of his eyes, things might have gone very badly indeed. But for whatever reason, as I stood there in all my naked, somewhat saggy glory, I did. I looked across the bed and past his not-remembering, and into *him*, and I saw it. I saw the warmth I had seen last night, I saw my companion, I saw my protector, and I saw the bond between us—still intact.

And then, before I could reconcile warmth with condemnation, the bedchamber door crashed open and a blur of blue fuzz streaked past me, followed by Keven's distant but enraged bellow of "*Harry!*"

The little dragon's body thudded onto the bed, a startled and naked Lucan leapt backwards out of the same, and Baba Yaga huffed into the room, indignation in her every line as she planted feet wide on the floor and planted hands on hips.

"Where is beast?" she demanded as Harry tried to burrow beneath the duvet. "Is bad, bad dragon!" She took one hand from her hip to wave the soup ladle she held at me as if I were to blame.

As far as distractions went, it was actually pretty epic. My mortification and shame—along with my nudity—forgotten in the heat of the moment, I put myself between the angry witch and the dragon wriggling under the duvet, attempting to draw her ire away from him.

"What did he do this time?"

"Is *bad* dragon." Baba Yaga spotted the blue body sticking out from under the covers and waved the ladle in Harry's direction. "Spill soup. Break dish. Make—" She stopped suddenly, and her gaze narrowed on me. "You stink," she announced, her nose wrinkling.

"I beg your pardon?" I blinked at her.

"Stink," she repeated. Her gaze flicked to Lucan, then back to me, and she *tutted* as she shook her head. "Magick stink," she said darkly. "Is not good. Is bad."

A shiver slid over me. Remembering my nakedness, I picked up the robe Keven had dropped on the bed and clutched it against my breasts. "I don't understand."

"Bah." The old witch waved both hands, ladle included, in a dismissive gesture. "Is too late now. Is already done." Harry apparently forgotten in my stench, she turned to shuffle out the door, muttering under her breath.

"Wait," I called after her. "What's too late? Why is—was—the magick bad?"

But the door banged shut behind Baba Yaga, leaving me alone with my now fully resurrected angst, Lucan, and—

"Who in the name of the goddess was that?" Lucan asked from the opposite bedside. "And what is that awful racket?" He jerked his head in the direction of the window.

"And *what*"—he pointed at the parts of Harry sticking out from under the covers—"is *that*?"

"That was Baba Yaga, and this"—I pulled back the duvet from the dragon—"is Harry. He helped get us back here from Camlann."

Harry sneezed and set fire to the duvet, and Lucan jumped forward to pat out the flames.

"You brought a *dragon* here?"

"A baby one," I said, pulling the robe over my head. "Or maybe a juvenile, now. I'm not sure." I thrust my arms into the sleeves and let the fabric slide down over my hips. My brain was still processing Baba Yaga's dark declaration, stitching it together with Keven's odd behavior. Along with

Lucan's own less-than-pleased reaction, a creeping, ominous feeling had begun to creep over me.

Especially when I factored in Freya's words from the night before: "... *magick without mutual consent is corrupt ... dark.*"

What had I done?

"And the noise?" Lucan asked, indicating the window again.

"Odin," I said absently, shooing Harry off the bed. I needed to find Freya. Now.

Lucan stared at me as if he suspected I'd lost my mind. "*Odin?*"

"And his cohort." I slipped a foot into a waiting slipper, then looked around for its mate, only to find Harry disappearing under the bed with it clamped in his jaws. "Damn it, Harry, that's my slipper, not a rat!"

"What the hell happened while I was gone?" Lucan was shaking his head, looking more than a little dazed by all the information, and a pang of sympathy went through me. Or would have, if I'd been capable of feeling anything other than the magick sizzling through me right now.

I clenched my fists. *Breathe,* I told myself. *You won't be helping anyone if you lose control.*

"A lot," I said, getting down onto my hands and knees to peer under the bed. I heard Keven's heavy tread on the back stairs as she returned, no doubt to remind me that the others were waiting. "A lot happened, and I promise I'll tell you about it later, but—"

The bedroom door opened behind me, and seizing his opportunity, the little dragon shot out from under the bed, past Keven, and down the corridor. With my slipper.

"For *fuck's sake,*" I growled. I pulled my head out from under the bed and pushed up from hands and knees onto my heels, then paused at the sound of raised, angry voices. Freya's and the Morrigan's voices, to be precise. Loud enough to be heard from downstairs and not just raised in anger ...

No, they were shrieking at one another in absolute fury.

Even though I had just woken up, exhaustion settled over me like a weighted blanket. I closed my eyes and toyed with the idea of crawling back under the bed and staying there. This whole being-in-charge thing was getting very old, very fast. I hadn't even had coffee yet, let alone dealt with Lucan's condemnation of last night's sex magick—or Baba Yaga's disgust, or Keven's silent disapproval, or—

The latter cleared her throat, and I took another deep steadying breath as, one at a time, I shut down my thoughts in favor of the greater good. Because as old as they might be getting, my responsibilities still existed and that damned, dogged resilience of mine wouldn't let me walk away from them.

Or hide under the bed.

I opened my eyes and pushed to my feet. "The Morrigan is back," I observed unnecessarily. "I don't suppose she brought any of the other gods with her?"

"Other gods?" Lucan asked. "What in the name of the goddess is going on?"

Keven glanced at the naked shifter, and her already-stony expression hardened visibly—a feat I might have marveled at in other circumstances—but she ignored the question and returned her attention to me.

"She did not, milady," Keven said.

"Of course not." I swallowed the question of whether the Morrigan had even tried to find the other gods, because that was my problem and not the gargoyle's, and instead nodded at the open door. "Should I ask what that's about?"

"I think it's best that you see for yourself."

Wonderful.

I headed toward the door, but Lucan's hand on my arm stopped me. "Wait. I should come with you."

I felt a small, pleased flutter in my stomach—and not just at his touch. Despite everything, he wanted to come with me?

That was a good sign, right? At the very least, it meant that he was feeling better, and maybe even that he—

Keven stepped into the doorway.

"No," she said. "You should not."

Her response—both barring our path and not *it's best that you stay*, but a flat-out *no, you should not*—gave me pause, but with the argument downstairs escalating in volume, I didn't have time to figure out why.

"We'll talk later," I told Lucan. "I promise. And Keven will fill you in on what's happened in the meantime." Then, not waiting for him to answer, I tugged my arm from his hand and jogged down the hall in my one slipper toward the staircase leading to the great hall.

Bedivere was closing the sitting room doors as I reached the foot of the stairs, his face more taciturn than ever. Given the muffled screeches coming from inside the room, I didn't blame him. For his expression, or for the way he ignored me, stalked across the great hall, wrenched open the front door, morphed into his wolf-form, and disappeared into the cold.

Frankly, I thought as I went to close the door and pick up the puddle of clothing he'd left behind, I wished I could follow him. I dropped his still-warm clothes on the bench beside the door and turned to walk back to the sitting room and the goddesses waiting for me.

Better yet, I wished I could just change into another form —a bird, maybe, or heck, why not a dragon?—and soar up and out of the house and—

And *fucking hell*.

I stopped short as realization buried itself in my gut like a fist. Frantically, I replayed the last few minutes in my brain. Not the Keven coming into the room or the me coming down-stairs part, but the part where the bedchamber door had banged open, Harry had shot onto the bed beside Lucan, Baba Yaga had stormed in on the dragon's heels, and Lucan had dived onto the floor ...

In human form.

In the face of a sudden, unknown threat, Lucan had remained human. He hadn't shifted. He hadn't tried to—

The sitting room doors burst open and the centuries-old war between goddesses spilled out into the hall.

CHAPTER 16

FREYA AND THE MORRIGAN STOOD NOSE TO NOSE IN THE center of the hall, the former tall and blond and as cold as the icy world she'd come from, the latter sharp-faced amid a cloud of crows that yelled in raucous accompaniment to her accusations.

"You *knew*! You *knew* what it would do," the Morrigan screeched, jabbing a talon-like finger out of the crow cloud and into Freya's chest.

The Norse goddess lifted her chin in her own special, haughty way, and looked down her nose at the other. "Of course I knew," she said. "Why do you think I did it?"

I tried to muster my thoughts and make sense of the goddess's words, but even if I hadn't still been reeling from my Lucan-realization, I was pretty sure it was a lost cause. I was going to have to ask. I cast a last, longing glance at the door Bedivere had escaped through, then sighed.

"Did what?" I asked. I braced for the answer, because nothing that made Freya look that smug could be a good thing.

For a moment, both goddesses ignored me, then the Morrigan's crows settled around her into a semblance of a gown, albeit one that flapped restlessly, as if it might dissolve into flight any second. She stared a challenge at Freya.

"Will you tell her, or must I?"

Freya shrugged, managing to look both careless and satisfied at the same time. She waved a hand at the Morrigan. "By all means, be my guest."

The Morrigan's scowl deepened. Darkened. It made me glad she didn't have control over all her power at the moment. More so when her glower was turned on me.

"That *magick* you created last night? It was a binding as well as a healing, and *she*"—an accusing talon-finger pointed at Freya—"knew it would be when she suggested it."

"A binding?" My gaze traveled between them. I didn't like the sound of that. "What kind of binding?"

"The kind that binds, you idiot! What other kind of binding is there?"

I raised an eyebrow at the invective but decided to ignore it—at least until I knew more. "Fine. Then what, exactly, was bound?"

Above the Morrigan's long, white neck, her jaw worked convulsively, clenching and unclenching as she strived for control. "My magick," she ground out at last, "has been bound to Earth through the shifter."

"Bound ... I don't understand. Bound how? And what does that mean?"

"*How* was in joining my magick with one of my constructs of this world," the Morrigan snarled, "and it means that my magick is trapped here with him. *I* am trapped here, and so are you."

It took a second to comprehend her words. Another to understand their ramifications. A third for the full impact of those ramifications to sink in.

Dear fucking goddess. I couldn't cross over to the Otherworld? I couldn't repair the divide? I ...

I turned to face Freya. A laughing Freya, her blond head thrown back in delight. No. Not delight. Revenge.

Delighted revenge.

She laughed, the Morrigan vibrated in impotent rage, and I—I couldn't form a coherent thought to save my own life right now, let alone the lives of every living creature in this world and all the others that the Between would devour.

Fuck, I thought distantly. Too late—far, far too late—I remembered how Lucan had held me at arm's length from the beginning. How he had acknowledged my *charms* but held himself aloof from them. How he'd said that magick had removed choice from the shifters and gargoyles.

How horrified—and angry—he'd been to find me in his bed this morning.

Had he known this would happen? Had Keven? But no—she couldn't have. She would never have agreed with Freya if she had. But Lucan ... Lucan had known.

And I would never unsee the look in his eyes or forget how he'd pulled away from me.

Fuckity, fuck fuck ...

Slowly, my gaze drifted past Freya's shoulder to the sitting room, where the Crones and Jeanne stood just inside the door. Their shock was palpable, hanging thick in the air. Their expectations even more so as they waited for my response. My reassurance.

But I had none. Not this time around, because if I couldn't cross into the Otherworld ...

The Norse goddess had stopped laughing and now sneered in triumph at the Morrigan. "Even when the human dies and your powers return to you," she said coldly, "even when your own construct dies, your magick will be bound to this world, and you with it. Let's see you try and break up another marriage *now*, shall we?"

With a shriek of utter fury, the Morrigan exploded back into a murder of crows, circled an unflinching Freya's head, and then streamed toward the door. Maureen raced across the hall to fling it open at the last second, the birds disappeared into the cold light of the winter day beyond, and a naked Bedivere stepped back into the house. Folding his arms over his hairy chest, he glowered at the goddess who remained, making no move toward his clothes on the bench.

Slowly, I swiveled on my heel. Freya held my gaze unapologetically, implacably, and with all the pettiness she'd once warned me that the gods possessed. More than I'd ever imagined possible. There was so much to unpack in what she'd done, I hardly knew where to start.

"You used me," I said.

"I did what was necessary."

"By tricking me into corrupting my magick? By forcing Lucan—" I choked on the words, unable to finish them. I'd been about to say *forcing Lucan to make love to me*, but there had been no love in that act. There hadn't even been awareness.

"Magick stink," Baba Yaga repeated in my mind, and I knew now what she'd meant. My entire being burned in shame at the thought of what I'd allowed Freya to do to Lucan. What *I* had done.

"That's what you're up in arms about?" The Norse goddess snorted. "He was entirely willing, believe me."

Anger quivered in my core. "How," I growled, "can he have been willing? How can he have consented to what he doesn't even *remember?"*

Freya heaved an exaggerated sigh. "The potion I gave him may have removed his … inhibitions," she allowed, "but the desire to connect with you was still there. The magick would not have healed him if it wasn't."

Removed his …

My jaw dropped. Fucking hell. She'd drugged him and had no concept whatsoever of the wrong behind that, and—

And that was just a teeny, tiny snowflake on the tip of the iceberg. I rubbed both hands over my face, let them trail down from my forehead over my eyes and then my cheeks, and then rested my fingertips against my lips while I regarded her in stupefaction.

"The sheer wrongness of that aside, do you realize what this means?" I asked her. "Have you *any* idea?"

"It means that I took the revenge that was my right," she retorted, her voice as haughty as the rest of her. She flipped her braid over her shoulder to lie along her back and crossed her arms over the polished armor covering her chest. "And I will not be questioned by a mortal."

"Not even if you just signed a death warrant for everyone in this world and your own?"

The ice-blue eyes narrowed a tiny fraction, and the blond eyebrows tugged together as she stared at me. "Explain," she said at last.

Weariness settled over me like a mantle made of stone. "The tear in the fabric of existence itself," I repeated her words back to her. "The one you claim that I created—where is it, exactly?"

Freya hesitated. A faint something flickered in the depths of her gaze—was that actual regret? I blinked, but before I could decide, pride snuffed out whatever it might have been, and the goddess drew herself up even straighter.

"What's done is done," she announced. "You will find another way."

The anger that had been simmering in my core exploded into wrath, and I threw my arms wide. "Damn it to hell and back, Freya!" I yelled. "Don't you get it? There *is* no other way."

The Norse goddess blinked at me in shock, and then her demeanor shifted. Haughtiness faded, and her expression turned stony enough to rival Keven's as an asynchronous energy rolled outward from her and rippled through the room. An unhappy vibration in the house's very foundation responded.

So did the Fire sizzling beneath my skin.

I clenched my fists against it as Maureen hurried to join the others. The five women drew back into the sitting room. Bedivere's shoulders tensed; his feet shifted wider.

Freya circled me slowly. Her power pressed against me. The magick in me pushed back. Could she feel it? I tightened my fists and locked my arms against my sides, grappling for control over that which still didn't feel like mine. If it got away on me ...

The house's vibration grew stronger. I locked onto it, stretched my senses toward it, and found Earth beneath it, hoping it might root me. That it might hold me and the magick together. It responded sluggishly—or perhaps that was at my end—but at last, it reached up to meet me. It wrapped around my ankles and crept into my limbs, and under its steadying touch, Fire subsided a little.

I allowed myself a small exhale of relief, then sent what I hoped was reassurance to the house. A silent promise to protect it. The vibration subsided into a low, unhappy hum, and Freya came to a halt behind me.

She leaned in to whisper into my ear, her breath hot against my neck. "Be careful, mortal," she said, her voice a menacing growl. "You forget who I am."

I held myself still, refusing to flinch or to turn to face the goddess. Refusing to give her the satisfaction. Beneath my feet, Earth's power grew, burgeoned. Fire seethed in my core. Air gathered, thick around me. Water began to pool in my fingertips. Bedivere morphed again into the battered remnants of his wolf and crouched at my side, a low rumble emanating from his chest.

Freya finished her circle of me, coming to stand so close that I could see flecks of gold in the ice-blue irises of her eyes, the lines at their corners, the pores of her skin. Bedivere's rumble became a snarl. Freya ignored him.

"Did you hear me?"

I flexed fingers that thrummed with power and tilted my head back to look up at the Norse goddess, weighing my options. My alternatives. My odds. And then I made my decision.

"I heard," I replied, hearing my voice as if it belonged to someone else. "And I know exactly who you are. I also know that you are no longer welcome in this house."

Freya's head snapped back in sheer surprise. Then she gave a harsh bark of laughter. "You think you can throw me out? Dear child—"

"Stop." I cut her off. "I am not a child, Freya, and you may not condescend to me. The Between is devouring the Otherworld as we speak, and if I can't get to the barrier, I can't fix it. And it won't stop with your world; it will come for this one, too. And then the next, and the next, and the next. Because of *you*. Because whatever I may have started? *You* are the one who just finished it."

I paused, letting her absorb the impact of my words while I checked in one last time with my own sanity. And then, because there were no good choices to be made here and I honestly had nothing to lose, I readied myself to protect the others as best I could and pointed out the window through which the crows had flown.

"Now get the fuck out of my house," I said.

CHAPTER 17

"I CAN'T BELIEVE SHE ACTUALLY LEFT," ANNE MURMURED beside me as Maureen pressed a cup of tea into my shaking, post-confrontation hands.

I couldn't believe it, either. I closed my eyes, my fingers wrapped tight around the heat of the mug as I relived the standoff with Freya. Long, tense moments had slid by while rage warred in her expression with—what? There had been something else there—something besides shock and disbelief —but I'd been so focused on holding onto the power roiling through me that I hadn't had the attention span to identify it.

Then, when she'd simply turned on her heel and walked out of the house, my focus had shifted to safely releasing the power I'd gathered to me and returning it to its sources—and to not folding onto the floor in a trembling mass of shell-shocked nerves. A soul-deep desire to feel Lucan's arms around me and hear his words of reassurance had coursed through me, but I'd remembered that was impossible, and then—

Then, a cold, hard knot had replaced the Fire in my core as I looked down at Bedivere's wolf beside me. Bedivere's, not Lucan's, because Lucan had not perceived the threat to me. Had not come to protect me. Had once again not shifted.

"Maybe Keven wouldn't let him," my Edie-voice said. *"Maybe he's not fully recovered and just needs time."*

Or, goddess forbid, maybe I'd been right about not all of him having come back from—

Hot tea splashed onto my hand, jerking me back to the present. Hastily, I lifted the mug up and out of the way of the not-so-little dragon trying to climb into my lap.

"Harry, no." Elysabeth reached to push him away. "You're too big for that."

"It's all right," I told her as Harry sprawled across me and leaned against my chest, rumbling with concern. "He just needs a little reassurance."

"Don't we all," muttered Maureen. Nia shushed her, but I sighed.

"We do," I said, including myself in the *we*. "And I wish I could give it, but …"

"You have no ideas at all?" Anne asked. "Not even wild ones?"

I shook my head as I looked around at my friends. Baba Yaga had come and ushered the midwitches out of the sitting room and down the corridor toward the kitchen in the aftermath of the standoff, and only my fellow Crones remained with me, along with Jeanne and Bedivere. All of them were looking to me for direction—for a plan to save not just them, but the entire world. But I had nothing. No plan, no way to undo what had been done or to stop what was coming. Nothing but a cold, empty dread at my very core, as if—

"Claire."

The entire room stopped breathing. Or maybe that was just me. The cold knot at my center tightened. Harry leaned harder against me, and his rumble grew louder. On the opposite sofa, Nia and Elysabeth exchanged a look. By the fireplace, Jeanne and Maureen did the same. Bedivere, his back to the room, stiffened, and Anne reached for the hand I rested on Harry's head.

"Lucan," she said, looking past me toward the sitting room doors. "It's good to see you awake."

"It's good to be awake," Lucan replied.

A taut little silence fell, and then Jeanne, bless her heart, addressed the elephant in the room. "And not good at the same time, I imagine," she said quietly.

"Yes," he agreed.

I heard his footsteps behind me as he walked around the sofa where Anne and I sat, heading toward the fireplace. His shadow entered my peripheral vision, and as if drawn like the proverbial moth to the flame, my gaze lifted away from the dragon lying across my lap and locked with his. A part of me wanted nothing to do with the forthcoming conversation, but time was too short—and growing shorter by the minute—to dance around what needed to be said.

As if reading my mind, Anne stood up and beckoned to the others. "We'll leave you to … discuss the situation," she said. "We'll be in the kitchen."

Crones and Jeanne filed out of the sitting room, taking their mugs of tea with them. Harry and Bedivere stayed, Harry's body tense against mine, Bedivere staring into the fire, his mangled hand braced against the fireplace mantel and the stump of his other arm hanging at his side. If there had still been a hand attached to the latter, I had no doubt it would have been curled into a fist.

"Bedivere?" I prompted.

Bedivere looked over his shoulder at his brother. "What the *fuck* were you thinking?" he snarled. "You *know* we cannot —" He broke off and turned his scowl on me. "And *you*," he said. "Do you have *any* idea what you've done?"

"Don't," Lucan told him, putting a hand on his shoulder. Bedivere shook him off.

"You cannot shift, Lucan." Bedivere's growl was part accusation, part betrayal. All loss. "You cannot *shift*." He slammed his fist against the heavy beam of the mantel and glared at me with so much venom that I caught my breath. The burly shifter had rarely looked at me with anything other than dislike, but this—this was more. Much more.

It was anger and hatred and despair and—

And I would have thrown the goddess out of the house all

over again if I could have done so. But I couldn't, and so I would do the next best thing. I tightened my arms around Harry and returned my gaze to the accusation in Bedivere's, only flinching from it a little. I straightened my spine.

"I'd like to talk to Lucan," I said. "Alone."

For a moment, I thought he might tell me what to do with my request, but then his attention snapped back to his brother, and he and Lucan stared at one another, too many messages passing between them for me to read. Then, with a final snarl under his breath, Bedivere swung around on his heel and stalked between me and the chest, treading without apology on my toes.

The doors to the great hall banged open, slammed closed, and Lucan and I were alone.

SILENCE DROPPED OVER THE ROOM LIKE A WEIGHTED BLANKET in the wake of Bedivere's departure. Lucan stayed by the fireplace, staring into the flames, and I played with the last tuft of hair that remained on top of Harry's head. The little dragon closed his eyes and rumbled with pleasure. I closed mine and gathered my nerve.

I was sixty years old, I reminded myself, and I was Crone. I didn't hide from what needed to be said. Not anymore. I opened my eyes again.

"You should have told me," I said to Lucan's back. "You should have told me why you—why I—you should have told me."

"You might not hide from what needs to be said," muttered Edie, *"but you're not exactly eloquent about it, are you?"*

Perhaps not, but Lucan understood. "Yes," he said. "I should have."

"I would never have …"

"I know." He half-turned, resting one elbow on the mantel and the opposite hand on his hip as he looked down at the hearth. His profile was no easier to read than his back had been. "But you did—*we* did—and now this is where we are. What we have."

"What we have?" I asked. Deliberately choosing to misunderstand him—because maybe I wasn't as forthcoming at sixty as I'd thought—I laughed a hard, mirthless laugh that made Harry jump back from my chest in alarm.

"Look around you, Lucan," I said. "We have *nothing*. The Between is coming, the gods are fleeing to Earth, the Crones have lost their Morrigan powers, my own powers are useless if I can't cross back into the Otherworld, and—and—" I summoned my last reserves of courage and spat it out. "And *I broke you*, damn it. Maybe not on purpose, but I did. What the hell am I supposed to do about that?"

"There's nothing you can do, Claire. There's nothing anyone can do. But you didn't do this, Freya did."

"Freya," I snapped, "was not in that bed with us last night."

To my annoyance, his lips twitched.

"It's not funny," I said. "None of this is funny, Lucan. I have done everything I was supposed to, everything I was asked to do, but no matter how hard I try, I just keep messing up, and—and—" I flapped a hand over my head in a wide, *just-look-at-this-unholy-mess* gesture, and Harry tilted his head to one side, watching me with jewel-eyed concern.

I patted the dragon's blue tuft and glared at the broken shifter, who still hadn't looked over at me. "How the *fuck* do I get us out of this?"

Lucan's lips twitched again. Irritation sparked in me, and Fire crackled down my arms. I slapped it away. *Not helpful*, I growled at it—at me—at whatever.

The no-longer shifter detached himself from his leaning post by the fireplace and came to shoo Harry off my lap. He took my teacup—how was I even still holding that?—and set it on the far side of the wooden chest. Then he sat on the same chest in front of me, rested his elbows on his knees, and took my hands in his. The dragon tried to nudge under my arm again, couldn't, and curled up with an aggrieved sigh beside me.

"You do know," said my protector—could I still call him that?—"that you are not solely responsible for the survival of the universe?"

I scowled. "But the Between—"

"Existed long before you did," he interrupted. "Long before any of us did. Perhaps even before the universe itself."

I tried again. "But I'm the one who tore—"

He raised his voice over mine. "Claire."

I snapped my teeth shut.

"You didn't act alone," he said.

"Actually, I'm pretty sure I did," I retorted, thinking about my lonely trek across the Otherworld to the Camlann splinter. Except for Gus, of course. I'd always had Gus, thanks to Kev—

My thoughts ground to a halt. I blinked, then zigzagged my way through the memories of my Otherworld trek. I'd had Gus because Keven had tucked him into my rucksack, and without the cat, I wouldn't have made it across the Otherworld to Camlann at all. Or found Harry. Or had the little dragon's help in Camlann to create a vortex for the portal back to Earth. And if none of those things had happened, I wouldn't have been able to destroy Morok, who had started this whole thing in the first place.

Morok and the Morrigan. Freya and Odin. Goddess knew who else.

Never mind the Between, all of *them* had happened long

before I had existed, too. Their exodus from Earth, their petty machinations …

Oh.

"I love the sound of a penny dropping," Edie commented cheerfully.

Just as cheerfully, I ignored her.

Less cheerfully, I frowned. "That's all well and good," I told Lucan, "but it doesn't change the fact that the world is about to end, and I still have no way of stopping it."

"You don't, if you keep pretending you're alone in this," he agreed. "But what if you let the rest of us help?"

The snort escaped before I could swallow it, and I winced at myself. "Sorry," I said. "That wasn't nice. But—and I mean no offense here—how? The Morrigan was supposed to round up the gods, and Freya was supposed to teach the Crones how to tap into the elements again and reconvene the Council, and now they're both gone, and I can't even cross through the portal anymore, and Freya taught the Crones *nothing.* Where, in all of that, is the way out of this mess?"

"You tell me." The amber gaze held mine, steady and certain. But certain of what? Me?

I scowled at him. He'd always believed in me—in my ability—even when I hadn't myself. His continuing confidence was nice, but it was seriously misplaced this time around. And more than a little irritating.

"Do you not think that if I had an idea—*any* idea," I grumped, "that I wouldn't be all over it? But we're talking about a handful of midwitches and former Crones with no pendants and no elemental training, Lucan. How in hell can a group like that even *hope* to stop something like—" I stopped short as a tiny spark of an idea floated into my mind.

Lucan's fingers tightened around mine. "You thought of something."

"I'm not sure." I closed my eyes and chased after the spark that was more like a speck. Not an idea, exactly, but the possibility of one. Or the impossibility, depending on how you wanted to look at it.

But it was still an idea. And it might provide the only faint hope that we had.

I opened my eyes again and wrinkled my nose as I regarded Lucan. "Please tell me you can still travel the ley."

"I'm not sure." He frowned. "Theoretically, I suppose I might. Why?"

"Because if I can convince Keven that she still has more of Morgana in her than she thinks," I said, "I'm going to need someone to help me rally the gods, and Bedivere might not be the best choice for ambassador."

WITH HARRY TROTTING BEHIND US, LUCAN AND I HEADED FOR the double doors leading to the great hall—I to find Keven and explain my plan to her, and he to test his ability to travel the ley that crisscrossed the clearing outside the house. But as we reached the door, he stopped.

"We might not have time for this later," he said, "and you need to know."

Sixty years of hard-won fortitude went up in a puff of smoke. With that look of seriousness on his face, no, I most certainly did not need to know whatever he—

"Freya was right," he said. "About my desire. It was still there, milady. It just should never have been acted upon."

My mouth flapped. Or hung open. Or made some other kind of weird movement over which I had no control, but I wasn't sure what as I gaped at him.

Edie cleared her throat in my head. *"All right, maybe you did need to know that,"* she said. *"Because I certainly did."*

"And now that it has?" I asked. "Been acted upon, I mean."

For a moment, the amber of his eyes turned molten, and a memory of last night's magick sang through my veins. His voice turned rough, sliding over me like raw silk. "Do I still desire you, do you mean? Milady, I will never stop."

"I—oh," I said, because apparently my eloquence knew no bounds.

Edie had no such problem.

"Well, holy hell and hallelujah and dear goddess," she said. A fluttering noise accompanied her voice. Was she *fanning* herself?

"Is it just me?" she asked, *"or did things just get awfully warm in here?"*

She *was* fanning herself.

"But it cannot be acted upon again," Lucan said. The heat in his eyes was gone, replaced by a grim determination—and a deep, sad regret. "The magick between us—"

"I know," I said. "There could be more repercussions."

"Yes." Seeming to consider the conversation done, he reached for the doorknob, but it was my turn to stop him.

"Wait," I said. "Before, when you said that this is where we are, now—what we have …" I took a deep breath. "Are you all right with it? With … everything?"

He paused, and a shadow crossed his face. "I'm alive," he said finally, as if that was answer enough.

It wasn't.

"That's not what I asked." I put a hand against the oak door to keep him from opening it. "This morning … last night …" I paused to gather my words and all sixty years of my courage. "Last night, I thought you remembered everything. All of it. Camlann. But this morning—" I broke off as Lucan's hand tightened on the doorknob, his knuckles going pale. The shadow that crossed his face this time was most definitely not a trick of the light.

"I remember," he said.

My mouth went dry. "All of it?" I pressed. My voice

cracked despite my best efforts to keep it neutral, and Lucan flinched.

"Everything," he said hoarsely, confirming what I'd been most afraid of.

For centuries, the shifter had carried with him the guilt of not being able to protect his wife and son in the war of Camlann. Now he would live with the memory of his wolf being chained in that hut beside their bodies, too. And of what that wolf had done.

"*Fucking hell,*" murmured Edie, all levity gone.

I searched for the words I needed, this time to give some kind of solace. A tiny modicum of peace. "That wasn't you, Lucan," I whispered.

He stared at my hand holding the door shut. A muscle in front of his jaw flexed, and the cords in his neck stood out beneath his skin. Agony radiated from him. I dropped my hand to cover his on the knob.

"*That wasn't you,*" I repeated fiercely.

His hand was as rigid beneath my fingers as Keven's granite claws were, and for long, interminable moments, he made no response. Gave no sign that he'd even heard me. Then, when I'd begun wracking my brain for what more I could say, he inhaled deeply and made a visible effort to unlock his jaw and drop his shoulders.

"You're right," he said at last. "It wasn't me. And last night," his gaze returned to meet mine, steady, direct, and refusing to make room for argument, "was not you."

Well, shit, I thought. A prickle of heat gathered at the back of my eyes, and I blinked it back.

"*He's got you there,*" Edie said, with more delight than I thought was warranted. But she was right. He had me there. I swallowed against the tears and conceded defeat.

"Touché," I said. I took my hand from his and curled my fingers into my palm, holding onto his fading warmth as he pulled the door open and stood back for me to precede him. I hesitated. "One last thing?"

"Of course."

"You and me," I said. "I'm not sure what we are anymore."

My not-protector and no-longer-shifter was silent for a moment, and then he heaved a great sigh. "Complicated," he said. "We're complicated, milady. Just as we've always been."

CHAPTER 18

"TEACH THE CRONES TO ACCESS ELEMENTAL MAGICK," KEVEN repeated, clawed hands planted on hips, soup ladle still gripped in one. Broth from the pot she'd been stirring dripped from it onto the flagstone floor while she stared at me as if I had grown a second head. Even Gus, wrapped around her shoulders, seemed to wear an expression of utter astonishment. "Me."

"Yes," I said, "so that they—"

"So that they can *maybe* hold back the Between if it arrives here while you're out trying to find the rest of the gods," she finished, still astonished. "I heard you the first time. I just don't know how you think any of that is even possible."

"You didn't think it was impossible when Freya suggested it."

"Because Freya was to teach the Crones what they needed to know, and the Morrigan at least stood a chance of convincing the gods to return to the Otherworld. But this? You?" Her eyebrow—or the place an eyebrow would have been, if she'd had them—lifted again on the *you*.

I didn't blame her, because the part about me gathering the gods and enlisting their help was definitely the fly in the ointment of my idea, especially if Lucan wasn't able to travel the ley, and we had to rely on Bedivere to help me.

But Keven teaching the Crones? That part, I was certain of.

Certain-ish.

"Huh," grunted Baba Yaga from beside the second wood stove that the house had installed in the kitchen for her. "Is interesting plan."

124

Keven shot her an impatient look. "It's an impossible plan."

"Is it?" I asked, lifting my chin in challenge. "I absorbed your magick in the Otherworld, Keven. I felt how powerful it was. I can still feel it."

The gargoyle's heavy stone brow furled into a scowl. "You took on the Morrigan's power at the same time. You're confusing the two."

"No. No, I'm not." I staggered under the weight of Harry as he leaned against my legs, unhappy with the elevated tension in the room. For a creature of such legendary ferocity, he was surprisingly sensitive. I gave him an absent pat on the head and pushed him away. The little dragon gave the high-up Gus a wistful look, then crept over to try to lean against Baba Yaga instead, but the witch growled at him under her breath—still hostile after the morning's soup incident—and he slunk back to curl up at my side.

I let him settle his head on my foot for comfort and returned to my argument with Keven. I needed to convince her, needed her help.

Needed her, period.

"I know exactly which magick came from which source," I continued. It was true, because hers I could manage in me, and the Morrigan's not so much, and the two posed a serious problem when they came together. But telling her about my control issues right now—my *magickal* control issues, I added for Edie's benefit—would hardly help win the gargoyle over to my idea. I pressed on. "And I know that you could manipulate the elements the way a god or goddess could."

She stared at me for a moment, then turned back to the pot on her own stove, stirred it again, and set the ladle aside. She picked up a cloth from beside the sink, but seizing the opportunity of her distraction, Harry had abandoned my leg to greedily lap up the soup she'd dripped on the floor, so she set the cloth down again and returned her attention to me.

"I couldn't," she said. "Not really. I was learning, perhaps, but it was a long time ago, and I was nowhere near a goddess's level of mastery. And it took me years, not days."

"Because you didn't believe in yourself." I tugged my foot from under Harry's head so I could go to her. I placed a hand on a rough stone forearm. "You were learning on your own, you didn't think you should be able to do what you were doing, and I very much doubt that your neighbors—or the Morrigan herself, for that matter—encouraged you."

A Crone's memories flitted across a gargoyle's expression; sadness followed in their wake.

"Perhaps that is true," she allowed. "In part. But that doesn't make what you propose any more possible. Even if I remembered what I once knew, I cannot hope to teach the others to connect with the elements in the time that we have. Not enough for them to be able to hold back what they cannot even see."

"You taught *me*."

Keven raised her non-eyebrow again. "Our memories about your lessons appear to differ somewhat, milady. And even if I did manage to teach you something, you had the Morrigan's pendant. They do not."

"Neither did you when you learned to connect."

"Which took years," she reminded me. She went to a wooden bin on Baba Yaga's side of the kitchen and scooped up a handful of potatoes. "Perhaps if you were to teach them your—"

The exterior door leading into the garden opened, cutting her off, and an ashen-faced Lucan came into the kitchen. Catching my eye as he stamped the snow off his boots, he shook his head, his mouth tight.

"I can travel the ley," he said, "but by every goddess who ever existed, the pain of doing so is like nothing I've ever endured. I'm not sure how many trips I can take."

Fuck, I thought, and Edie concurred in my head.

My shoulders sagged. "That's what happened to me when I lost my magick in them."

"I can still—"

"No." I shook my head. He might have enough magick in him to travel, but he hadn't fully recovered yet, and I had too many questions about what else our ... night together ... had done to him. "No, I'd rather you stay here to keep an eye on things, especially with Odin next door. I'll take Bedivere with me, and Keven ..."

The gargoyle, her fist full of potatoes, stopped at the sound of her name, and Harry peered up hopefully at the bounty just above his head. Keven lowered her ponderous head and closed her eyes for several long seconds. Then she heaved a sigh.

Unfortunately, the air that gusted from her tickled the nose of the dragon at her feet. Harry sneezed, flames spurted from him, the potatoes turned to crisps of black, and Gus leapt down from the gargoyle's shoulders with an ear-piercing yowl and his tail on fire. Lucan caught the cat in mid-air and snuffed out the flames. He might no longer be able to shift, but his reflexes remained lightning quick.

"That thing is a menace," he growled, pointing at Harry as he set the smoldering cat on the floor. Gus bolted from the room, and Harry waddled to the table and crawled under it, head and tail drooping. He looked so woebegone that even Baba Yaga took pity on him, tossing a scrap of meat his way, but Harry only sniffed at it and then curled up into the smallest ball that he could.

"He doesn't mean to be," I defended the dragon. "He's still just a baby."

Keven *hmphed* as she dropped her handful of potato remains into the scrap bucket by the sink. "The mutt is right," she grumbled. "It doesn't belong in a house."

"Well, a certain god who shall remain nameless has a certain relative of that menace on the wall of his Otherworld lodge," I responded tartly, "so if either of you is thinking he should be put outside to fend for himself, the answer is no. Am I clear?"

"Well. Look at you, pulling rank and being all bossy," Edie said. *"Good for you. Besides, I rather like the menace."*

I did, too, not to mention that I was responsible for him, having brought him from the Otherworld with me. And now … now, I needed an answer to my question. I turned my back on Lucan's surprise at my new-to-him display of authority and squared off against the squat displeasure that was Keven. Might as well harness my bossiness while I could, right?

"I need you to do this, Keven," I said. "We have no other options."

The gargoyle placed claws on haunches and glowered at me. I glowered back. From my perspective, it was an epic battle of wills. I had never stood up to anyone quite like this before—well, anyone that I liked and respected, I amended, thinking of my battle with Morok—and it took every ounce of stubbornness I possessed not to fold under Kevin's disapproval.

From the corner of my eye, I saw Lucan cross his arms across his chest and lean back against the door to wait for the outcome. Harry lifted his head from under his tail to watch, too. Even Baba Yaga stopped what she was doing at her stove and gave us her undivided attention.

And then, just as I felt the edges of my determination begin to crumble, damned if Keven didn't fold. Kind of.

"Fine," she snapped. "If you can convince the Crones that your *plan*"—she growled the word—"is possible, then I will teach them what I can."

Piece of cake, I thought, allowing myself to unclench the fists I'd wrapped in my robe. Edie snorted.

Lucan straightened away from the door. "Would you like me to speak with Bedivere for you?"

Gratitude rushed through me, hot on the heels of relief.

The Crones, I could handle. The shifter who had glared at me with such hatred earlier? I preferred not to even try. I nodded. "Please," I said. "And Baba Yaga——"

"I teach uzzers," she informed me. "Zey be better witches when I am done. More powerful."

I would take all the help—and the power—we could get.

"Thank you," I said. "I'll tell the midwitches when I go up to talk to the others."

And just like that, we had a plan again.

Until, of course, we didn't.

"So what you're saying is that any of us"—Elysabeth poked a hand out from under her ever-present wrap and waved it to encompass the room—"all of us—are goddesses?"

I shook my head, frustrated by my lack of ability to make myself clear—and by not having enough information to do so. Oh, how I wished I'd asked more questions of Freya in the Otherworld. I sighed.

"Not really," I said, "although I suppose any one of us *could* be, if enough people believed in them, but I suspect that would take centuries. Or at least decades. It's more like we can all access the same power, the same magick, as any of the goddesses or gods can."

My fellow Crones stared at me in perplexity. Jeanne, like I'd lost all my marbles. I tried to keep my frustration focused on myself and not let it spread to them. There had to be a way of convincing them. And myself, I thought, as doubt crept along the edges of my mind.

"But isn't that the same thing?" Anne asked. "Doesn't it still come down to belief?"

"Well … yes and no. I think your own belief will allow you to tap into the same power—to connect with the elements in the way that the goddesses do—but you would need the belief of many others to magnify that power to a goddess level."

"You think. But you're not sure."

"I only know what Freya told me—that the gods were once as human as any of us, but they knew magick. They could manipulate the elements. She said that it was the belief of others that fueled their power and made it more. I think ..." I paused and assembled my scattered thoughts as best I could. "I think," I repeated slowly, "that others have had that power over time, too. That we have it now. All of us. But it's been suppressed by those who fear it—who fear us."

"The witch hunts," Nia murmured as I paused, and I nodded.

"Yes," I said eagerly, seeing their skepticism hover on the brink of turning to speculation. "Yes. The witch hunts and the later Inquisition and a hundred other times they tried to put us down. To stifle us."

"The entire patriarchy?" Anne suggested, her voice dry.

"In a sense, yes. And because of it, we've forgotten how much we once knew, forgotten to trust ourselves, forgotten that we still have it. The power, I mean. *Our* power."

"And Freya told you all of this," said Anne.

"Not ..." I trailed off and sighed, then finished my admission. "Not exactly. I was focused on other things at the time and didn't ask enough questions, so I'm afraid a lot of this is ..." I spread my hands and lifted my shoulders in an apologetic shrug.

"Extrapolation," Maureen finished.

"Yes."

The four Crones exchanged long looks with one another before Jeanne asked, "And if you're wrong?"

"If I'm wrong, the gods win," I said. "For a while. And then we all lose. I've seen what the Between does to a world, and it won't stop at the Otherworld. But if I'm right, we at least stand a chance."

"*Sure,*" muttered Edie. "*Just like a snowball has a chance in hell.*"

I wondered if she could go back to being an imaginary voice.

"You do remember that Freya already tried to teach us how to connect with the elements again, don't you?" Maureen asked. "And that it didn't work? She said—"

"Freya," I said, "has a vested interest in you not realizing how powerful you are. Just as the Morrigan did."

A faint undercurrent of objection rippled through the room at my inclusion of the goddess we'd once served, but no one gave louder voice to it. Another long silence—there had been many in this conversation—fell over the room, punctuated by the snap and crackle of a pine log in the fire and underscored by the relentless party that was Odin's camp.

Odin, who was one of the gods I would have to convince to return to the Otherworld. But that was a future-me problem. Present-me still had to contend with—

"You really think Keven—a gargoyle," said Elysabeth, "can teach us what a goddess could not?"

"I know she can," I said, and I only crossed the fingers of one hand under the folds of my robe. "You just have to trust her. And yourselv—"

From out in the great hall came the crash of the front door slamming open. A man's familiar voice, filled with anguish, bellowed, "*Mom!*" and everything I'd been about to say, everything I needed to do, vanished from my brain in one panic-stricken, primal thought.

Because, Paul.

CHAPTER 19

My thoughts came in staccato bursts as I strode across the sitting room, my son's words ringing in my ears.

Shades

In Confluence.

Attacking the downtown core.

And Natalie was there.

I plowed through the double doors and into the great hall. My steps hitched as I squeezed my eyes shut against the images my mind wanted to conjure of my daughter-in-law's lifeless, mutilated body. I forced them away and resumed my stride across the flagstone floor. Natalie was still alive, Paul had said, or had been when he'd taken Braden and fled, and I needed to believe that I could get to her in time.

I *would* get to her—

I came up short against a hard chest as Lucan put himself between me and the front door I was aiming for.

"No," he said. He put his hands on my shoulders and held me away, looking every inch the protector I remembered. So much so that I faltered and, for a split second, dared to hope.

But no. While Bedivere had morphed into his wolf-form when Paul and Braden had stumbled into the house, Lucan had not. He still couldn't shift, he couldn't protect me, and we remained—as he'd said—complicated. I tried to pull away.

He held fast.

"You cannot go alone," he said. "Not against that many shades."

I wanted to assure him—to assure them all—that I was more than capable. That, after destroying Morok himself, I could manage a handful of shades. Because with more than half the power of a goddess running through me, I should have been able to. In truth, the power could absolutely take them out. One uncertainty loomed large, however: I struggled to control—no, full disclosure, I *couldn't* control—it.

Hesitation held me captive. What would happen if it got away on me in town? I'd flattened an entire forest when I'd been starting out in this magickal thing, and I'd had a fraction of the power then that I had now. My track record clearly demonstrated that I was capable of as much harm as I was good—perhaps more so.

My gaze went over my shoulder to the sitting room doors standing open behind the silent, watchful friends who had followed me. It settled on the man huddled in a blanket by the fire, misery etched in every line of his body as he clutched the mug Keven had given him. For a moment, every fiber of my being ached to return to my son and hold him and comfort him. But that was not what he needed from me.

What he needed from me was to find his wife—the mother of his child—and bring her back to them.

They'd been having lunch at the Java Hut when the attack came, Paul had said. A dozen flying monsters—black, with yellow eyes and razor-sharp talons that tore through the metal of car roofs and shredded their occupants, that latched onto pedestrians and carried them into the air only to drop them, bleeding, onto the icy pavement.

Natalie had thrust Braden into his arms and shouted at him to run, to find me, and before he could stop her, she'd disappeared into the mayhem of the street to—

My heart had crumpled in on itself, and the rest of his words had turned muffled, buried beneath the pounding of my own heartbeat in my ears. The rush of terror through my veins. Because what could Natalie, who wasn't even a midwitch, hope to do against shades? What could anyone in Confluence do?

"I should have stayed," Paul had muttered, self-loathing written in every shocked line of his face as he bowed his head. "I should never have left her. What kind of man am I, leaving her behind like that?"

"The smart kind," Maureen had assured him when I hadn't been able to muster either words or voice. "You came to us for help."

And help he would get, I told myself fiercely. I would find a way to harness the power, because I had to. I curled my hands into fists at my sides and turned back to Lucan, who had released his grip on me. I was done arguing. I might not be Confluence's best chance of survival, but I was its only one, and I *would* get to Natalie, and—

I blinked as he took my cloak from a hook over the bench and held it out to me.

"Bedivere and I will come with you," he said. "The others will keep Paul and Braden safe."

"But you can't shift," I objected. A collective inhale from the Crones and Jeanne reminded me that they hadn't known about that particular glitch yet. Hell.

"They were going to find out sooner or later," Edie observed.

Yes, but it still didn't change Lucan's inability to—

The snick of metal against hardened leather sliced through the thought, and I recognized—thanks to Freya—the sound of a sword being drawn. Instinctively, I summoned Fire to my fingertips and whirled. A glint of metal sailed toward my head, and in a display of the same lightning-fast reflexes that had caught the burning Gus, Lucan's hand flashed up to catch the glint, and then he and the sword spun away from the fireball that left my hand.

Fire smashed into the wall above the staircase, narrowly missing a naked Bedivere's head where he stood beside one of the suits of armor. In the shock that followed my little perfor-mance and accompanied Keven's wordless shuffle to snuff out the flames, my gaze locked with the burly shifter's.

"You've forgotten what he was before the Morrigan changed him," the shifter said. "What we both were."

My gaze dropped to the newly unarmed armor. I *had* forgotten, except that wasn't quite the right word—how could it be, when I'd gazed up at Arthur's fabled castle with my own eyes and stood on the blood-soaked battlefield amid the bodies? It was more like I'd never stopped to think about what it meant. The implications. The realness. The—

"A knight," I whispered. "He was a knight. You both were."

"Of the Round Table," Bedivere agreed.

I turned back to face Lucan again. A tall, broad-shouldered, grim-faced Lucan who had the light of battle in his amber eyes and whose every loose-limbed line held the supreme confidence of a warrior. A Knight of the Round Table. A protector.

My protector.

In spite of the gravity of the situation, a tiny corner of my heart smiled. I nodded at the sword he gripped in his right hand, its tip not quite touching the floor. "Is it enough to stop a shade?"

"I don't know. But it's enough to distract one," he replied. "And to take care of the ones who called them."

The ones who called them.

"*Fucking Mages,*" muttered Edie.

The reminder added another layer of impossibility to the whole situation, another weight to the ones already threatening to drag me under. Because where there were shades, there could well be Mages, and we would be leaving the house unprotected against them as well. The house, my friends, my son, my grandson.

We were on our own in this. Freya had failed to teach the Crones what I'd asked her to, and the Morrigan was gone, and—

"Bah." Baba Yaga emerged from the kitchen corridor with

Braden settled comfortably on one broad hip, Harry trotting at her side, and the ever-present soup ladle in her hand. Her wrinkled face was calm and her faded blue eyes steadfast as they met mine.

"Shades is nussink," she said. "You go. Baba Yaga and Keven take care of assholes here."

Nussink ... nothing. A tiny hope kindled in my breast. "You can defeat them?"

"We hold off," she replied equably. "You hurry."

Lucan opened the front door. I took my cloak from him. We hurried.

BEDIVERE'S WOLF SET A FIERCE PACE ACROSS THE CLEARING, BUT even with Lucan's strong, steadying grip beneath my elbow, my own progress was frustratingly slow. The frozen crust of snow broke under my every step, scraping my shins and plunging me knee-deep into the powder beneath. By the time Lucan and I joined Bedivere at the tree line, my breath came in gasps and my ribcage felt like a bellows. It would have been easier—so much easier—to step into one of the ley lines dancing and twisting around us as I'd planned, but Lucan had pointed out that to do so risked one or more of the shades retracing our journey back to the house and its occupants in our absence.

And while Baba Yaga said they could hold them off, we had every reason not to tempt fate. Or at least, *I* had every reason, I thought. And so, slow and painful though it might be, we would travel on foot to Confluence.

Once in the trees, Bedivere broke trail with his chest as he plowed ahead of both of us, and Lucan kept his stride short so that I could follow in his footprints. At first, the noise from Odin's encampment swallowed the sound of our steps:

raucous laughter and whoops and yells, the sound of an ax biting into wood, the muffled *whump* of a tree hitting the snow. I clenched my teeth at the latter, hating that the god was injuring what I had come to think of as my own forest. The sooner I talked him back into the Otherworld with his comrades, the better.

The sounds of destruction faded as we continued, becoming first a backdrop to our progress, then a distant, barely there underscore that I had to listen for. The afternoon sun slanted through the bare trees surrounding us, casting long shadow lines across the snow, like bars on a prison. Ahead of me, Lucan glanced over his shoulder, his breath coming in puffs of steam and one eyebrow raised in silent query. Was I doing okay?

Despite the burn in my thighs and ache of my hips from lifting my feet high out of his deep boot prints—and the rapidly fading feeling in my frozen shins—I nodded. He turned back to the path his brother was forging, and we struggled on.

My cloak snagged on a branch a few steps later, and I stopped to disentangle it, grateful for the brief respite. A whisper of sound caught my ear, like snow sliding against snow, or perhaps dropping from a branch, and my fingers stilled.

A flash of memory jolted through me of another time when Lucan and I had taken this path, after the gnome attack when I first became Crone and shards of the broken creatures had kept coming after me. My skin crawled at the remembered sensation of a ceramic head collapsing beneath my boot, and I cast a quick, furtive look around me at the snow-covered forest with its prison-bar shadows. Nothing moved except Bedivere and Lucan, however, and they were now far ahead.

I gave my head a shake, freed my cloak, and hurried to

catch up. We had enough to worry about with real threats. We didn't need me imagining more.

CHAOS.

That was the only way to describe Confluence's main street.

The coffee shop where I'd once met with Paul had been demolished, tables and chairs and window glass scattered across the sidewalk where Lucan had stood watch. If Natalie —or anyone—was in there now, she couldn't be seen from our vantage point. Cars were strewn up and down the street, their roofs torn open. Crimson splotches stained the snow.

On the side of the street where Bedivere and Lucan and I stood, the town hall's clock tower lay in a pile of rubble at the base of the venerable stone building. A police car was skewed across the pedestrian walkway with its doors open and two officers sheltering behind them. More police cars, similarly open, interspersed the wrecked civilian vehicles. Right in front of the coffee shop, a dozen heavily armed and armored officers bailed out of a tactical van and ran to take up position behind what little protection the ruined building offered.

I shaded my eyes and looked skyward, following the point of their weapons, and felt my blood turn cold. A dozen shades wheeled above the remains of the town hall, circling and dipping through the air, each pass bringing them closer to the ground. I flinched from their sheer numbers. I knew only too well the damage a single creature could inflict with its talons and toxic, razor-sharp feathers. Knew, too, how hard they were to kill. One or two would have been challenging enough, but *twelve?* Over a town filled with vulnerable people?

"Fuck," I whispered.

"I see them," Lucan responded grimly. And then the gunfire began.

Semi-automatic guns spat hundreds of rounds of ammunition into the air, and for a moment, I could hear nothing else. I stuck my fingers in my ears against the din. Like a child, I wanted to squeeze my eyes shut until it was over, but I didn't. I couldn't. I needed to see what effect, if any, guns had against the creatures.

The answer, of course, was none.

I had no doubt that at least some of the bullets had found their mark—with that number of them being fired, it would have been impossible for them not to. But not a single shade fell from the sky or so much as wobbled in the air to signal that they might have been winged.

I'd expected as much, but my heart sank, nonetheless. It really was going to be us against all of them, wasn't it? My gaze went to the cops readying for another barrage, and then to the sword-bearing man and the wolf at my side.

And we were going to have to do it in front of everyone. We were going to have to expose magick.

The knowledge deserved a hearty round of *fuckity fuck fuck*, but I had no time to utter it. Not when the damned magick decided to seize control of me instead of the other way around.

Fuckity fuck became a surprised roar of "Jesus fuck!" as a white fireball rolled off my fingertips and sailed into the midst of the shades. The creatures shrieked in equal surprise—and one in agony as it dropped to the lawn of Town Hall.

Lucan shot me a startled look, then sprang toward the downed shade twitching in the snow and severed its head from its body as I struggled to contain a second fireball. Black fluid squirted upward in a steaming geyser from the shade's neck, and its companions flapped about in confusion overhead. One dipped too low, and Bedivere's wolf sprang upward with a roar.

Wolf and shade rolled across the snow-covered Town Hall lawn in a snarling, screaming tangle of fur and feathers, and Lucan spun away from his kill, sword at the ready. I focused on the remaining shades in the sky—all ten of them—as I wrestled with the elements rampaging through me and demanding their release.

I had more than enough magick in me to take out the creatures, but I didn't dare. Not like this. Not with Fire snarling through me as if it had a mind of its own, and Earth struggling to root me to the ground where I stood—and sure as hell not when Air hurtled toward me in a blast of wind that thundered down the street, tossing cars and cops aside like dried leaves as it drove a wall of snow before it. Snow swirled around the fallen shade and encased it in ice, then reached for the open-jawed police officers across the street.

Gritting my teeth, I ignored the threatening shades that had now zeroed in on me and focused instead on clawing back the sheer immensity of the power twisting through me—and toward the cops.

"Claire!" Lucan's bellow filtered faintly through the wind. I ignored him, too. The wind-driven snow wall was halfway across the street, but it was slowing. My feet, however, remained rooted to the ground—goddess, but I hated it when that happened—and Fire still raged at my core. I tried to center myself. To narrow my focus.

"One element at a time," Edie coaxed. *"Just—"*

"Maman!"

The familiar voice did in a millisecond what I hadn't been able to do myself, and my magick went *poof*. The snow wall dropped to the street, my feet came unstuck so quickly that I would have fallen if Lucan hadn't caught hold of my arm, and my core went cold.

"Natalie," I whispered. I pushed Lucan away as my frantic gaze probed the street, the wrecked buildings, the scattered cop cars.

"Watch out!" Edie shouted in my head. The warning almost deafened me from the inside out, but I ducked in time to dodge the incoming shade and the answering slash of Lucan's blade. He missed, and the shade wheeled away unharmed. Another started toward us, talons outstretched. The remainder lined up in a ragged formation in the sky.

The fuckers were organizing to take turns at me.

"Maman!" Natalie called again, and my head snapped around as Lucan deflected the incoming shade. This time I saw her. My daughter-in-law crouched in the narrow, pedestrian alley running between buildings to the left of the ruined coffee shop, and—

"I'll get her," said Lucan. "Wait here."

"No." I caught his arm as he began striding away. "Get her out of here," I said. "Take her back to the house."

"But milady," he objected, reverting to my title in sheer surprise, then he pulled me close with his left hand and swung his sword with the right. Something hot spattered against my cheek and a shade shrieked in pain and fury.

My stomach heaved as I swiped the back of my hand over the spatter, then wiped it off on my cloak. "Please tell me shade blood isn't as toxic as their feathers," I muttered.

"It's not."

"Good. Then go. Take Nat back to the others and wait for us there."

"I cannot leave you and Bedivere alone with"—Lucan waved his sword, scowling—"this. There are too many."

"Maman!"

My insides vibrated at the sound of Natalie's voice, and I curled my fingers into my palms as I tried to curb my panic. My impatience. The magick that wasn't mine.

"Lucan, I can deal with this, but the magick—it's complicated. I need to focus, and I can't as long as I'm worried about Nat."

And you.

141

Across the street, the gunfire started up again. I ducked my head and hunched my shoulders, but I didn't dare put my fingers in my ears this time. Not the way they were tingling right now—or with the memory of that white fireball still fresh in my mind. A glance at the sky found the next shade inbound, and I pushed away from Lucan.

"Go," I shouted over the guns. "Please! Get her out of here before—"

A new commotion reached us—whoops and hollers that sounded vaguely familiar, and ... a horse's neigh? I stopped in mid-bellow at Lucan, not believing my ears, and spun around to look for the source, because was that ...?

My jaw dropped.

Jesus fucking Christ. It was.

"Shit," I muttered. It was bad enough that my own magick was about to be revealed along with that of Bedivere and a dozen shades—but hey, who was counting, right?—now Confluence was about to meet an asshole of a Norse god as well?

"It's Odin," I said to Lucan, who hadn't yet had the pleasure. Odin, complete with Viking butler, Valkyries, Thyra, and his giant black horse—all armed and armored for battle.

Lucan tensed beside me, adjusting his grip on his sword as the Norse god pulled his horse to a stop in the center of the street. "Is that a problem?"

All of the cops' guns swiveled toward the newcomers. Oh, it was a problem, all right.

"Fuuuuck," breathed Edie in my head.

Flanked by his entourage, Odin dropped the reins and removed his helmet, gazing down at the heavily armed cops with an air that by Odin-standards seemed almost benevolent. Unfortunately, I was the only one who thought so.

"Greetings, humans," he called out. "I am Odin, come to your aid."

His words acted as a catalyst, and my heart landed with a

thunk beside my toes as, swiftly, a half-dozen police officers left the shelter of their vehicles and surrounded the Viking group, their weapons ready and their shouts menacing.

"Get down! Get down *now!*"

"Throw down your weapons!"

"Put your hands in the air!"

The orders came fast and furious, and Odin's brow darkened with each of them. Slowly, deliberately, he turned his head and stared at me, as if he'd known all along that I was there. He shook his head at me, shrugging as if to say, *"I tried, but they didn't want to listen,"* and my breath caught in my throat as he flexed his right hand and rubbed thumb against fingertips.

He wouldn't ... would he?

The air around the god darkened, and a rumble of thunder made the cops take a startled step back. Odin raised outstretched fingers toward the sky and a jagged bolt of lightning ripped into a police vehicle down the street, bouncing it skyward in a blinding shower of sparks.

Fuck. He would.

Armored cops dived away from the group and into the meager shelter of their vehicles, and shots rang out once more. One of the Valkyries spun about as if an invisible hand had reached out to her. She dropped to the ground, and without pausing to think—or overthink, as was my habit—I gathered Water in both hands and threw it between cops and Vikings. It formed as a tall, glistening wall of ice into which the hundreds of rounds of gunfire slammed harmlessly.

I paused to make sure it would hold, then threw up a second wall between me and the circling shades, turned to Lucan, and pointed across the street.

"Go!" I snapped, "Get Natalie and get out."

Without argument, Lucan plunged through the snowbank between us and the street. Everything in me wanted to watch until he got my daughter-in-law safely out of the alley, but the spit of semi-automatic weapons, a bellow of rage from Odin, and a yelp from Bedivere wouldn't let me.

I would have to trust my no-longer-shifter-but-still-protector, because I needed to end this. Now.

Pulling back my shoulders and straightening my spine, I called my full focus to bear and, with teeth gritted and sweat beading on my forehead, began to harness the power seething through me.

CHAPTER 20

I LIKED FIRE. I HADN'T ALWAYS, NOT WHEN IT HAD RESIDED IN me for years as "hormones," without me knowing what it was or what it could do. Now, however, it was familiar, and I found comfort in that familiarity. As far as one could find comfort in an inferno, anyway.

The more important thing was that I knew from experience that Fire could wound a shade; the one lying on the ground told me that it could kill one, too. And so Fire was what I called. Fire, in all its glorious, seething heat. In its tempestuousness. In its indescribable, untethered, wanton power. I called it. I held it. I contained it. I spoke to it. It was like the mother of all hot flashes ... until I released it in a rolling sweep of white-hot flames.

The eleven remaining shades—the one Bedivere had tackled had flown up to join its compatriots—didn't stand a chance. There was no escape. Even if they'd had somewhere they could fly to, they would have had no time to get there. My flames melted the ice wall between us, engulfed the shades, became them, and in an ear-splitting, shrieking instant, destroyed them—

And then—then the flames no longer belonged to me. Something bigger, something not mine seized them and wrenched them away from me, sending them out beyond the oily, black tendrils of the shades' remains in a horrible, all-consuming roil that I was powerless to stop.

I watched, horrified, as what I had conjured wreaked the very havoc that I'd feared. First, snow and ice melted into a lake of water that spread across the town hall lawn and then became a river that flowed down the street. Then the ice wall between Odin's party and the police dissolved into the river, carrying Valkyries and Odin's horse with it, swelling it into a roaring torrent that shattered storefronts and picked up cops and vehicles, tossing them about like bits of flotsam. Screams pierced the air—and my heart.

"Holy mother of—" Edie whispered into the bedlam of my head. *"Do something!"*

Her voice cut through my inertia, and I yanked my attention away from the grim scene unfolding before me. Gritting my teeth, I closed my eyes and turned every ounce of focus I possessed inward. The power was there, and it was oblivious to me. Instinctively, I turned away from what I didn't know— didn't understand—and called again on the familiar. The elements. *My* elements.

Earth rooted to me; Water rippled through my veins; Air swept into my lungs; Fire burned at my core … and then the four came together into one, a single knot of magick that unraveled into a voice that was all but swallowed by the rush of water.

"Stop," it said, and I caught my breath at its familiarity.

It was *my* voice, but bigger. My voice, but filled with the voices of the ones who had come before me. My voice, meshed with those of the ancestors. And at the sound of it, the power hesitated.

I centered myself and spoke again. "Stop," we said.

This time, the voice cut through the water and the screams of the police and the furious bellows from the Valkyries, and the power shrank a little. Then a little more. Then a little more.

"Enough," the voice said, and just like that, the last of the power retracted back into my center as utter silence fell over the street.

The last of the oily, black, fried-shade tendrils drifted earthward and settled onto the puddles. Valkyries and cops climbed to their feet. With a screech of metal on metal, a police vehicle slipped off another that it had landed on and hit the street with a thud. A steady *clop clop* heralded the return of Odin from wherever the river and my power—my *not* power—had carried him.

And the gazes of all those who had borne witness to my magick began to turn to me. I felt the impact of each and every one of them, along with the burgeoning fear behind them.

Well. The fear behind the cops' gazes, anyway.

Odin's gaze held only cold fury as he stopped his soaking-wet mount a few feet away and stared down at me. No. Fury and something else, something dark and absolute and—

Before I could identify what it was that I saw in the Norse god's eyes, he jerked the horse's black head around, slapped his booted feet against the massive sides, and galloped back down the street from where his company had come. The Viking butler picked up the injured Valkyrie and slung her over his shoulder, the remaining five women warriors sheathed their swords, Thyra stooped to retrieve the fallen one's weapon, and the entire company jogged in the wake of their overlord, their feet splashing through the remains of the river.

And then the cops trained their weapons on me.

"*Shit,*" said Edie.

I concurred. It would have been good to stay and search for the Mages who were undoubtedly behind this, but caution seemed the better part of valor right now, especially when there was no wall of ice to protect me—or Bedivere, whose wolf had come back to stand at my side. I wasn't at all sure I could conjure another before the bullets flew again. I was even less sure that I should try.

I put my hand out to rest on the thick fur of Bedivere's shoulder. "I think we should go," I murmured.

As if sensing our intent, a shout rose from among the officers. "Stop! Stay where you—"

Bedivere morphed back into human form, naked and

hairy at my elbow, cutting short the command. "Yes," he agreed, "we should."

He pulled me into the ley line writhing parallel to the sidewalk, and together we dissolved.

Once, ley travel without the protection of a magickal being had damned near killed me, and only the power that had seeped into me from the pendant of the Fifth Crone had made it possible at all.

Now, even though I hadn't been in the protective circle of Bedivere's arms, it barely ruffled my hair. Between that and the performance I'd put on just now in downtown Confluence, I was beginning to suspect that I had absorbed more from the Morrigan and Morgana than I'd thought. Or something other than their powers.

It was an unsettling idea.

Judging by the oblique, narrow look Bedivere slanted in my direction as we stepped out of the line again in the woods facing the house, I wasn't the only one who thought so. But dwelling on it would change nothing. Dwelling rarely changed anything.

For instance, I thought, trying hard to distract myself, I'd been over and over the Lucan conundrum a hundred times in my head since Freya had dropped her little bombshell—

"A hundred and five," Edie grumbled. *"At least."*

My lips twitched in spite of myself. Irritating as she could be, it was good to have her back. I'd missed her more than—

"I missed you, too," she said gruffly.

But that didn't change anything, either. Freya's deceit meant that I still couldn't cross over into the Otherworld to seal the breach I'd created, she and the Morrigan had both deserted us, I was the only one among my company—except for Baba Yaga—who had any power to speak of, and the gods would keep fleeing and the Between would keep coming. I'd faced a lot before this, and I had no intention of turning tail and running, but I honestly, truly could see no way out of this.

Especially not when I couldn't trust my own—

I gave a yip of surprise as a figure suddenly stepped out from behind a spruce tree to block the path. The sound hadn't even died away before Bedivere morphed and launched at its throat. In the same instant, I recognized one of the Valkyries —and the glint of metal in her hand. I reacted with a gust of Air that caught Bedivere in the side and sent him wide of his mark—and of the sword that had been aiming for his throat.

The wolf landed with a snarl in chest-deep snow that slowed him not at all. He sprang up and around, ready for another attack.

"Bedivere, no!" I cried.

Bedivere checked his wolf and changed course, landing back on the path in front of me, haunches tensed and head low between his shoulders as he snarled. The Valkyrie ignored him and looked down her nose at me.

"Odin will speak with you," she announced.

I glanced through the trees behind her at the house in the clearing that contained all I cared most about. Goddess, how I wanted to be there. I wanted to be sure that Lucan and Natalie had made it safely back, and that Natalie was okay. I wanted to learn more from her about what had happened in town. And I desperately wanted to get out of my robe and cloak that stank of dead shades, and—

"Now," the Valkyrie added.

And I really, really didn't want to see Odin again.

Really.

I considered telling the warrior where Odin could put his "invitation," but I hesitated. With Freya and the Morrigan both gone, I needed help. And Odin was the only potential for that help that I knew where to find. Well. *Potential* might be too strong a word. It was more of a possibility. A vague one.

At best.

But I had to try.

I stepped forward until I was abreast of Bedivere's wolf and put a hand on his shoulder. Muzzle drawn back in a snarl, he looked up at me, then morphed into his human form. The snarl stayed.

"Out of the question," he said, though I hadn't yet spoken.

"It wasn't a question."

The shifter crossed hairy arms over a hairier chest and sent a withering look at the Valkyrie before returning his glower to me. "I cannot allow—"

I lifted my chin. "I wasn't asking permission, either."

His scowl deepened. "It is a foolhardy thing to—"

"Odin is waiting," the Valkyrie interrupted, and the shifter morphed back into a crouching wolf again.

"Bedivere," I said, putting all the command I could muster into his name and willing him to stand down. After what had happened in town, I suspected things would be tense enough with the Norse god without deliberately provoking him.

Bedivere shifted again and whirled to face me. Then, sending a fierce look at the Valkyrie that dared her to stop him, he grabbed my arm and marched me a dozen feet down the path. When we were far enough away to satisfy him, he turned me so that my back was to Odin's messenger, and he could glare at her over my shoulder.

"By the goddess herself, milady," he growled at me, "you cannot be serious. I saw how the god looked at you in town, and you are all that *they*"—he pointed at the house with his stump—"have left. If something happens to you, they are lost."

My gaze followed his point back to the familiar lines of the house, this time letting it linger on the sturdy stone walls, the snow-covered slate roof, the smoke curling up from the many chimneys, the mullioned windows that glowed in the fading afternoon light.

I thought about the people behind those windows. My son and grandson and Natalie. Keven and Baba Yaga. The Crones and midwitches and Gus and Harry. Lucan. I thought about how some of them were willing to fight an unwinnable battle at my side, and how all of them were sacrificing for it. I thought about how Bedivere was right, and how it would be easier to agree with him. To let him convince the Valkyrie to let us pass, to follow him across the clearing and into the house, to let myself be folded into the warmth of those I loved and who loved me back.

So much easier.

For a little while, anyway. But then … then it would be anything but.

"The shades are only the beginning," I said quietly, still watching the house.

"Yes."

"And you know what is coming for us."

"I do."

"I can't stop it by myself, Bedivere."

"The others—"

"They can't stop it by themselves, either. Or with me. We're not enough."

For long seconds, the shifter said nothing. Then I heard him sigh.

"And you trust Odin?"

I snorted, raising an eyebrow in the direction of the waiting Valkyrie. "I don't trust any of them as far as I can throw them. But I have to try. And I think I can at least handle him if he tries anything. You saw in town what I can do."

LYDIA M. HAWKE

"I did," he agreed. "Forgive me if that fails to instill me with confidence."

"Welcome to the club," I muttered, sidling past him to follow Odin's warrior.

CHAPTER 21

VALKYRIES, IT TURNED OUT, COULD NOT TRAVEL THE LEY BY themselves, and this one recoiled as she might have from a medusa when I suggested that Bedivere or I could take her. So instead of taking the practical way, we walked back the same way she had come. Although *walk* wasn't the best choice of word for the sheer slog required to follow the warrior.

She backtracked easily, stepping into the footprints she'd already made, but her stride was too long for me to do likewise, and she made no effort to shorten it. Bedivere's wolf, seeing my struggle, moved in front of me and did his best to break trail, but I still sank up to my knees with every step, and the snow's crust still scraped shins that already felt raw from our earlier trek to town.

By the time we stood at the edge of the Norse god's camp, my trembling legs felt like they weighed a thousand pounds each, my lungs were burning, and *cranky* didn't even begin to describe my mood. For the sake of both my body and the upcoming negotiations, I stopped and leaned against a birch tree to catch my breath.

If the Valkyrie noticed, she gave no sign. She continued following her tracks out of the trees and across the clearing, and a raucous shout went up from her fellow warriors when they spotted her. Bedivere, however, did stop. Then he retraced his steps to join me and morphed back into his hirsute self.

"Are you all right?" he asked, and I had to consciously not raise an eyebrow at the unexpected solicitousness.

Still wheezing, I nodded instead of answering and took the opportunity to study Odin's camp—although *camp* was a serious understatement for what the god and his cohort had wrought in the heart of my woods.

The Vikings had been here mere days—I didn't have the brain capacity to stop and count how many—and already they had created a massive clearing in their construction of a log lodge that rivaled the size of the one Odin had occupied in the Otherworld. An enormous bonfire blazed before the building, with stumps arranged in a circle around it and a log chair —no, a throne—in their midst.

Odin occupied the throne, of course, while half the Valkyries—including the messenger—and Thyra sat on some of the stumps. The Viking butler stood beside the god, refilling his tankard from a leather flask, and the remaining Valkyries worked at butchering the bloody remains of a deer.

Bedivere grumbled something under his breath that I suspected echoed my own thoughts. Because freaking hell, the Norse god hadn't wasted any time in staking a claim here, had he?

I heaved a sigh and glanced at my companion. "Ready?" I asked, because there was no point in putting off the inevitable.

Wordlessly, the shifter slipped back into wolf-form and fell in at my side as I stepped out of the trees and into the clearing. Frozen branches, all that remained of the many trees that had been sacrificed for a god's ego, crunched under my booted feet. We had made it a third of the way across the clearing when, as if triggered by some unseen signal, Thyra, butler, and Valkyries all left their stumps and butchering to form a protective semi-circle around the fire between me and their god. All of them held weapons at their sides—including the Valkyrie who bore a rough bandage over the shoulder that had taken a bullet in town.

I paused for a moment as Fire flared in my core, then forced my feet to carry me forward, stopping out of sword-reach to meet Odin's gaze.

"You requested a meeting?" I said.

The enthroned god regarded me through the fire's dancing flames, his eyes narrowed, one brow raised, and his mouth tight. So, he hadn't liked my use of the word "requested?" Good. Because I hadn't liked being ordered.

I crossed my arms over my belly, physically holding on to the powers that roiled in me. I was supposed to be negotiating a treaty of sorts, not starting a whole other war.

"You interfered between me and the humans," he said finally. "I did not ask for your help."

"And I wasn't there *to* help," I retorted. "At least, not to help you."

Six swords and two spears lifted, and eight Vikings took a single, unified step toward me. Sheer stubbornness kept my feet rooted to the ground as I ignored them.

"So this is what saber-rattling looks like," Edie muttered.

Hush, I told her. *Let me focus.*

Across the fire, Odin got to his feet. He drained his tankard and tossed it aside, and it rolled across the packed snow to join a pile of others, all carved from yet more trees. My lips tightened.

"You are bold for a human," he said, and I didn't think he meant it as a compliment. He walked around the fire and the protective semicircle of Vikings and came to stand in front of me, close enough that I could smell the beer on his breath—and the stench of what smelled like rotted meat.

But I would not—could not, in what had become a silent battle of intimidation—step back. As subtly as I could, I switched to mouth-breathing through barely parted lips, but that only led to me being able to taste rotted meat as well as smell it. I gritted my teeth and tightened my arms around myself.

Odin leaned in closer, the stubble along his jaw brushing against my cheek.

"Except that's no longer what you are, is it?" he murmured in my ear. "You're not human anymore, are you?

Not entirely, anyway. You're not … you, anymore. You are … more."

And you are less.

The retort sat on the tip of my tongue, but Edie hissed, *"Inflammatory!"* in my head, and with no small amount of effort, I grudgingly caught it back. Cooperation, I reminded myself, not alienation.

"You're wrong," I said. "I'm still Claire Emerson, and I'm as human as I ever was. Which is why I've come to talk to you. I—"

Odin cut me off with a snort. "On the contrary, Claire Emerson who is not as human as she pretends, you are here because *I* wished to speak with *you.* What you did in your town, the power you drew on when you killed the shades … one wonders where that came from."

I didn't need the press of Bedivere's wolf against my leg to tell me that I was treading on thin ice here. Or the low rumble of a growl beneath his ribs. Given the history Odin had with the Morrigan, I wasn't about to tell the god about my acquisition of the goddess's powers. On the other hand …

One of the Valkyries standing behind the god shifted her grip on her sword. Another widened her stance. Thyra hefted her spear. I swallowed … hard.

On the other hand, I wasn't about to get away without telling him something.

"It's complicated," I said.

Odin reached out and gripped my chin with hard fingers. "Then I suggest you simplify it," he said softly. "For my sake."

"Shit," said Edie, as the power Odin asked about swirled through my veins at his touch.

Shit, I thought, as I grappled to keep it there.

Bedivere's rumble became audible. I put my hand on his shoulder, willing caution into him. Into myself. The magick swirled across my vision—*that* was new—and I blinked it away and met Odin's gaze with all the steadiness I could muster.

Simple, I told myself. *Keep it simple.*

"There was a witch once," I said. "A powerful one. Her name was Morgana. When I got to Camlann, I found her magick there, and it became part of me."

Odin's eyes narrowed, and his nostrils flared wide as I held my breath, and he weighed my words. Sparks exploded at the edges of my vision, and my skin felt as if it had taken on a life separate from mine. If the god didn't accept my explanation, if one of the Valkyries decided to attack—

A shadow crossed the god's expression, and for a split second, the gray eyes looked almost black. Then, as quickly as it had arrived, the shadow was gone, and he released his grip on me.

"See?" he said. "That wasn't as difficult as you thought. Now, what was it you wanted to speak with me about?"

I gaped at the sudden change in topic and sagged at his sudden letting-go. Only Bedivere's support kept me from stumbling, and I let myself lean against him for a moment. That was it? That was all Odin was going to say? Or ask? But—

"Gift horse," Edie muttered.

"What?"

"Stop looking a gift horse in the mouth, Claire. You need to get yourself and Bedivere out of here."

She was right. But I'd had my own agenda in coming here, and while I didn't think I would succeed after Odin's display just now, I had to at least try. I curled my fingers into Bedivere's thick fur.

"I came to tell you that you can't stay here," I began. Odin didn't let me get any further.

Chuckling, he crossed his arms over his armored chest. "On the contrary," he said, "I can and *will* stay here. By your own invitation, remember? We made a deal, Claire Emerson. Your safe passage through my lands in exchange for a favor."

"You misunderstand. I don't mean *here* here"—I took a

hand from the warmth of my robe and waved it at the lodge behind him—"I mean here in this world." I waved a wider circle over my head, narrowly missing his, which was still too close for comfort. "You can't stay on Earth at all, Odin. You don't belong here anymore. None of the gods do."

"And yet," he replied equably, "here we are." He studied me with the kind of curiosity one might direct at an insect before squashing it. "You do know that we originated here, right? That we created this world that you claim as your own?"

"But that's not entirely accurate, is it?" I asked. "You didn't create the world, the world created you. And then you left."

"Be that as it may, I'm back."

"But you can't be. The Between won't stop at the Otherworld, Odin. It will come here, too. You and the others have to—"

"Have to what? Go back and fight it?" This time, Odin didn't just chuckle, he put his head back and bellowed with laughter, and so did the Valkyries ... and Thyra ... and the butler ... and freaking hell, was that the horse nickering in its makeshift corral?

"And what," the god said when he'd caught his breath, "if I don't want to?"

My own breath snagged like glass in my throat. The shadow had returned to Odin's face, and the black to his eyes, starting at the edges of his irises and working its way toward the pupils until it had swallowed them—and what the hell *was* that?

Odin laughed again.

The power uncoiled in my chest.

CHAPTER 22

ODIN'S LAUGHTER FOLLOWED US ALMOST ALL THE WAY BACK through the woods before the Valkyries began partying again and their noise drowned it out. Predictably, I had not gained his cooperation.

On the upside, however, I had managed not to unleash the magick that seemed bent on testing every constraint I placed on it. I had Bedivere's wolf to thank for that, because sensing my rising anger, he'd bumped into my leg and knocked me off balance just as the power's tentacles had slithered down my arms and spread into my fingers. The distraction had been enough—just—to let my brain direct me to turn and walk away instead of knocking Odin's supercilious ass onto the ground where it deserved to be.

"*I dunno,*" Edie muttered. "*I personally think you should have done it.*"

"Not helpful," I replied.

Bedivere, a few steps ahead and in human form, had stopped to peer into the darkening forest, his head tipped back as if testing the wind the way his wolf might. He looked over his shoulder at the sound of my voice, his ever-present scowl in place. Damn. I'd spoken aloud, forgetting that only Lucan and Keven knew about my friend's ghost, although they didn't yet know about her return. I supposed my lapse could be forgiven under the circumstances—because shades and Odin, and what the *fuck* had I seen in his eyes back there?—but unless I wanted to explain Edie as well as all my other issues—

Edie *harrumphed* in my ear. "*I'm an issue now, am I?*"

"*You know what I mean,*" I told her, using my inside voice this time. Ahead of us—me—Bedivere turned back to the trail

159

and continued plodding through the snow, his breath leaving a lingering vapor trail.

I wrapped my cloak more tightly around me and followed the naked, barefoot shifter. How could he not feel the cold?

"It's all that hair," Edie said, and I caught back a snort.

"Be nice," I told her.

"Sympathy for Mr. Grumpy-pants? When did that happen?"

"He's—grown on me," I said. *"He has a good heart."*

"A good heart."

"He stayed, Edie. He stayed when the others left. And he's acting as my protector in spite of … everything." In spite of what I'd done to his brother.

"Huh," grunted my ghost. Then she sighed. *"Fine. I'll leave the surly shifter alone. But you, on the other hand …"*

"What about me?"

"Exactly. What about you? Specifically, what about those other issues you lumped me in with? More specifically, that power you don't seem to have much of a grip on."

"More like *any* grip," I muttered, as much to myself as to her.

Bedivere had stopped to wait for me, and as I drew abreast of him, I saw that we'd almost reached the clearing. We were home again. Through the last fringe of trees, the house waited for us, the lights in its windows holding back the dark of encroaching night, the wards sparkling in a net above it. It felt present, welcoming … safe. I drew a deep breath, held it a second, and then released it in a sigh of gratitude.

Whatever was coming, whatever we had to face, I at least had this. This house, these people, this moment—

And then, as it had done earlier on our trip into town, snow shifted against snow in the woods behind us.

The sound was as innocuous this time as it had been when I'd heard it earlier, but for some reason, it made the hair on the back of my neck stand on end. I glanced at Bedivere to my right and found his wolf standing rigid, nose lifted and sharp gaze fixed on the shadowed forest.

"Do you see something?" I whispered. "Is it Odin's—"

A slow, rhythmic drumbeat began, bouncing off the trees and echoing through the woods. I couldn't pinpoint its source, but it wasn't Viking-generated. Oh, no. It was worse than that. Much, much worse.

Memories flooded my veins with ice water.

"Bedivere?" I croaked. "Is that what I th—"

Before I could finish, shards and chunks of ceramic erupted from beneath the snow all around us and began fusing together—but in all the wrong order. I watched in stunned disbelief as a beard slammed into a shoulder where an arm should have been, a half-missing face replaced a torso, arms went where legs should have been on bodies that faced the wrong way, and bright blue eyes clicked onto the top of a broken hat.

Disbelief turned to appall as the bits and pieces became grotesque caricatures of the creatures they had once been. But their appearance mattered not at all to the gnomes that were coming for us. They closed in on us from every direction, limping, crawling, lurching …

And there were hundreds of them.

"Fucking hell," Edie said.

Bedivere snarled a warning and launched his wolf at a one-eyed, one-armed gnome leading a mini-charge on our left flank. I focused on the right, where an enormous figure towered above its companions, built of dozens of gnomes that had piled together. Multiple broken faces grinned at me from its seven-foot height, and countless arms and misplaced feet waved cheerfully at me as it lumbered toward us. A frisson of horror ran through me—not at the attack itself, but at the gruesomeness of its soldiers. The sheer wrongness.

The drums grew closer, and the rhythmic sound of hundreds of tiny feet marching in unison joined them. Reinforcements. Awesome.

I sent a wave of Air at the multi-gnome. Ceramic parts fell away from one another and rained to the ground. Almost immediately, they came together again in another gnome, and another, and another.

From the corner of my eye, I saw Bedivere go down under a pile of the creatures, and I sent another blast of Air at those, pushing them back and shattering them against one another. Bedivere bounded to his feet and threw himself back into the fray.

The gnomes reassembled.

I switched to a combination of Air and Fire. A blast to shatter them, then Fire to melt the shards. Broken bits of gnomes picked themselves up from the battle-scarred snow and reunited with melted globs of gnomes.

"Fuck," I muttered under my breath. I called on Water and threw up a wall of ice, encasing them in a tomb; they broke free in seconds. The drums were almost here. So were the marching feet.

"I don't think it's working!" Edie shouted over the crash and tinkle of ceramic bouncing off trees and ice.

Light spilled across the clearing from the front door of the house, and through the trees, I caught a glimpse of Keven framed in the doorway, with Baba Yaga behind her—and then my gaze settled on Lucan, sword upraised, racing across the snow toward us.

My heart stalled in my chest for an instant, and then I remembered that the gnomes couldn't cross the clearing. The house and its occupants were safe. Lucan was, too, as long as he stayed—

The former shifter crashed into the woods, sword swinging

wide and decapitating—again—a half dozen gnomes. I opened my mouth to order him back, then snapped it shut again. First, because there was no way he'd listen, and second, because his presence at my side gave me strength. Calm. Focus.

But none of those helped against the steady stream of horror coming at us. The gnomes were an endless, relentless tide, forming and reforming as fast as Bedivere, Lucan, and I could knock them apart, and if I unleashed more power …

I cringed from the very idea. The only magick that would stop the gnomes entirely might well get away from me—again—and stop everything else, too. The woods and the creatures who lived in it, even in winter. The trees that I had already once destroyed and vowed since to protect.

The wards that protected my family and friends.

Lucan's back pressed against mine, and I felt the surge of his shoulders as his sword swung left, then right. In the shadows before me, Bedivere's snarls grew increasingly furious. And the drums were almost here, sounding as if they were angling to come between us and the clearing. If they cut us off, we'd be out here indefinitely, stuck between the figurative rock and hard place unless I did the unimaginable.

"We cannot hold them, milady!" shouted Lucan behind me.

I made my decision.

"Bedivere!" I shouted. Bedivere's wolf tossed an armless, faceless gnome against a tree and looked to my voice. I pointed at the clearing with one hand and with the other, sent Air at three more gnomes about to land on his back. They sailed into the shadows.

"House!" I yelled.

His sides heaving, Bedivere's head dipped between his shoulders—in agreement, I hoped—and he turned back to the battle. This time, however, instead of holding his ground, he fell back step by step, letting himself be pushed back to the edge of the trees, controlling the influx but not trying to stop it. At my back, Lucan did likewise, slowly taking me with him, clearing the path for me.

It felt like it took an eternity, but it could have only been minutes, because we made it before the drums did. And then Edie was yelling, *"Go!"* in my head, and the three of us were turning tail—Bedivere, literally—and bolting toward the house.

Then, and only then, I saw that hundreds of creatures had encircled the entire clearing. Whole ones, cobbled-together ones, hideously disfigured ones. They stood shoulder to shoulder, a veritable wall of grinning ceramic, and then the wall took a step forward, out of the woods.

My own steps faltered. For one heart-stopping moment, I thought we had made an awful mistake. That *I* had made an awful mistake. And then four Crones, a dozen midwitches, Jeanne, and Baba Yaga all spilled from the house, their voices raised in chant and hands joined above their heads, and in a blinding flash, the net of wards fused together, lit up the night, and held.

We were safe. For now.

But who in hell had brought the gnomes back to life?

CHAPTER 23

KEVEN PEELED AWAY THE BLANKET AROUND ME UNTIL SHE found a hand to thrust a mug of tea into. "Drink," she said.

"I'm honestly okay," I told her, because I was. Lucan had picked me up and carried me into the house over my protests; Maureen and Anne had stripped my ruined cloak from me, given it to Baba Yaga for repair, and wrapped me in not one but two blankets; Jeanne had stoked the sitting room fire; and the midwitches had taken Harry and Braden—both of whom wanted to share my lap—out to the kitchen for snacks and distraction.

I was as cared for as anyone could possibly be, but I really didn't need it.

Keven glared at me. "Drink," she growled again, pointing at the mug. Wrapped around her neck, Gus glared, too.

I drank.

Only when I had finished the last dregs—and shown the gargoyle the empty cup—did she allow any of us to speak. As if by unspoken agreement, the others yielded to Lucan, who hadn't stopped scowling and pacing since he'd put me down on the sofa.

"Odin?" he asked.

I shot a quick look at Paul and Natalie, wondering if I should send them to join their son before we got into this. Natalie looked exhausted after her own ordeal, and Paul might know about my magick, but he didn't *know* know, and I wasn't sure I was ready to share it with him. I wasn't sure I was ready to share it with anyone.

On the other hand, after my display in town, I supposed that ship had sailed. I pulled the blanket closer.

"Odin is ..." I hesitated.

"A dick?" Maureen muttered. "Enough of one to bring the gnomes back and try to take over the world?"

"I like her," said Edie.

"I don't know," I answered Maureen. "Maybe, I suppose, but it doesn't seem like his way of doing things. He's too arrogant. Too sure of himself. If he's planning to take over the world, he's going to want everyone to know that it's him. Which makes him—"

"A problem," Bedivere interrupted on a growl. "A serious one."

Lucan's scowl deepened, and his gaze traveled between me and his brother. It settled on the latter. "Explain."

Briefly, Bedivere told the gathering how Odin had threatened to turn on the police, and how I'd thrown up a wall of ice between them ... and how furious he'd been when I'd destroyed the shades. Judging by the darkening of Lucan's expression, that part of the story alone was bad enough. The rest—the part about being waylaid by the Valkyrie and my chat with Odin—was worse.

The entire room was silent when Bedivere finished his story, and I wondered idly who would find what part of the tale to be the most unsettling. Would it be Odin's high-handedness? The fact that magick—mine and a Norse god's—had been so thoroughly outed in the public eye? Or—

"Eleven shades," murmured Anne, "and she took them all down at the same time?"

Or that.

"Indeed, milady," Bedivere said, before I could deflect the question ... or hedge my answer ... or maybe just pull the blanket over my head.

On the opposite sofa, my son's mouth opened as if to speak, but Natalie's fingers, entwined with his, gave a quick squeeze and he subsided back into silence. I tried to catch his eye and give him a reassuring smile, but his gaze slid away from mine, and he stared steadfastly into the fire, wrestling with this new aspect of the world—and his mother. The rest of the group's gazes, however …

"It's not that big a deal," I told the Crones, preferring to address their shock over Lucan's disapproval. "They were all clustered together in the sky. They were an easy—"

"Claire." Elysabeth leaned forward on the opposite sofa, resting her elbows on her knees. "We're fighting for our lives here. Our very existence. We need to be able to trust you."

I bristled at the implication. "You *can* trust—"

"If we had secrets," Nia broke in, "would you trust us?"

Touché.

But how did I tell the ones who depended on me, on my magick, that I had somehow become the least predictable thing in their lives? How—

For the second time that day, the front door in the hallway crashed open, Bedivere morphed and Lucan didn't, and I leapt to my feet.

IT WAS A GOOD THING THAT THE FORM IN THE GREAT HALL outside the sitting room belonged to a goddess and not a human, given the fireball that left my fingertips before I could snatch it back.

Or maybe not, given that the goddess stepping out of the blue flames and dodging Bedivere's wolf was Freya. I scowled and readied another blast, torn between being terrified at the speed of my powers and the desire to test them further.

Specifically on her.

"Hold!" The goddess waved something aloft, as she might a flag, but this flag was black rather than white, and it squawked furiously.

No. It didn't squawk, it cawed. And it flapped. And it appeared to be trying its damnedest to take out the Norse goddess's eyes. I choked on my own breath. Freaking hell, it was the Morrigan. Freya had captured the Morrigan and—

Freya slammed the door shut behind her with one foot and turned a triumphant gaze on me. "I've returned your goddess to you," she announced, "so that you may save your world and ours."

And with that pronouncement, she released the bird into the air. The Morrigan, her remaining powers no longer contained by the Norse goddess's hold, exploded into a dozen black furies. Freya pulled her sword from its sheath at her side and waved it in a wide circle around her head.

"Please," she invited the Morrigan between clenched teeth. "I dare you."

Bedivere's wolf snarled a warning, Lucan drew his sword and strode across the room to join him, and I hastily dropped my blanket on the couch and slipped past Maureen and Nia to follow him. In the great hall, I stood not with Lucan, but with Bedivere, resting my hand on the raised ruff of fur along the wolf's spine in silent caution. I had no idea whether Freya's power was enough to kill him, but I had no doubt it could at least do significant damage—and he had suffered enough of that on my behalf.

Bedivere's growls subsided, and he morphed back into human form, turning a look on me that demanded to know what I was going to do about the goddess hostilities taking place. It was a good question.

My first inclination was to turn around and go back to tea in the sitting room, leaving the two of them to fight it out, but the house didn't deserve the havoc they would likely wreak. Which meant I had no choice but to intervene and—

Keven beat me to it.

"Desist!" Her gravelly roar rumbled through the great hall with the force of a minor earthquake, sending a tremor into the house's very foundation and bringing a rain of dust down from the ceiling timbers onto Freya's head and the crows circling it.

Abruptly, the crows came together as the Morrigan. She and Freya stood side by side, staring in shock at the gargoyle who had joined us. Freya recovered first.

Her blue eyes narrowed to slivers of ice as she regained her composure. "You *dare* speak to me that way?" she demanded of Keven, her voice a dangerous hiss of sound. "You dare disrespect—"

"Respect," Keven snapped back, looming over the goddess, "is earned. And you, Freya of the Norse, have done nothing to earn it in this house that does not belong to you."

They might have come to actual blows, then, my gargoyle and Freya. A striking of sword against stone, perhaps, or one goddess's magick against the product of another's—with who knew what outcome. They might have, if the power I'd grappled with all day hadn't quietly, simply, and once more eluded my grasp.

It happened so fast that I had no time to even think a warning, let alone give voice to it. One minute, six of us—me, Keven, Freya and the Morrigan, Lucan, and Bedivere's wolf— were standing almost toe-to-toe at the foot of the stairs in the great hall ... the next, we were being buried in a hail of timbers, splinters, and dust that all but swallowed Edie's roar in my head of, *"Claire, no!"*

Thank the goddesses—all the ones not present, anyway— that the only others standing in the hall were magickal creatures of one sort or another, able to survive my inadvertent tantrum. Perhaps fittingly, it was I who suffered the greatest impact ... and the most damage. The center beam landed directly on top of me, pinning me against the flagstone floor. Only the fact that it was held up at one end, where it had also landed on Keven, kept it from crushing me entirely.

For what felt like an eternity, I couldn't breathe, couldn't move, couldn't even feel anything beyond shock. Then the pain set in.

Holy mother of everything and everyone that had ever lived or would live or might live, but it hurt. My ribs, my shoulders, my skull, my legs—even my eyes hurt when I dared to blink against the grit filling them. Or maybe that was my eyelashes that hurt. I wouldn't have been surprised if it was.

At one time, not all that very long ago in the timeline of my life, panic would have gained the upper hand and magnified the pain a thousandfold, but in the last months, I'd been through too much—*lived* through too much—to feel much bother at the mere dropping of a ceiling on myself. The beam, perhaps strategically dropped by the house itself, had saved me from death, and I knew from the same months of living that I would heal, and so not even the baseline of pain took much attention.

Which, as I resigned myself to waiting for rescue, left plenty of time for the foreboding in my belly to send tendrils snaking into my chest and around my heart. I wanted to believe that I'd lost control just then, but the truth was that I hadn't had any control in the first place. Not over whatever that had been. I'd been trying to hold back the Morrigan's power, yes, but what had slipped from me had been different. Been other. I hadn't summoned it, hadn't wanted—

"*But you did,*" whispered Edie's voice in my head. "*You did want it. Oh, Claire …*"

What little air remained in my lungs left me in a hiss, but before I could reflect on the truth of my friend's words, the beam shifted suddenly sideways and hard fingers seized my upper arms. With no thought—or perhaps just no care—for my injuries, Freya yarded me upright and shook me until my head snapped back and forth like a puppet's.

"Where?" she demanded. "Where did you get power like that?"

CHAPTER 24

THEY SAY CONFESSION IS GOOD FOR THE SOUL. IT ISN'T, however, always a good thing for personal safety. Especially when that personal safety is being threatened by a goddess.

"*No* control?" Freya demanded. The expressions flitting across her face alternated between disbelief, horror, and something I didn't care to identify but that made me glad I had Lucan, Bedivere, and Keven here for backup.

The Norse goddess and I stood before the fireplace. Or perhaps faced off was a better phrase for it, given that she had sword in hand and I could feel Fire clawing at my belly. Keven stood behind me, her solid presence at my back helping me hold myself upright, and Lucan and Bedivere's wolf were behind the goddess. Both were primed for a fight. The Morrigan paced restlessly in front of the window beyond them. The four Crones had crowded onto one of the sofas flanking the hearth, Natalie and Paul had taken the other nearest me, and Jeanne …

Jeanne hovered halfway between us and escape.

Conscience stabbed my heart. The poor woman looked as harried and exhausted as I'd ever seen her, and I could only imagine the regret she must be feeling at having chosen to throw her lot in with mine. I made a mental note to talk to her —maybe tomorrow, after I'd recovered somewhat from my day from … huh.

My weary mind toddled off in a random direction as I wondered if hell actually existed somewhere in the Otherworld, and whose domain it would be there. Would it belong to Satan? Lucifer? Hades, who had apparently returned to Earth? Huh. If that were the case, would hell have followed him here? Who knew? Maybe Hell on Earth would become an actual thing.

Freya hissed in annoyance, jerking me back to the present. I sighed and repeated what I'd already told her. Twice.

"No control *sometimes*," I enunciated the words as clearly as I could from between teeth clenched with the effort of holding onto the Fire that had almost slipped through my fingers.

"Distraction bad," Edie muttered.

"No shit, Sherlock," I grumbled in return.

Freya stared down her nose at me, blue eyes narrowed in suspicion. "And other times?"

Like now? The words sat on the tip of my tongue, but I bit them back when Edie intervened again.

"Probably not helpful, my friend. Just saying."

I sighed again, managed not to roll my eyes, and said instead, "Other times, it happens before I can stop it."

Freya's gaze flicked over her shoulder to the Morrigan, barely visible in the deep shadows away from the fire. Night had settled, but the house had refused to turn on any of its lights. I was pretty sure it was a protest against what I'd done to it—again. Keven had dug into her stores and found a handful of candlesticks but no lanterns, Freya didn't seem to care enough to provide additional light, and I wasn't sure the Morrigan could, anymore.

I might have been able to provide light myself, but it hadn't escaped my notice that no one had suggested the idea. Least of all me.

"Is this normal for your powers?" Freya demanded of her cohort.

"None of this is *normal*," the Morrigan snapped back. "Including you taking me captive."

"Well, if you hadn't left in a temper—"

"*Me?*" The Morrigan's shadow stopped pacing. "You blame *me* after *you* rendered my powers next to useless?"

"Oh, for fuck's sake," Edie and I said together.

Freya turned her wrath on me again, her scowl telling me that an apology was in order—or at least expected. I suspected the Morrigan's expression was equally fierce, but I didn't give a rat's patootie at this point. Between shades and Odin and gnomes, I'd had a bitch of a day all around, and I'd had more than enough of Freya and the Morrigan's bickering.

The strain of not unleashing Fire and simply ending their squabble had become painful. I had a massive headache, I was tired, I was hungry, my legs wobbled precariously beneath my robe, and I desperately wanted nothing more than to fall into bed after hugging my grandson. I started around the sofa where Paul and Natalie sat, heading for the doors.

"I'm done for tonight," I told the goddesses. "Keven will prepare a room for each of you"—assuming the house cooperated and expanded enough after my latest incident, otherwise the two of them could camp out in the cellar, for all I cared—"and we'll continue tomorrow at breakfast."

I looked over my shoulder to the gargoyle for confirmation, and Keven nodded.

"Of course, milady."

Their expressions visibly and uniformly relieved, the Crones and Paul and Natalie all scrambled up from the sofas to accompany me—and escape the goddesses—and Lucan and Bedivere brought up the rear. Unsurprisingly, Freya's voice followed us.

"We are not done, Crone," she called, "until *I* say—"

"Oh, in the name of the Weaver herself, Freya," interrupted the Morrigan wearily as I reached the double doors, "give it a rest."

Jeanne opened the double doors, scurried through them ahead of all of us, and then slammed them closed again, shutting the two goddesses in with the incredibly forbearing Keven, to whom I would express my eternal gratitude later.

Resting her back against the doors for support—or perhaps to make sure they stayed closed—Jeanne shook her head. "Jesus Christ on a cracker," she muttered. "That one is a piece of work, isn't she?"

Edie did a double-take in my head. *"Did she just say …?"*

I was just as surprised as she was by the words I'd never thought I'd hear Jeanne speak, but I had no capacity for reacting to them. That, like everything else, would have to wait until morning. Right now, I was entirely, totally focused on getting to the sleeping grandson I so desperately wanted to see and then falling into bed. I started for the stairs.

Or tried to.

But without warning—or without *more* warning than their wobble so far—my legs had just … stopped.

I stood for a moment, perplexity clouding my thoughts. Had I inadvertently triggered the Earth element? I wouldn't put it past myself tonight. I felt around inside myself, but no, there was no sensation of anything holding me to the ground. No tendrils wrapped around my ankles, no roots—

I lifted my robe away from my feet and peered down at them to be certain, even though elemental Earth magick was invisible when it joined with me. As expected, my feet looked fine. They just weren't moving.

"Huh," I said.

"Claire?" Lucan sheathed the sword he'd kept at the ready until now. "What's wrong?"

"My legs," I began, and then multiple hands reached for me as I crumpled toward the floor. Lucan's were the ones that caught me. His grip on my shoulders was as gentle as it was strong as he guided me to the beam still lying across the ceiling-littered floor and pushed me down to sit on it. Then, without a word, he crouched before me, took both my hands in his, and simply held them as the others gathered around us.

Maureen sat down on one side of me and Jeanne on the other. Anne, Nia, and Elysabeth picked their way through the rubble to stand at my back, and I closed my eyes as someone's hand settled atop my head. Four more hands settled onto me, covering my shoulders and my forearms, and a slow warmth that was not my own and—blessedly—not the power's spread over me. The warmth of healing.

For a moment, I tensed against that which my friends offered. *I* was supposed to be the strong one, I told myself. *I* was the one with the power of a goddess and the magick of the first Crone, and—

"Yes," said Edie, *"but yours isn't the only magick, and you're not the only one who cares. Let them in, Claire. Let them do this for you."*

My breath hitched as the healing began to sink beneath my skin, to reach for my bones, my heart, my center. My eyes squeezed tighter as I steeled myself to accept the gentleness and the love that was behind it. I didn't expect that my friends would be able to fix whatever problems plagued me, but maybe—just maybe—they could take the edge off the day so that I could sleep and let my subconscious do the work that my conscious could not. Because one way or another, somehow, I *needed* to learn to own the power that wanted to own me.

At first, I had to hold myself still. But slowly, oh so slowly, my hands began to relax in Lucan's, my shoulders softened, my breathing deepened, and my heartbeat slowed, and then ...

The sound of a knock broke the spell—literally.

My eyes snapped open as the warmth that had enveloped me abruptly, jarringly withdrew. Momentary panic replaced it as I struggled to get my bearings. Bedivere had replaced Jeanne in leaning against the sitting room doors, and at first, I thought the knocking had come from one of the goddesses wanting to get out. Even as Edie reminded me that such manners seemed beyond gods and goddesses in general, however, the knock came again—from the outside door.

In the blink of an eye, the hands that held me all dropped away, Bedivere morphed into his wolf and launched himself across the great hall in a snarling blur of teeth and fur, and Lucan followed with sword drawn.

The front door—that poor front door—crashed open yet again, shifter and knight disappeared into the dark, and all remnants of fatigue fell away from me as the Morrigan's unbridled power surged unbidden once more.

CHAPTER 25

SOMEHOW, I MANAGED TO LEASH THE POWER ON MY WAY TO the door and not destroy the rest of the hall. Leashing Bedivere and Lucan was another matter. By the time I got to them, the wolf was crouched on top of a prone figure spreadeagled on its back in the snow at the edge of the flagstone porch, Lucan's sword rested against the same figure's throat, and whoever that throat belonged to was in serious danger of expiring.

"Stop!" I ordered.

Lucan slanted a brief glower at me over his shoulder but kept his sword in place. Bedivere just snarled some more.

Swiftly, I assessed the form, taking in the worn boots, the threadbare clothing, and the bare, dark-skinned hands resting in supplication on either side. A woman's hands. A woman who had gotten through the wards and therefore posed no threat.

"Huh." Edie grunted. *"You're forgetting that Odin and Freya got through, too."*

She had a point, but we'd given both of them a chance to speak, and—

"And look how that *worked out."*

It was too freaking cold out here to hold any kind of interrogation. My fingers already stiffening up, I stepped out onto the frozen porch and tugged on Lucan's sleeve.

"Help her up," I told him.

Lucan hesitated, then grunted and stepped back to resheath his sword. Bedivere issued a last, deep grumble, his breath a cloud of steam over the woman's head, and then leapt aside and morphed into human form. With an unhappy look at me, Lucan stretched out a hand. The woman—no, not

177

a woman, because Edie was right, no woman could have gotten past the wards the way she had, not to mention the gnomes still beating their damned drums in the woods—the *goddess* hesitated and then reached up to accept the offered assistance. Lucan pulled her to her feet.

I pulled together my resolve—because freaking hell, the last thing I needed was another goddess right now—and took a deep breath.

"Who are you," I asked, "and why are you here?"

Brown eyes skated over Lucan, settled briefly on the naked Bedivere, and then met mine. "I'm Mary," she said quietly. "Mary of Magdala, and—"

A muffled gasp came from the open door behind me, and I glanced back to see Jeanne sinking to her knees in the hall.

"Jesus Christ," she whispered, only this time, I suspected she meant it exactly as she said it and not as an epithet, because—

"Mary *Magdalene?*" she croaked, confirming my shocked recognition of the name.

Shocked, because Mary Magdalene had been an apostle, not a deity, and—

"Says who?" asked Edie dryly. *"The almighty male-dominated church that tried to destroy her gospel?"*

My gaze returned to the woman, taking in the dark skin, the long brown hair peeking out from beneath a head scarf, and the steady, unflinching, most profoundly soulful eyes I'd ever seen as I tried to reconcile the possibility.

"You know this makes this akin to a second coming, right?" Edie added.

"Not helping," I growled at her. But in a sense, she was right, and judging by the other Crones' faces—and those of Natalie and Paul, who had also been drawn in by the commotion— she wasn't the only one thinking it.

To say that our company was stunned by the woman's— the goddess's—appearance on our doorstep would have been akin to calling Freya and the Morrigan mildly annoying. But that was neither here nor there at the moment, because pain was etched in every line of her face, and she was reaching a thin, brown hand toward me, her fingers trembling.

"I seek sanctuary," she said. "Please."

And then she collapsed on the flagstone porch.

Lucan—bless his heart, because my brain had simply stalled—took immediate charge. He hoisted our unexpected guest into his arms and headed back toward the sitting room, barking instructions over his other shoulder. In response, Nia scurried down the corridor toward the kitchen to summon Baba Yaga, their fellow Crones scattered in search of blankets and supplies, Bedivere opened the sitting room doors for Lucan and bellowed for Keven's assistance, Natalie took Paul's arm and steered him back toward the stairs and their bedchamber, and Jeanne ...

Jeanne looked up at me from behind her red-framed glasses with stricken eyes. "*Mary Magdalene* is one of them?" she whispered. "She's a *goddess*? She lives with the others? But *how*? And does that mean—does Jesus live there, too? He's not real?"

I pushed the front door shut against the drums and the endless Odin-party and then crouched beside her, choosing my words carefully, knowing what lay behind her questions. Knowing that, in the world she'd grown up in, what I was about to say would be blasphemy. And honestly not knowing quite where to even start.

I settled on the Jesus issue, given that I suspected he was the crux of Jeanne's inner struggle. "He is real," I said, "inasmuch as they all are—or were, at some point in time. We made them real, like I explained."

"But he's different," she objected. "He's supposed to be different. He's the son, Claire. "The son of *God*. Does that mean *God*...?" She trailed off, her expression flummoxed.

Briefly, wistfully, I thought about the grandson I still

wanted to hug—and the bed I longed for—and then I sighed and settled myself on the floor with her. The cold of the flagstone seeped into hips that ached with weariness. Would this day ever end? Would this *nightmare* end? Putting an arm around her shoulders, I gave my friend a squeeze.

"I don't know for sure," I allowed, "but ... yes, I think so. I think they were us once, the way Freya said, and then, because we didn't know better, we built them into something more. It's not a bad thing, really, it just ... is."

"I'm not sure she can do this," Edie muttered. *"Not without her brain exploding."*

"Be kind," I told her, forgetting to use my inside voice. Jeanne gave me a slow blink, then sighed.

"She's back, isn't she?"

I thought about denying it, but really, what was the point? Nia was right, I reminded myself. No more secrets.

"Yes," I said.

"I wish I could hear her, too," Jeanne said wistfully. "I miss her." Her face turned hopeful. "Does she have anything she wants to say to me?"

Edie groaned. *"Yes. Tell her she just took all the fun out of this, damn it."*

I repeated her words to Jeanne, and our former neighbor and mutual friend smiled, chuckled, and then dissolved into tears in my arms.

"That's what she needs," Edie said, her voice suspiciously tight, *"a good cry."*

She wasn't the only one, I thought as I sat on the floor and rocked Jeanne to the muffled beat of the gnome drums outside. But some of us would have to wait for a while.

ELYSABETH CAME TO MY RESCUE SOMETIME AFTER JEANNE'S sobs had died away. I'd been contemplating the possibility of moving for the last several minutes, but my friend's head rested on my shoulder, and the arm I had around her had seized up, as had my hips, and I wasn't sure my various body parts would cooperate with the idea. By the time Elysabeth's hand settled on the shoulder not cradling Jeanne, a low-grade panic was beginning to set in.

"She's awake," she whispered to me, nodding toward the sitting room and our guest. "I'll take Jeanne up to her room so you can go see her, if you'd like."

I did not like. I did not like at all. I would have preferred never to lay eyes on another goddess so long as I lived, at this point, in fact, but …

I nodded at Elysabeth, and she reached down to help Jeanne up from the floor. My arm slid away from my friend with an audible, crackling protest from my shoulder. The Crone paused.

"Are you all right?" she asked. "Do you need help up?"

"I'm fine," my pride replied. And then it waited until Elysabeth and Jeanne were halfway up the stairs before it attempted actual movement.

Difficult movement.

Freaking painful movement.

Magick, I decided, would be a great deal more helpful if it could at least make me feel younger on occasion instead of older.

"You do know that pride goeth before a fall, right?" Edie said.

"You don't happen to come with an off switch, do you?" I growled from my hands and knees as I pondered stage two of my rising. A hand appeared in front of my nose, scarred and misshapen, and I closed my eyes. Bedivere. Of course it would be Bedivere. I should have taken Elysabeth's help.

"Told you," said Edie.

I opened my eyes, lifted one hand from the cold stone, and

reached for Bedivere's hand. His thumb and two remaining fingers encircled my wrist, and he pulled me effortlessly to my feet. Well, effortless on his part, anyway.

"Thank you," I said, pulling away from his hold as my body settled into the idea of being upright again.

He grunted. "Lucan sent me," he said.

His way of letting me know that my protector was watching out for me? Or that helping me wasn't his idea? I pushed away the uncharitable thought that was likely born of pain and fatigue—or maybe just plain grumpiness. Bedivere had gone above and beyond in looking after me, I reminded myself. General irascibility aside, he deserved better from me.

"Well," I said, "thank you anyway."

The shifter shrugged and turned back toward the sitting room. I hesitated, casting a longing glance at the stairs leading up to my bedchamber. Then, with a deep sigh that felt like I'd dredged it up from my toes, I shored up my flagging reserves and shuffled after him.

Mary Magdalene lay on one of the sofas, her head scarf gone, shoulders propped up on pillows, and feet toward the fire. The others—Lucan, Keven, the two goddesses, and the Crones except for Elysabeth—stood ranged around the room in various aspects of hover-mode. Baba Yaga sat on the chest that served as a coffee table, bowl in one hand and spoon in the other as she fed our guest.

"Eat," she urged. "You skinny since we last meet."

My shuffle-steps hitched. "You know each other?" I looked to Freya and the Morrigan for confirmation of acquaintance. Both of them shrugged, but I wasn't sure if that meant *yes, no big deal*, or *no, never seen her before in my life*.

Baba Yaga, on the other hand, smiled happily, the creases in her weathered face deepening. "In Uzzerworld," she agreed. She dropped the spoon into the bowl and leaned forward to pat Mary Magdalene's cheek with what appeared to be great fondness. "Is good girl."

I processed the declaration, decided it was a good thing Jeanne wasn't witness to it—lest her brain actually explode as Edie had suggested—and continued into the room to stand at the foot of the sofa. And then ...

Then my own brain froze.

More accurately, it went to war with itself, because Jesus Christ on a—*Mary Magdalene*?

Soft brown eyes met mine, their depths haunted. "Lady Claire," the apostle-slash-goddess said.

"Claire," I said. I cleared my throat. "Just Claire."

"And I'm just Mary."

The words—almost a plea—struck a chord with me, and I nodded back. "Noted," I said, "but what in the world are you doing here?"

CHAPTER 26

JUST-MARY'S ARRIVAL ON OUR DOORSTEP HAD BEEN SHOCKING enough. The story of *how* she'd arrived there?

That was definitely unexpected.

"A cavern," I repeated when she'd finished. "You came through a door into a cavern."

"Yes," she said, pulling a hand from beneath her blanket to point west. "It's that way, behind a—"

"It's behind a waterfall," finished Maureen. "Where three rivers meet."

"Yes. You know it?"

"We do," Anne said, her voice grim with the memories we all carried.

"Wait," I said, feeling like my brain was still playing catch-up in the conversation. "You're telling us that you came to Earth here? In Confluence?"

"If that is the name of this place, then yes. We all do. It is the only way."

"The only—" I stared at her, then turned to gape at Freya, who lounged on the opposite sofa, taking up the entire thing in what I'd begun mentally referring to as a goddess-spread. "Seriously?" I demanded, clutching my mug harder so that I didn't "accidentally" pitch it at her. "There's only one door between our worlds and it's practically in our back yard? Why didn't you say so?"

With all of the nonchalance one might expect from a goddess, Freya shrugged. "You didn't ask," she said. "I didn't know it was important."

"*Not important?* Freya, we could have—" I stopped as the ludicrousness of what I'd been about to say hit me. Freya snorted.

"You could have what? Stopped us?" Her gaze—her very speaking gaze—traveled the room, encompassing what was admittedly a motley crew at best. Four Crones—Elysabeth had returned by now—a damaged shifter, a shifter who could no longer shift at all, and a gargoyle who couldn't leave the house whose magick gave her life. There was no point in even including the midwitches who remained with her, and the way I'd been operating lately, I was a wild card at best.

I abandoned my indignation and settled back against the sofa cushions beside Mary. Another question came to mind.

"When you got here—to the house, I mean—you claimed sanctuary. From what?" I asked the newcomer.

She tucked her hand back beneath the blanket and hunched her shoulders. "Coming here was a mistake," she said. "I'd forgotten about the voices. They are so many, and they all want something from me that I can't—"

"From *you*?" The question escaped before I could stop it, and a bitter kind of sadness crept in to join the weariness in Mary's eyes.

She stared past me into the fire. "We were one, once, you know," she said. "Jesus of Nazareth and I. We lived together, taught together, helped together ..." She shook her head. "We were equals then, but what you call the patriarchy is a powerful machine, Just-Claire. Its version of history wrote me out of my own life. I was lucky to survive at all."

"I ..." I didn't know what to say. I wasn't surprised by any of her words, of course. Certainly not the part about the patriarchy, and not even about the voices.

When I'd first met Freya in the Otherworld, she'd told me much the same thing—how she and the other gods had left Earth because there had simply been too many demands, too many expectations. A hardness behind her expression as when I glanced at her now said that she had not forgotten.

Centuries had passed—millennia, in some cases—and humanity had made incredible advances, but at its core, nothing had changed. We still wanted others to fix the problems we'd created for ourselves.

"I will, of course, make my way back to the cavern and the Otherworld, if you wish," Mary said after a minute or two, "but if I may stay for a day or two, I would be grateful. It is quiet here."

From over by the window came a loud snort.

"Wait," Bedivere's voice advised darkly. "That will change, believe me."

The fact that he was right was both funny and sad, but it was mostly just true. The weariness I'd been fighting for days suddenly felt insurmountable. I still had questions—so many questions—and we still needed a plan, and we still had gnomes and shades and Mages to deal with, and—

And I just didn't have it in me to care anymore. Not tonight.

For tonight, we were safe beneath our wards, Mary would have her peace and quiet—except for the gnome drums and Odin—and that was enough. Because it had to be.

I levered myself up from the couch.

"I'm going to find my grandson," I told everyone in general and no one in particular, "because I need a hug. And then I'm going to bed. I suggest you do the same, because Bedivere is right. Tomorrow, it's going to get noisy around here. Very noisy."

I MADE IT PAST THE HALL THIS TIME, AND ALL THE WAY UP THE stairs without assistance, although Lucan stood careful watch at the foot of them until I did. I didn't, however, get my hug, because it was beyond late, and Braden was already fast asleep.

I stood at the side of his bed, listening to the distant drums beyond the window and the crackle of the fire behind me as I stared down at the soft, relaxed little-boy face, lit by the lamp on his bedside table. While we'd been listening to Mary's story in the sitting room, the house had recovered from my earlier tantrum and had begun putting itself back together again, starting with electricity. Or what passed as the magickal version of electricity, considering that we were about as off-grid here as we could get.

But the fact that we had lights again didn't improve my mood. Neither had the fact that the house had mostly repaired the front hall by the time I'd left the others to come upstairs. I blinked back a watery sheen. The truth was, not much *could* help—not when I was feeling more than a little sorry for myself. Which, for the record, I felt entitled to do, because Jesus Christ on a cracker—

"Actually, according to Mary, he's still back in the Otherworld," Edie said.

I scowled at her unwelcome humor—and at her intrusion on my pity-party. "Go away," I muttered, sniffling.

Her sigh whispered through my head. *"Oh, hon,"* she said. *"I know you're tired, but—"*

I scrubbed away an escapee tear. "Do you? Do you, really? I went through the Otherworld to Camlann and destroyed fucking *Morok*, Edie. I absorbed the power of a goddamn goddess"—which was an antithetical statement if I'd ever uttered one—"and brought Lucan back from the splinter, and I've lost count of how many times I've fought one monster or another, and tired doesn't even *begin* to describe how I feel. This was supposed to be *done*. Over. I did what I was supposed to do and then some, and *I'm* done, damn it!"

"I know," she murmured. *"It doesn't feel fair, does it?"*

Her voice held the sympathy that my self-pity craved, but it was underscored by something else. Something sad and nostalgic and …

Fuck, I thought as memory drove a fist into my gut. How

could I have forgotten? How low did I have to sink *to* forget? To whine about my lot in life when I at least still had a life, but Edie …

Edie had already lost hers.

"Oh goddess," I said. "Edie …"

"It's okay," my friend said. *"What happened to me doesn't negate what's happening to you, Claire, and you're right. It should be over, and you should be done. But you're not. Not yet. The world still needs you, my friend. He still needs you."*

Through a blur of tears, I saw Braden's hair ruffle slightly against the pillow, as if lifted by a breeze. Or by a friend's gentle fingers.

My entire being ached as I stared down at my grandson— my arms for the feel of his small body tucked against mine, my senses for the scent of soap and childhood, and my heart for his unencumbered, unconditional, "I love you, Grandma."

But most of all, my soul for the lifetime he would never know if I didn't pull myself together. I took a deep, shaky breath and scrubbed at my cheeks.

"That's better," Edie murmured. *"Now get some of that sleep you were talking about, because you have a lot of people expecting you to lead them tomorrow."*

I snorted through my residual tears. "But no pressure, right?"

My forever-friend chuckled. *"Are you kidding? All the pressure, my friend. All."*

"Mom?" The deep tones of my son's voice announced his arrival in Braden's room behind me. "I heard you talking to someone. Is Braden awake?"

"He hasn't moved," I assured him as he came to drape an arm over my shoulders and look down at his son. "I was just … talking to myself."

Paul glanced down at me and snorted. "I'm not surprised, given everything that's been going on." He drew back a little and studied me, concern tugging between his brows. "Are you all right?"

I summoned the same smile I'd always given him when he'd asked that question. The smile that would give him the reassurance he asked for, that would hide a mother's vulnerabilities from her son and let him live his own life without worrying about her. About me. But then, for the first time ever, I let the smile fade, and I shook my head.

"Not really," I said. "I'm not."

He took a moment to absorb this new twist in his no-longer comfortable reality, then he lifted his arm from my shoulders and twined his fingers with mine. "Natalie—" He broke off and cleared the gruffness from his throat. "Natalie told me everything. It's been hard to wrap my head around."

"I'm familiar with that feeling."

"So it's all true, then. You're ... not just my mom anymore."

I choke-snorted. "I suppose that's one way of putting it."

"But ... how? How did this happen? And why you? I mean, you're—" Paul's gaze slid away, ostensibly to look at his son, but more to avoid looking at me as he broke off abruptly.

"No one?" I finished for him. I laughed wryly. "You're wrong, you know. I've always been someone. You just didn't notice."

My son half frowned, half raised an eyebrow. "I don't understand."

"Don't you remember? *Someone* needs to do the laundry? *Someone* needs to make dinner?"

"Well, of course, but—"

"I kept the house running for decades," I said. "I fed you, and raised you, and helped the neighbors when they needed it, and I was on the school parent committees, and I was there for Grandma when she was dying, and I did the million and one other things that needed to be done every day of my life *because* they needed to be done. And now, this needs to be done."

"That's hardly the same thing," he objected.

"Isn't it?"

Paul stared down at the sleeping Braden, his jaw flexing and his fingers playing with mine as he wrestled with my words. Then he shook his head and grunted. "It's still weird."

"You have no idea," I muttered.

Braden flopped onto his back in his sleep, throwing an arm out from under the covers and across the pillow under his head. For an instant, he looked exactly as his father had done at this age, and my two worlds—my then and my now— collided behind my temples. I blinked away the stab of unreality and the stir of panic and set my teeth against the accompanying stir of magick.

As if sensing my sudden tension, my son folded my hand between both of his own, drawing my attention back to him. His brown eyes were determined in the lamplight—and surprisingly calm. He had come a long, long way since my coffee shop magick trick, I thought. I was glad he'd been able to grow—for Natalie's sake, as well as for his.

"How can I help?" he asked.

Not just *can I*, because the answer to that would have been an automatic *no*, but *how can I*, which made me hesitate and give the question more consideration than I would have otherwise. I thought about what was coming for us—what we faced, what we would have to fight, what we couldn't hope to beat if we didn't come up with a plan.

And, my heart heavy, I knew there was no place in that fight for Paul—but there was for Natalie.

"You can look after your family for me," I said.

"That's it?"

"That's all I need."

Paul dropped a kiss on the top of my head and released my hand. He leaned down to tuck the duvet around his son's shoulders, then lifted the corner of it nearest me and motioned me toward the bed.

"You have my word," he said gruffly. "Now crawl in and get some sleep while you can, Grandma. But be warned, he kicks like a mule."

CHAPTER 27

I CAME AWAKE WITH A JOLT AND THE SENSATION THAT I WAS being watched. It took a moment to get my bearings, because nothing was familiar. The walls were wood paneled instead of stone, the light coming in around the edges of the curtains at the window was all wrong, and there was the sound of … purring?

I rolled onto my back in the bed that I had deduced wasn't mine and stared at the two forms at the foot of the bed, one dragon-shaped and the other a boy. The night of having Braden snuggled into my side—and being kicked, as Paul had warned—came rushing back, and my heart swelled with grandmotherly love.

"Good morning," I said, propping a pillow up behind me so that I could see them better. The fire in the hearth had died down to embers, which meant that neither Keven nor Braden's parents had been in yet. It was early, then. Very early.

"You snore," Braden replied to my greeting. "Why are you in my bed?"

I laughed at the blunt honesty of childhood. No secrets here.

"I was lonely," I said. "I missed you."

"I missed you, too. I like your dragon." Braden slapped the top of Harry's head affectionately, bouncing it up and down in his enthusiasm. Harry purred louder.

"I like him, too."

"Can he fly? Can I ride him? Can we fly to the moon?"

"He can fly, yes. But he's too little to carry you, I'm afraid, and dragons can't go to the moon."

"Oh." Braden regarded his new friend in disappointment,

then shrugged. "It's okay. We'll go when he grows up. Will he get very big, do you think?"

I thought of the dragons I'd left behind in the Otherworld, the mother that had died defending her young, and the father that I'd killed defending my cat and his newly hatched dragon companion.

"Very big," I replied, which begged the question of what I would do with him at that point—if we made it that far.

A knock sounded at the door, and Keven came into the room. She seemed unsurprised at finding me there, so presumably Paul had told her. She also wore a grimmer-than-usual expression.

"Milady," she said.

The ease of the morning slid away, and I sat up straighter in the bed. I was about to ask what was wrong, and then it registered. The drums. I couldn't hear the drums anymore. Or anything from Odin's camp. I swung my legs out from under the covers and stood up.

"Braden, I have to go, sweetheart. Baba Yaga and Keven will give you your breakfast. Can I have a hug?"

My beloved grandson threw himself across the bed and wrapped his arms around my waist with his usual enthusiasm, hugging me fiercely. I leaned down so that my face pressed against the top of the blond head, inhaling deeply, absorbing his scent, his warmth, his love. Imprinting my love on him. I wanted to stay like that forever, but almost six-year-olds had little patience, and he was already wriggling, and the ominous silence outside was demanding my attention, and ...

I gave my grandson a final squeeze. "I love you," I whispered.

"I love you, too, Grandma," he replied. "Hey, Harry, let's race to the kitchen!"

The blue dragon tumbled off the bed and galloped after the boy, and just like that, my little bubble of peace was no more.

"The dining room?" I asked Keven. She nodded. Then she went down the back stairs in the wake of Braden and Harry, and I went down the main ones to face the day.

"So it's decided," said Freya's voice as I entered the dining room. I paused in the doorway, searching for her as multiple heads nodded around the table. It looked as if everyone was here—the Crones and all the midwitches, Bedivere and Lucan, Just-Mary and Baba Yaga, Jeanne, Paul and Natalie, and … yes. There they were—both goddesses at the head of the table, with Freya seated in the position of obvious authority and the Morrigan standing a little behind, at her elbow.

I tried not to bristle—too much—and turned to Lucan, who leaned against the wall beside the door. "What's decided?" I asked.

He opened his mouth to respond, but despite the fact I'd clearly directed my question at him, Freya answered anyway. Because of course she did.

"The gnomes have pulled back," she said, "and our scout—"

"Scout?" My voice was sharp. I told myself that it was out of concern rather than irritation with the Norse goddess, but Edie snorted in my ear and Lucan raised an eyebrow. I scowled at the pair of them.

A midwitch at the far corner of the table near Freya raised a hand. "Me, Lady Claire. I went into town this morning, and—"

"The ones you call Mages have gathered there," Freya's voice overrode her, "and the ceramic creatures have surrounded the town center. An attack is imminent."

I frowned. Did she mean the gnomes? But how? I looked at Lucan again.

"I thought they couldn't leave the trees," I said.

"These trees." He nodded toward the window overlooking the clearing and the forest beyond. "Because of the wards around the clearing. But their natural habitat is——"

"Gardens," I finished, even as my brain skewed a little sideways at the idea of gnomes having a natural habitat. "Of course. And gardens are open."

He shrugged. "They travel across the open all the time. It's how they move."

So Confluence was a sitting duck waiting for them? Awesome. Just fucking awesome.

Lucan touched my arm. "Are you okay? You've gone white."

"Apart from wishing I'd stayed in bed?" I muttered. "I'm just peachy, thanks." Except for the part where my brain was diving down one rabbit hole after another, pursuing reasons the Mages might be planning another attack on the town, imagining the outcomes if they did, bouncing from one awful scenario to another worse one.

I curled my fingers into my palms and drew a deep breath as I looked across at the woman who'd spoken. I wished I'd paid more attention to names and faces, because if there was a time to address someone by her name, it was when she'd laid her life on the line for the good of humanity while I'd been napping.

"How many?" I asked.

"Seven that I could tell for sure. Nine others that are poss——"

Freya *ahemmed* loudly, and the midwitch shrank in her seat a little bit.

"Nine others that are probable," she amended.

Fuck, I thought.

"Shit," whispered Edie in my head.

I reached for an empty chair beside Anne and lowered myself into it. Sixteen Mages. That was not good. On the other side of the table, Jeanne stood and went to a sideboard. She poured steaming liquid from a teapot into a mug, then came around the table and set it in front of me. I murmured my thanks as I wrapped cold fingers around its heat. She squeezed my shoulder and returned to her seat.

"All right," I said. "So what have you decided we should do?"

This time, I directed my question to Anne. I was still determined to cut Freya out of the leadership role she was intent on playing. Something about the goddess—her arrogance? her patronizing tone? everything?—rubbed me the wrong way, and I wanted to make it clear that she was *not* in charge around here.

Anne cleared her throat, her gaze avoiding mine as it traveled around the table to settle on the goddess I didn't want to talk to. "I think Freya should explain," she said. "It was her idea."

Freya's idea? Wonderful. Just freaking wonderful. I scowled, and the magick that had so far lain dormant this morning sizzled to life under my skin. I gripped my mug harder, pressing my fingertips against the ceramic to hold the sparks in, disliking on sheer principle whatever the goddess was about to say. I met the ice-blue gaze at the end of the table and braced myself for her disdain.

But for once, Freya's voice held none of the notes that grated on me. Instead, it was level, quiet, and matter of fact. "I'm dividing my powers between your Crones," she said, "so that they may cross into the Otherworld in your absence."

Only Anne's quick reflexes saved my mug and its contents from ending up in my lap. She set the vessel on the table while I stared open-jawed at the Norse goddess, not quite believing my ears.

Oh, who was I kidding? I didn't believe my ears at all. Not

in the least. And yet, all around the room, the resolute gazes that met mine confirmed Freya's words. Somehow, she'd convinced Crones and shifters and midwitches alike that this was a *good* idea?

"But—but—how?" I sputtered.

"*She*"—Freya jerked her chin toward the Morrigan—"has agreed to show me."

I turned my gape on the black-gowned goddess who had moved to stare out the window, aloof and apart as always—at least when she wasn't shrieking at her nemesis. *The Morrigan* had agreed …?

"*Huh,*" said Edie. "*Who woulda thunk?*"

I hushed her as Anne cleared her throat.

"As soon as Freya has divided her powers, she'll take over our training from Keven," she said. "Her magick is different from the Morrigan's, so there will be some adjustment. The midwitches will continue working with Baba Yaga so they can help us open the portal, and Mary"—she nodded across me— "has agreed to be our emissary."

"Emissary?" I looked to the quiet, dark-skinned woman beside me. If she'd slept last night, it didn't show. The weariness I'd seen before was stamped more deeply into her features than before, and her eyes—

"Someone has to bring the other gods back to Confluence. We've agreed that I'm the best choice," she said.

With the plan at hand, she really was the only choice, I thought, but it didn't stop a pang of compassion from shafting through me. "What about all the voices?" I asked. "And the demands?"

"What about the Between?" she countered. "It seems to me that we will all make great sacrifices in this war."

Except me, of course. I would get to sit in my nice, comfortable stone cottage with my nice gargoyle servant and my not-shifter protector while my friends trotted off to undo my mistake, and—

"*Perhaps* that *is your sacrifice,*" said Edie. "*Sitting on the sidelines is never easy.*"

"Then what?" I asked Freya, in part because I wanted to know the rest of the plan—even if I wouldn't be participating —but mostly because I needed to distract myself from telling Edie what to do with her platitudes.

"*Ouch,*" whispered my friend.

"When the gods are here, I will reconvene the Council," Freya said, "and we will return with the Crones to the Otherworld to repair the tear."

I frowned. "But if you're all going back, why are the Crones needed?"

"To undo what you did, of course. You will tell them how."

And just like that, yet another fucking plan fell apart.

CHAPTER 28

"HOW CAN YOU NOT KNOW WHAT YOU DID?" FREYA THREW her arms wide as she paced the hearth in front of the sitting room fireplace. Eight strides one way, spin around on her heel, eight strides the other way. "*How?*"

We'd left the others in the dining room—or rather, Freya had left them there and I'd been hauled along by one arm with no say in the matter—but the doors remained open between us, and the Crones and Jeanne were standing inside the dining room ones as they listened without apology. I thought about sending a puff of Air to close them, but—

"*No secrets,*" said Edie.

"Well?" demanded Freya. "Have you nothing to say for yourself?"

I threw my own hands wide. "For goddess's sake, Freya, what do you want me to say? I was in the middle of a battle— how the hell am I supposed to know what I did? I split Morok from Lucan, I trapped him in some kind of bubble-thing, Harry started flying in circles and created a vortex, the Between started eating the edges of the splinter—"

"Stop." Freya leapt over the sofa between us and seized my shoulders in an iron grip. "Say that again?"

On the other side of the great hall, Bedivere's hand stopped his brother's sword halfway from its scabbard as I yanked away from the goddess's hard fingers. "Say what again? I'm telling you everything I—"

"The dragon," she ground out. "Tell me about the dragon."

My eyebrows twitched together. "Harry? What about him?"

"He did something. His magick and yours together—it did something."

"Harry has magick?"

She looked at me as if I'd become the stupidest creature in the universe—which I suddenly felt, because I'd seen that vortex with my own eyes, and I had wondered even then. The fluffy little blue dragon had flown in circles above his beloved muzzer, faster and faster, then moved up the hill to continue the circles above the stone that had once held Arthur's sword, and—

"He's a *dragon*," Freya snapped. "Of course he's magick."

Of course he was. But he wasn't *that* magick ... was he?

I didn't ask aloud—I didn't dare—but Freya answered anyway.

"Dragons are among the most magickal creatures in the Otherworld," she said. "It was rumored that Zeus bred them from the creatures of the Between. I can't even imagine what their magick might do if it were to be unleashed somewhere other than ..." She trailed off, and we both fell silent, because she didn't have to imagine, and neither did I.

The Norse goddess's lips went tight. "We're taking him with us."

"No." I shook my head. "He's just a baby! You can't expect him to—"

Freya grabbed me again, this time by the shoulder, and spun me about to look out the door into the great hall, where a tautly coiled Lucan stood with Bedivere holding him back, the Crones crowded into the dining room doorway, and there, between all of them, sat Braden.

He was seated on the bottom stair, at the feet of the suit of armor, reading a book to Harry, who lay on the step behind him, chin resting on my grandson's shoulder.

"And him?" she demanded. "Is your own flesh not a baby, too? What will he do when the Between comes for your world after ours? How will you explain to him that you chose a dragon over him and all the other babies in this world?"

Again, I wrenched away from her hold. "Stop it!" I snarled. "Just ... stop. Please."

On the stairs, Braden turned the page, Harry nuzzled his ear, and I listened to his giggle. Remembered Harry's softness, his antics, his devotion to Gus.

My heart began a slow, irrevocable collapse in my chest.

"He won't understand," I whispered. "Gus and I—we're all he's ever known. He'll be so lost without us. He'll be afraid."

Freya exhaled a long sigh behind me. In a rough, not-unsympathetic voice, she said, "I'm not suggesting we sacrifice the beast, Claire, only that we take him back to the world he belongs in so that he can help save it—and save you."

As if he'd heard, Harry lifted his chin from Braden's shoulder and turned it toward us. His jeweled gaze met and held mine, and then—

"Did he just nod his head at you?" Edie asked.

"Yes," I replied. *"I think he did."*

WITH THE MATTER OF HARRY SETTLED, IT WAS TIME TO return to the plan that had been hatched in my earlier absence. The midwitches and Natalie had departed to the kitchen for lessons with Baba Yaga, and Freya and the Morrigan had disappeared down the stairs into the cellar to work on dividing Freya's powers, leaving the rest of them to fill me in. We sat around the dining room table as Lucan— who appeared to have been accepted as team leader—laid out the details for me, mostly with respect to the part I would play.

Which, as it turned out, involved taking on sixteen Mages, the gnome army, and whatever shades came through from the

Between to attack the town, all without accidentally destroying the town myself.

That would teach me to oversleep and miss the staff meeting.

"You're joking," I said at first. No one was laughing, however, so I followed up with a flat, "No," and scowled at Lucan for good measure. "Absolutely not. You didn't see what I almost did in Confluence, Lucan." I turned to the other shifter for help.

"Tell them, Bedivere. Tell them what I almost did."

But Bedivere merely looked thoughtful—or maybe it was belligerent. It was hard to tell with him sometimes. I switched my gaze to Keven, certain she would support me, because she knew better than anyone the kind of unpredictable damage I could inflict when I wasn't in control of my magick. "Keven?"

The gargoyle's jaw shifted, but she said nothing.

My panic edged up a notch. One wrong move in Confluence, and—

"The key word is *almost*," Lucan said, "because you didn't lose control. You took down the shades and saved the town."

"I *regained* control," I corrected, "*that* time. But what about the next time? I can't trust myself—"

"Then trust me. And know that *I* trust you. We all do. You can do this, Claire. You've always been able to do this."

"But—" I cast a semi-wild gaze around the room, looking for support, sympathy, an ally—just one would do—but the stoic faces that stared back at me reflected nothing but the same trust that Lucan's did. The kind that said they believed in me more than I believed in myself. That they trusted me to figure it out.

Or that they were desperate enough that they had no other choice.

Either way, I was going to town to find sixteen Mages and their army of gnomes.

Fuck.

GATHER THE GODS, CONVINCE THEM TO GO BACK TO THE Otherworld, send Harry and the Crones with them to repair the divide. Gather the gods, convince them to return, send Harry and the Crones with them. Gather the gods …

I recited the plan over and over in my head like a mantra as I followed Bedivere across the garden toward the ley line that would take us into town—in part to convince myself of its simplicity, but mostly to keep from thinking about how many things could go wrong.

Because those things were a multitude.

I stepped across a row of carrots and paused beside a hill of potatoes, distracted for a moment by the weeds around the latter. I'd long since stopped marveling at a garden that could feed the household year-round, regardless of the season, but I still marveled at the miracle of growth in general, and I missed tending to that growth. And I couldn't help but wonder whether this particular growth would survive the multitude of things.

If anything would.

Bedivere looked back at me, and I hurried to catch up. I tried to return to the recitation of the plan, but it was too late. My concentration had been broken, and all the things that could go wrong had risen to the surface.

The most obvious question was whether Mary would be able to gain the cooperation needed from the other gods and goddesses. We didn't necessarily need them all on board, but it was definitely a case of the more, the better, and we at least needed *some*.

By Freya's estimate—supported by the latest newspaper Natalie had been clutching when Lucan rescued her from the shade battle—ten others had come through from the Otherworld in addition to her, Baba Yaga, Mary, and Odin.

She'd spat the last name with a particular kind of venom, and I couldn't say I blamed her, but we'd gone head-to-head yet again when she'd tried to cut him out of the plan.

"You mean, leave him here?" I'd asked in unfeigned horror. Her gaze had shifted away from mine, and once again, I'd found myself saying, "No. Absolutely not," to the Norse goddess.

And I'd meant it. I didn't care if I had to hog-tie Odin and his entire cohort and drag them to the cavern myself, they were leaving Earth. Especially after our last encounter and whatever that darkness was I'd seen in his eyes. Odin would not, *could* not, stay.

In the end, Freya had refused to discuss it further, but Mary had joined me as I yanked on my boots, assuring me that she would do her best to convince the Norse god of our plan as well.

I was pretty sure it would still require hog-tying.

But that was neither here nor there at the moment, because of the multitude of other potential problems we would face before we got to the crossing-over part. Freya and the Morrigan had still been down in the cellar when Bedivere and I left, and we had no idea whether the Norse goddess's plan to divide her powers would even work. Or whether the Crones would be able to master those powers in the time we had. Or, indeed, exactly how much time we had.

Because our other problems included sixteen Mages, a gnome army, and me.

Bedivere stopped beside the ley and waited for me to join him. I stood at his side, watching the graceful, undulating ribbon of energy that would carry me and my unpredictable powers into Confluence. Ahead of me lay battle. Behind me, the friends and family who relied on me to win.

Lucan had remained to protect them, because if Freya's division of magick *did* succeed, she and the others would be vulnerable to attack until the Crones could learn to wield it.

He hadn't been happy about letting me go alone—Bedivere notwithstanding—but we were both growing accustomed to his new role in my life. His complicated, not-protector but not-not-protector role. I sighed.

Then, in answer to my traveling companion's raised eyebrow, I nodded, because Confluence and the Mages were waiting, and I was as ready as I would ever be. We stepped into the ley.

"I've been wondering," said Edie, who had been uncharacteristically quiet since my last confrontation with Freya—and, of course, had waited to ask until I began to dissolve into the ley's magick. *"Why do you suppose the Mages are in Confluence in the first place? Why not somewhere else?"*

CHAPTER 29

"IT DOESN'T MATTER," BEDIVERE GROWLED WHEN WE STEPPED out of the ley into a narrow space between two buildings, and I asked him the same question. "We stick to the plan."

But Edie's musings had made me hesitate, and I caught his arm to prevent him from stepping out onto the sidewalk. "But it does matter. Someone brought the gnomes back, and now we have Mages, too, but why here? Why is all of this happening in Confluence? We can't just beat up all the Mages without trying to find out."

Bedivere gave me a dark look. "Who said anything about beating them up?"

I stifled my reflexive recoil from the shifter's flagrant disregard for life. We were long, long past trying to keep enemies alive in this war. Besides, my role in this was to contain the Mages' magick while Bedivere took care of ... well, the messier details.

"Fine," I said. "Then you can't *kill* all of them without finding out—"

"*Fine*," Bedivere mimicked, his annoyance escalating. "I'll let one stay alive until you can get your answers. But we stick to the plan."

I would have liked to argue further, but now was not the time to start changing things. Not with a gnome army roving the woods and shades being brought from the Between, putting the entire town of Confluence under threat. Our first order of business from a tactical perspective, Lucan and Bedivere had assured me, was to stop the magick that fueled them—and that meant taking out the Mages. The belly of the beast, so to speak.

"The *plan*," repeated Bedivere through clenched teeth.

"The plan," I agreed, "with one kept alive."

The shifter's shirt and pants—he hadn't even bothered with boots this time—dropped to the snow as he morphed into his wolf. I tucked them into a crevice at the base of one of the buildings on the off chance we might come back this way when we were done wreaking havoc. Then I confirmed that my magick was in check and joined Bedivere on the sidewalk.

At Lucan's suggestion, we'd taken a different ley line into town to avoid what Maureen had bluntly—and accurately—termed the scene of the crime. With a bit more tact, Lucan had pointed out that there could be clean-up crews, as well as heightened security, around the ravaged town hall. Bedivere had growled under his breath at the inconvenience, but he had scoped out other possibilities and settled on this one, which had landed us here.

The intersection was vaguely familiar, but I hadn't been downtown in what felt like forever, so I paused to get my bearings. The street leading away from us was barricaded a couple of blocks down, and I glimpsed yellow police tape fluttering in the wind. That would be town hall, then, which put Confluence's center about three blocks away to our left, which meant—

I turned to the left, and my gaze immediately settled on the familiar facade of my ex-husband's office building across the street. Yup. We were exactly where I thought we were. But why was it so quiet? It was only what—maybe noon? I wasn't sure on which day—I'd long since lost track of those—and yes, it was cold out, but regardless, there should have been at least a few people about. Or cars moving. Or something. My gaze went back to Jeff's office building ... third floor up ... corner ... no lights on.

"*Fucking hell,*" muttered Edie. "*I hope that's not some kind of omen.*"

Landing in front of Jeff's office, or the lack of people? Either way, *"Likewise,"* I replied.

I turned my attention to the wolf who had none-too-gently grabbed my hand with his teeth. Bedivere's ruff stood on end, and his gray eyes shone with urgency. He released his grip on me and took a few steps toward the town center. He'd sensed something.

Fire uncoiled in me, and flames flickered at the ends of my fingertips.

"Easy," Edie said.

I didn't need the warning. I pressed my lips together and fell into step behind the shifter, pulling my hands into the folds of the cloak that Baba Yaga had repaired and returned to me as we'd left the house. On second thought, perhaps it was a blessing that the street was devoid of traffic. The last thing we needed right now was a twitchy pedestrian calling in a flaming woman and her wolf. Getting in and out of town completely without notice was unlikely, given what we were here to do, but doing so without collateral damage was preferable—and an encounter with the police after the shade incident would make that almost impossible.

Sixteen practitioners of dark magick gathered together in one place gave off a peculiar—and strong—energy. I began sensing it after two blocks. It intensified with every step after we turned a corner onto Main Street. By the time Bedivere stepped across my path with his lips drawn back in a silent snarl, I'd already homed in on the source.

A sense of *déjà vu* settled over me as I stared across the street at the glass, oak, and brass entrance of a heritage stone building that housed the ritziest hotel in town. I remembered all too clearly another luxury building that Mages had occupied. That time, I'd had Keven and Lucan with me, and I'd fought my way past shades and the goliath to get to Morok and rescue the Crones. It had not ended well.

Foreboding joined the *déjà vu*, but I shook it off. It was

different this time. This time, it was just me and Bedivere, the Crones were safe, and there was no more Morok.

Only sixteen Mages and whatever monsters they had with them.

Piece of cake.

Bedivere nudged my leg. I took a moment to look up and down the street for signs that we had been noticed—or of more concern, that we were being watched. But here, too, the street remained deserted, except for the cars parked along it. Farther along, a few vehicles crossed at a controlled intersection, but here on Main Street itself?

Nothing moved at all.

Not even in the ritzy hotel.

Bedivere nudged my leg again.

"I know," I said. "It's—"

The word *weird* died on my lips as the first shade erupted seemingly from midair above the street. The second, from the building behind us. Air moved through me with a speed that left me breathless—no pun intended—and struck both creatures with a shock that drove them hundreds of feet down the street and into the intersection. Tires shrieked against pavement, horns sounded, and metal crashed into metal—and crunched into feathered flesh.

Avoiding notice was officially finished.

And then the gnome drums began.

"Jesus fuck," Edie said. *"They were waiting for you."*

They were. And where there had been no sign of them seconds before, they were suddenly everywhere. They came out of hiding in droves—from behind parked cars, out of buildings, down from rooftops. In seconds, we faced a wall of them, and I faltered. They were so many … and more would be coming. How could we hope to find the Mages, when it would take everything to fight their creatures? To keep them from attacking Confluence and the people I'd lived beside for more than thirty years?

"The belly of the beast," Edie said.

I closed my eyes against the decision facing me. Then, in my mind's eye, I saw Harry lift his chin from my grandson's shoulder and turn his jeweled gaze on me, then incline his head as if accepting his role in our fight. As if he knew his importance.

Know, the Book of the Fifth Crone had once said to me. *Accept. Trust. Be.*

I inhaled a centering breath, drew back my shoulders, and channeled my inner dragon.

I touched Bedivere's shoulder. "Can you hold them off?" I asked, and his lips drew back from his teeth in a smile that assured me he could—and made it clear where the term *wolfish grin* originated. I turned and grasped the ley line to my left, which ran straight through the crowd of gnomes and the hotel's entrance.

I'd barely had time to dissolve into the line's magick when it was time to step out of it again in the lobby. Changing back and forth that quickly left me disoriented as my body reassembled itself. My confusion lasted only an instant, but it was long enough for the Mages to launch their first volley.

Shock engulfed me first, then pain, as a dozen fireballs hit my unprepared body. My hair caught fire, and my eyeballs felt like they were dissolving in their sockets. For a moment, coherent thought fled in the face of agony. From a great distance, I heard Edie's voice calling me, but I couldn't respond. And then—

Know, whispered the book in my memory. *Know your magick.*

Water flooded my body and filled my eyes, dousing the magical flames engulfing me and bringing blessed, cool relief in its wake.

Accept, said the book. *Accept that this is what you must do.*

Fire uncoiled in my center and snaked along my veins, gathering in my palms as I held them out to my sides and spread my fingers wide.

Trust.

I could see nothing through eyes flooded with Water, but I didn't need to. I knew exactly where the Mages stood, all sixteen of them, and I had no doubt that my magick would find its targets.

Be. Be the power, Claire Emerson.

Earth reached up through the floor to wrap around my ankles and root me to the ground beneath. To the strength of a world.

The Mages unleashed a second volley of fire. I released mine first.

I won.

"Yes!" yelled Edie in my ear. Her voice startled the hell out of me and broke into my thoughts—or rather, the lack of them, because dear mother of all, I'd done it again. The lobby was aflame, fire was licking up the walls and crawling across the ceiling, the lights flickered as wiring melted, the tempered glass doors had turned to pebbles held together only by their frames, and the brass accents on the front desk were beginning to puddle on the floor.

Horror engulfed me, and I wanted to fold up on the spot, but something new and ruthless in me shoved aside the weakness. It called back the Fire rolling outward from me and tamped it down inside. It summoned Water from the walls and ceiling of the building itself to put out what it had done—what *I* had done. And then, as distant sirens wailed closer, it turned and walked through the smoldering embers toward the fractured glass doors.

We—it and I—were halfway across the ruined lobby when I remembered I needed to talk to a Mage. I forced my feet to stop moving and struggled to regain the upper hand over the relentless force gripping me.

"Stop, damn it," I muttered to myself under my breath. "A Mage. You need to find a Mage."

Whatever it was sitting in my driver's seat dragged me

another three steps toward the exit. I dug my heels in, metaphorically speaking, because literally doing so was impossible on a marble floor. What the hell was going on? This didn't feel like my usual one-part-of-me-vs.-another dilemma.

Something new from the Mages? A possession of some kind? But it didn't fit with what I imagined possession would feel like. I was too aware. And I was still me.

Wasn't I?

I closed my eyes, curled my hands into fists, and brought every ounce of my concentration to bear, delving inward. My magick lit up at my touch, each of the elements responding as they should, each tangled with the extra that had once belonged to Morgana. The Morrigan's power was there, too, seething beneath my surface as it always did. But they weren't all that was there anymore.

There was something ... else. Something that wound through everything else like the strands of a spider's web. Something ...

But even as I reached for it, the strands withdrew from me, dissolving beneath my awareness and vanishing.

"What the fuck," said Edie slowly, *"was that?"*

An animal's scream of pain came from outside before I could answer. Bedivere. I had to get to—

"Mage," Edie reminded me.

Right.

Shit.

I hesitated, torn between going to Bedivere's aid and looking for signs of life among the crispy Mages. Then I whipped around and jogged back toward the sixteen blackened lumps at the back of the lobby, between the elevators and the remains of the reception desk.

CHAPTER 30

I FOUND SIGNS OF LIFE IN THE THIRD BODY. THEY WERE THE bare minimum, but they were enough to make me grip charred shoulders and shake them. Chunks of blackened flesh sloughed away, leaving me holding glistening bone, the white a sharp contrast to the rest of the Mage. I gritted my teeth against the gorge rising in my throat and shook again. Eyes that had no more eyelids rolled down from inside the skull and slowly focused on me through their shock.

My heart contracted sharply, because Mage or no Mage, this was—or had been—a human being, and oh, dear goddess ...

"Chin up," Edie said, her voice hard and soft at the same time, as if she wrestled with the same compassion I felt. *"You can do this."*

Her words gave my backbone the steel it needed.

"Why are you here?" I asked the Mage. "Why are all of you here in Confluence? Who brought the gnomes back to life?"

A rasp of air wafted toward me as the living corpse ... chuckled? My fingers tightened, but the bone was unyielding. I shook again.

"Answer me! Who?"

" ... late."

The Mage's voice was a mere thread of sound, not even a whisper, and I leaned in closer, my eyes watering and throat burning from the stench of burnt flesh and hair. "What's late?"

"You," the Mage croaked. He gave another feeble chuckle. "You're too late. He's already back."

Another shriek of pain reached through the shattered

doors and across the lobby. Bedivere. I had to get to Bedivere. Any lingering compassion for the Mage left me, and I gripped the shoulders with all my strength and shook until the charred, hairless, mostly skinless head flopped back and forth.

"Who is? Who's back?" I demanded. "Answer me, damn it!"

But the Mage was gone. No life remained in what I held, and there would be no more answers. I had to go. I had to help Bediv—

A small noise—the rustle of fabric—reached my ears, and I looked up from my death grip on the Mage's corpse into the terrified eyes of a man cowering behind the hotel desk. Our gazes locked, and for an instant, I saw the tableau around him through his eyes. The ruined hotel, the war between Bedivere and the gnomes and shades outside, the sixteen lumps of charcoal on the floor, and the wild-haired, robed woman who was crouched over those lumps, shaking the remaining life from them.

Edie grunted. *"Look at it this way, my friend. If you and Bedivere don't make it out of here, at least you'll be a legend. Now get out of here and go help that poor boy."*

THE "POOR BOY'S" WOLF MET ME ON THE SIDEWALK IN FRONT of the hotel. Pain glazed his eyes, a gash ran along his ribs, his jaws were bloody, and the first thing I saw beyond him were the remains of a shade, still twitching. The second, the wall of gnomes he'd managed to hold at bay. So far.

My gaze darted back to the gash in his side, and I noted how he swayed on his three and a half legs. If that wound had been shade-inflicted, his gnome-fighting abilities were about to be severely limited when the toxins took hold—and the ceramic horrors were still coming.

"Why in hell are they still coming?" Edie growled. *"The Mages are dead. Shouldn't their magick be, too?"*

It should have been, yes, but it wasn't. And I didn't want to use mine after the way it had behaved in the hotel, but if I wanted to save Bedivere, I had no choice.

I cautiously gathered Air to me and pushed it at the gnome-wall, sending the creatures tumbling to the other side of the street and shattering them into pieces.

My stomach tied itself into a dozen knots as the Mage's words echoed in my brain, *"He's already here,"* because I could only think of one *he*, and I had destroyed him in Camlann. I'd watched him squashed out of existence as the sphere closed around him and the Between came to devour him and—

Broken gnomes reassembled, and their wall advanced again. Bedivere staggered at my side. The toxins were taking their toll. He needed healing—and we needed to get out of here.

I scanned the street, cataloging our situation. What had felt like an eternity inside the hotel had been only minutes, and Confluence's first responders were just beginning to arrive. A fire truck turned onto the street a block away and lurched to a halt in the sea of gnomes. Two police cars careened around the corner in the truck's wake and plowed through without slowing down. They would be here in seconds.

Swiftly, I assessed the ley lines surrounding us. I didn't know how many transitions Bedivere could make, wounded as he was, so we needed to be as direct as we could. The ley running beside us and into the hotel had an unfamiliar energy to it, so that one was out. The one that would take us back to the house was too far away to reach with a posse in pursuit and gnomes in the way.

We'd passed another a half-block away, however—in the opposite direction from the approaching emergency vehicles

—that had felt familiar. Not house-familiar, but woods-familiar. It would have to do. We just needed to get to it.

I leaned down, one hand resting lightly on the shoulder of Bedivere's wolf and the other pointing down the block. "Go," I told him. "I'm right behind you."

Limping and lurching, the wolf pushed into the gnomes, winding around and between them as best he could. I tried to follow, but gnomes filled the street from sidewalk to sidewalk and surrounded me in seconds. I couldn't put a boot down without stepping on one.

Bedivere reached the ley, and I yelled at him to go, but he ignored me and instead tossed aside a gnome heading past him in my direction. It was clear that he wouldn't leave without me, and so I stepped up my efforts to get to him.

I wanted to use my magick again, but the Morrigan's power seethed in me, urging me to call on it, too, and the very fact that it wasn't my idea spelled the potential for another disaster. Grimly, I resorted to kicking gnomes aside to clear a narrow path. Step by step, kick by kick, shattered head by shattered limb, I pushed toward the waiting shifter.

The sirens wailed into silence behind me, and doors slammed, but I didn't look back. Voices shouted at me to stop. I kicked harder.

"Um, you might want to listen to them," Edie said. *"They—"*

The voices interrupted her, louder this time, and angrier. The sound of a gunshot ricocheted off the buildings that lined the street, bouncing from one side to the other as it traveled and then fading into the winter afternoon. My steps faltered. I gauged the distance I still had to go—twenty feet at least— and weighed it against the speed of a bullet, the twitchiness of the cop who had fired the first shot, and the chances that I'd been recognized from the town hall incident the day before.

The odds were not in my favor.

And Bedivere wouldn't leave without me.

And *damn it.*

"Do it," Edie whispered. *"But be careful."*

Again, I had no choice. I closed my eyes and called Earth, gathering it beneath me, feeling its power, its might. Its tendrils reached up and wrapped around my ankles, steadying me, holding me. Another shout came, followed by the sound of ceramic breaking under an advance of heavier boots than mine. I held my hands out to my sides in a gesture of surrender, then gritted my teeth, tore one foot from Earth's grip, and brought my heel down on the icy pavement.

For a moment, nothing happened. Then a swell began beneath me, lifting me gently with the street. Earth released its remaining hold on me, and I slipped and slid down the rise toward Bedivere. The swell continued to grow. The voices grew alarmed, then confused, then alarmed again, and I shot a glance over my shoulder.

A hill a dozen feet tall had risen in the middle of the street where I'd stood a moment before. Frozen pavement had shattered, and with it, the water main below. Water gushed upward in a fountain, flooding down both sides of the rise and freezing on contact.

It would be a minor catastrophe for the merchants and residents of the street, and it would take days to repair, but for now ... for now, it had caused the gnomes to roll away, leaving me a clear path to Bedivere and escape.

I ran.

CHAPTER 31

I'D BEEN RIGHT ABOUT THE FAMILIAR ENERGY OF THE LEY, AND we arrived in the woods, halfway along the path between Odin's camp and the house. Bedivere staggered as we emerged, his breath coming in ragged pants that made his sides heave like bellows. Dark red blood dripped from the gash along his ribs.

I lifted the hem of my cloak and tore a wide strip from it. Then, ignoring his snarls and one snap that came dangerously near my shoulder, I wrapped the cloth around his body, covering the gash.

"Hush," I told him between his growls. "I need to stop the bleeding, and the cloak's magick might slow the toxins."

The shifter's teeth remained bared, but he submitted to my first aid. I twisted the ends of the cloth strip together and tucked them under the bandage, then levered myself up from the snow and brushed off my knees.

"We'll go slowly," I said, "and you rest when you need to. And I'll go first and try to pack down the path a bit more to make it easier for you."

I held the remains of my cloak and the robe beneath it out of the snow and started down the path, but before I could take more than a couple of steps, the shifter crowded against my knees, forcing me back one step, two, three …

"Bedivere, stop," I said. "The house is—"

"On the other side of my territory, I believe," said a familiar and most unwelcome voice.

"Oh, for fuck's sake."

Multiple swords emerged from scabbards with a rattle as I turned to look up at the Norse god sitting astride his massive black horse.

Odin raised an eyebrow, his gaze distinctly frosty. "Excuse me?" he said.

"That wasn't me," said Edie. *"That was you. But for what it's worth, I concur."*

Hell.

The injured Bedivere put himself between me and the sword-toting Valkyries flanking the god. Power crackled through me, making my fingertips tingle with magick—or perhaps that was just anticipation. I scowled at Odin. I wanted to tell him—rather desperately—that our house wasn't on the other side of his anything, because the land belonged to me, not him, but Bedivere's hind legs were already quivering with strain. He wouldn't be able to stand up for a drawn-out discussion, let alone to do battle of any kind, should an all-out altercation take place.

Pride was a bitter thing to swallow. Sarcasm made it a tiny bit sweeter.

"With your permission, oh great and powerful Odin," I said, "we would like to pass so that we may seek healing for my companion. If it pleases your lordship, of course."

Odin's expression darkened, and his mouth went tight. So did the Valkyries' grips on their swords. Bedivere rumbled a warning deep in his chest, and for an instant, I thought I'd gone too far. But to my shock—and watery-kneed relief—the god let out a bellow of laughter.

"You, Claire Emerson, continue to surprise me. Under other circumstances, I think I might have liked you."

Watery-kneed relief hesitated. "Other circumstances?"

"Such as when you didn't lie to me."

"I—you think I lied?" I frowned. "About what?"

"Your plan to reconvene the Council. You made no mention of that when we spoke yesterday."

I blinked in surprise. Mary had already talked to him? That had been quick. And perhaps the discussion had not been as informative as it should have been, because there was no way that Freya would allow Odin to be a part of the Council. I tried to deflect the god.

"When we spoke"—how was it even possible that it had only been yesterday?—"you made it clear you didn't care about our plan, and so—"

"If there is to be a Council of the Otherworld, I will be on it," he said.

"That might be difficult," I hedged. "Freya—"

"I will be on it," he repeated, his voice calm and matter of fact, "and I will be the head of it. And I will go with you to the Otherworld."

I opened my mouth to tell him that I wouldn't be going to the Otherworld myself, but I was distracted by the return of the shadow to his eyes. A creeping black that started at the outside of his pupils and slowly moved to cover their centers, like—

Bedivere's hindquarters buckled, dropping him almost to the ground. He pushed himself upright again, but he was fading fast. He needed Keven's healing. Now.

Talk about being caught between a rock and a hard place. I sifted quickly through my options. Freya would be livid, but—

"But you need all the help you can get," Edie murmured. *"And this saves you having to hog-tie him."*

But we needed all the help we could get, and yes. That.

Sensing my capitulation, Odin straightened in the saddle again and gathered the reins. The shadow had receded. "Good. You will send a messenger to me when you are ready, and I will meet you in the cavern."

As quickly as he had arrived, he was gone again. I stared after him. That was …

"Weird?" Edie suggested.

"Weird," I muttered. A faint, niggling *something* floated along the edge of my mind—something I thought I should know but couldn't quite grasp, but Bedivere was panting at my side, and I had no time to chase it.

I tugged gently on the thick scruff of the wolf-shifter's neck. "Bedivere, we need to go. We need to get you back to—"

Unbidden, the memory of Edie's earlier question surfaced in my mind. *"Why do you suppose the Mages are in Confluence?"* she whispered.

"... already ... returned ..." answered the Mage in the hotel.

My fingers tightened on Bedivere's fur as a thousand fragments of thought—a thousand impossibilities—exploded in my brain, all wrapped up in realizations that had seemed unconnected—that I hadn't had time to connect.

Until now.

"Why...?" Edie's question repeated, and suddenly, I knew.

I knew, because Odin was in Confluence, too. Because he'd stayed when all the others—with the exception of Freya—had simply passed through. Because he'd demanded sanctuary from me when it wasn't needed, and there had been an ugliness in his eyes when he had claimed that sanctuary, and there was a shadow that kept creeping over those eyes from the outside in, like—

"Like someone else taking him over," Edie said now. *"But that's ..."*

"Impossible," I whispered, and then Bedivere sank onto his side in the snow.

TIME TURNED SURREAL.

Or maybe it was just me.

He's already back.

We made it back to the house, Bedivere and I, but I couldn't remember how. One minute I was helping his wolf to stand up from where he'd fallen in the woods, and the next, Lucan was meeting us halfway across the clearing, demanding to know what had happened, if I was okay, if I could walk the rest of the way by myself.

Impossible.

I must have answered, because he hefted his brother into his arms and strode back to the house, leaving me to follow on my own. And I must have done that, too, because suddenly I was in the great hall, and a worried Jeanne was *tutting* as she stripped my ruined—again—cloak and boots from me and steered me toward the dining room, away from where Keven tended the injured shifter in the sitting room.

I saw him die.

And then I was sagging into a chair, and Baba Yaga was pressing a mug into my hands, and Harry was trying to crawl into my lap, and Jeanne was shooing Braden upstairs, and—

I saw him ...

I jolted to my feet, spilling tea across the table and over the dragon's head wedged under my hands. Magick surged through me, and the mug exploded. Because I *hadn't* seen him die. I'd trapped him in a sphere, and I'd seen the Between devouring the edges of the Camlann splinter, and I'd opened a portal in the vortex Harry had created, and I'd left. I'd taken Lucan and Gus and Harry, and I'd left ...

But I had not seen Morok die.

I looked down at the spreading puddle of tea on the table and the wet, highly insulted Harry stalking stiff-legged out of the room past Jeanne and Baba Yaga, who were both staring at me in concern.

"Get the others," I told Jeanne.

"Right now? But they're down in the cellar with—"

"Get the others," I repeated, my mind working furiously now that it was back online, "but only the Crones. Not the goddesses. Tell them that Morok is back. Tell them ... tell them that he's Odin." I didn't wait for anything more than her sharp inhale before I looked at Baba Yaga. "Can you travel the ley lines?"

"Not need ley lines," she replied. "Use house."

Damn. I'd been going to send her after Mary, but—

"House in woods," she continued. "I hide. You want I should get?"

"You brought your house—" I stopped and shook my head at my surprise. At my ability to *be* surprised anymore. "Yes," I told Baba Yaga, "I want you to get your house, and then I want you to go and find Mary for me and tell her we need her back here."

"What about uzzer gods?"

"Will they listen to you?"

"Mebbe. Mebbe not." She shrugged.

"However many you can find," I said, "as fast as you can find them. And take them straight to the cavern."

CHAPTER 32

"You're certain," Anne said. "Absolutely certain."

I wished I could say otherwise, or at least prevaricate, but I could do neither. I had never been more certain of anything in my life. Ever. "It's him," I said.

"But Freya—how did Freya not know?" Maureen asked. "Odin was her husband. She's a goddess. How can she not have noticed?"

"Deceit," murmured Nia. "Morok is the god of deceit."

The five of us—me and the four Crones—sat at one end of the table in the closed dining room, talking in hushed tones, while Jeanne remained by the door to listen for anyone coming. Keven and Lucan remained with the injured Bedivere in the sitting room, and Baba Yaga had quietly vanished from the house back to her own magickal one, after tasking the confused midwitches with making dinner for the household in her absence.

"He is," I agreed. I shuddered at the memories of both Kate's and Lucan's possessions by Morok. How I'd once thought that I should have known, too. "And he's very, very good at it."

"We'll have to tell the others," Elysabeth said, pulling her wrap closer around her shoulders.

"We should figure out what he's up to, first," Maureen said. "I mean, why Confluence? Why the gnomes and the Mages? Why does he want to be part of the Council?"

"Revenge." The word slipped out before I'd even registered it, but I knew its truth as soon as I spoke it. "I've defeated him twice. He wants revenge."

Silence met my words, and shock sat across every woman's expression. Shock, knee-jerk denial, and then … acceptance.

Morok was the god behind the lies and deceit that had held our kind down for centuries, after all, and we'd all seen it happen before—if not in our own lives, then in a friend's, an acquaintance's, the news. Because there was always someone who needed, for his own ego, to keep us where we "belonged," and who would do anything—*anything*—to prove himself superior.

Morok was the epitome of a stalker, a bully, and an abuser all rolled into one—on a cosmic level.

"So what do we do?"

"We stick to the plan," I said, "but we don't include Od— Morok. He stays here, and I deal with him once and for all."

Objections were immediate—and loud.

"What? But, Claire—" began Elysabeth.

"No!" Nia interrupted.

"You can't—" Maureen said.

"Shh!" Jeanne hissed from where she kept guard at the door. Maureen scowled but dropped her voice.

"You can't possibly go up against him on your own," she muttered. "That's how the divide got torn in the first place!"

"No." I shook my head. "That was something else—separating him from Lucan, maybe, or creating the portal. I won't be doing those things this time. I'll just be ..."

"Killing him," Anne said.

"Yes," I said.

"But ... can you?" asked Jeanne.

"Yes," I said. "I can."

The power in me stretched like a cat trapped beneath my skin, curled up into a ball, and settled again with a contented thrum of agreement that vibrated through my body.

"That's *not creepy as fuck*," said Edie. I pretended not to hear, and she snorted. "*You know I can hear you not hearing me, right?*"

I ignored that, too. Placing my tingling hands on the table, palms down, I looked at each of the others in turn. "Morok's whole purpose right now is to crush me. He will do everything he can to stop me from going through to the Otherworld to repair the divide, and—"

"But you're not going to the Otherworld," said Maureen.

"He doesn't know that, and we need to keep it that way. So, no one outside this room—not the goddesses, not Keven, not even Lucan—can know. And when Baba Yaga gets back with the others, we're going to move as fast as we possibly can to—"

The dining room door opened abruptly, sending Jeanne flying with a startled squeak, and Keven stood in the doorway, her expression thunderous.

"Morok lives?" she demanded. "And you didn't think it was important to tell us?"

BEST-LAID PLANS BEING WHAT THEY WERE, MINE REQUIRED significant tweaking. Before we were done, both the goddesses had joined us and we'd waited out Freya's histrionics, which swung wildly between grief for the husband she'd once loved and savage joy at seeing him suffer.

Goddesses, it was becoming clear, weren't always the benevolent—or well-balanced—beings we liked to think they were.

We did eventually reach agreement, however, in part because Freya and the Morrigan both sided with me. We would not, as Odin had ordered, send a messenger to him when we were ready to convene the Council and have them and the Crones cross into the Otherworld. As set as the Morok part of him was on getting revenge against me, there was too high a chance that, if he was in the cavern when he discovered that I couldn't cross into the Otherworld myself, he would do everything he could to interfere with our plan just to spite me.

"Gods are really that petty?" Anne murmured at one point.

I'd almost choked, trying to hold back my snort, and Freya had given me a filthy look. Keven, bless her stone heart, had steered the conversation into safer territory—specifically, the need to keep Lucan out of the loop.

"He wasn't in the room when Bedivere told me," she said, "so he doesn't know. I think it best we keep it that way, for his own safety."

Keeping secrets from my protector after all we'd been through went against every fiber of my being, but I couldn't argue with her wisdom in this case. If Lucan knew that Morok was back and in the body of Odin, he wouldn't even hesitate to go after him—and there would be only one outcome. Around the table, the Crones and Jeanne nodded their heads.

Even the goddesses agreed. Now that things were getting real, an air of somberness had settled over them, softening them, subduing them.

"Damned if I don't miss the arrogance," Edie muttered.

Damned if I didn't, too.

"So it's settled, then," Nia said, breaking the silence we'd fallen into, each of us lost in our own thoughts. "As soon as the gods and goddesses arrive, we're doing this."

"Yes," I said. "We are."

It was far from ideal, our plan. It meant that the Crones would be learning to wield their new Freya-powers in the Otherworld after they'd crossed over, rather than before they went. Freya assured them—and me—that the crossing would still be safe, but oh dear goddess, talk about a leap of faith. It also meant that they would be doing it all without me.

Going to the cavern with who knew how many deities, including some they'd never met. Facing Cernunnos again. Crossing into a world that would be as foreign to them as it had been to me. Relying on Freya, who now had only one-fifth of her powers, to keep them safe.

Taking Harry with them.

I put a hand to the ache in my chest. I would be losing them all, and I might never—no, I would likely never—no, I would almost certainly never see them again. Because of Morok.

The power sitting in my core stirred and stretched lazily again, and for the first time, I found myself glad of its presence. Embracing it. Because if anyone deserved to be on the receiving end of the magick it wielded—that *I* would wield—it was the god of lies and deceit.

He wanted revenge?

I would show him fucking revenge.

CHAPTER 33

THE HARDEST PART OF THE PLAN FOR ME WAS WAITING FOR Baba Yaga and Mary to arrive with the gods. I'd never been very good at waiting, and every hour that passed—every second—meant another chance that Odin-Morok would realize that I'd figured out who he really was, and I would lose any element of surprise.

The second-hardest part was the goodbyes. I'd never been very good at those, either.

First came my family. To keep Lucan from guessing at what was going on—and to keep me from having to outright lie to him, on top of keeping Morok's secret—I asked him the following morning to take Paul, Natalie and Braden home and to watch over them there, where they would be safely out of the way. And where Natalie couldn't decide at the last minute to join the midwitches in helping to open the portal.

Lucan wasn't pleased with the idea, but when Bedivere stepped in with a promise to personally see to my protection, he agreed.

Bedivere, it seemed, didn't have the same qualms about keeping secrets from his brother as I did.

Natalie, of course, tried to object. "What if you need me?" she asked. "We should have everyone there that we can. Cernunnos—"

I cupped her face in my hands. "We don't even know if this will work, Natalie. We don't know if any of this will work —if the Crones can get through, if they can stop the Between, how much time they'll have. None of it. The best thing you can do is be with your family. I need to know that Paul and Braden will have you if … I just need to know, all right?"

There had been tears, then hugs, then more tears, but she

had agreed. Then there had been more hugs from Paul, along with blinked-back tears, and an even more tearful parting between Braden and Harry, and then Lucan had hugged me, too—fiercely—and murmured to me to be careful, and then they were gone.

My family.

My trusting protector.

Most of my heart.

Harry had followed me around like a lost puppy the rest of the day, and sensing something amiss, Gus had in turn abandoned Keven's shoulders in favor of following the dragon.

"Me and my shaaa-dows," Edie sang softly as the three of us sat before the fire in my bedchamber, and I smiled sadly. I would miss my little menace.

Edie stopped singing and sniffled. "We'll *miss him,*" she corrected.

Harry had crawled into my lap while Gus curled up on the hearth, as near to the flames as he could get without spontaneously combusting. I stroked the dragon's head gently. "I'm so sorry, little one," I murmured. "It's such a lot to ask of you."

Too much to ask of a baby who still had tufts of fluff sprouting in odd patches from his new, leathery dragon skin. My only consolation was the ageless, timeless wisdom that seemed to gaze back at me from the jeweled eyes. Perhaps I imagined it for my own sake. I hoped not. Harry settled his head on my shoulder, closed his eyes, and purred the way he'd learned from his muzzer. Gus rumbled back from the hearth.

Edie sighed. *"You know it's for the best, though, right? That he needs to go back, even if he can't help them?"*

I did. But he would still be taking another part of my heart with him.

He … and the Crones. Elysabeth, the former Earth Crone I'd rescued from the cell that Morok had trapped her in. Nia, the Fire Crone who epitomized the divine feminine. Maureen, the Air Crone, whose fiery spirit and shocking red hair always made me think that *she* should have been Fire. And Anne, the Water Crone, whose ancestors had known long before we had that Confluence was a place of power.

With our timeline sped up, Freya had suddenly turned serious about passing on her knowledge to the bearers of her newly created pendants. The Crones had been down in the cellar with her and the Morrigan—who had discovered a helpful side of herself that surprised everyone—since long before dawn, and an empty dining room on the second morning signaled another day of the same.

I hesitated in the doorway for a moment, then turned and headed for the kitchen and Keven, who was alone in there now that Baba Yaga was gone. And now that I'd sent Jeanne and the midwitches away.

The goodbyes had been hard, despite the women's stout assurances that they would all look me up when this was over. Jeanne, of course, meant it. I hugged her long and hard as I told her where I'd hidden the key to Edie's house.

"Are you sure?" she'd asked. "I can always ask Gilbert—"

"I'm sure," I'd replied, "and don't you dare."

Bedivere had seen each of them home for me. He had recovered from the shade wound as quickly as Lucan had healed way back in the beginning, on my first night here in this house. Between his virtual immortality and Keven's poultice, he'd been back to his usual surly self by the following morning. Mostly.

Mostly, because it had been he who offered to transport the midwitches in the first place, and he had done so with neither rancor nor impatience, allowing me to thank each of them in turn before they left.

And not once commenting on the fact that I still couldn't remember their names.

With Harry following closely enough to step on my heels, I

pushed open the door to the kitchen and walked inside. The room's familiar warmth wrapped around me as Keven turned from the woodstove, and sudden nostalgia glued me to the floor. How many meals had I eaten in here with Lucan and Keven? How many revelations and cups of tea and crises of confidence? And now—

Now it would be just us again.

Assuming I survived round three with Morok.

I realized that Keven wasn't alone in the kitchen as, from the corner of my eye, I saw Bedivere rise from the bench at the table. He pushed away a partial bowl of what Keven liked to call porridge, but the rest of us knew as half-set cement.

"Milady," he said. "I'm done, if you were looking to sit in here today."

"Stay," I said, crossing to the table to sit across from him. "Please."

He hesitated, then resumed his seat but didn't pull the bowl back. I didn't blame him, honestly, and when Keven asked, I told her I would just have tea. Bedivere's lips pulled tight.

Keven set a steaming mug of black liquid before me, and I looked up. "Coffee?" I asked, because I'd been expecting some kind of fortifying herb mixture.

"The witch taught me," she said. *The witch* … Baba Yaga. Just as *the mutt* was Lucan when Keven needed to distance herself.

"We'll miss having her here," I said.

Keven grunted and lumbered back across the kitchen. I watched her set an enormous bowl of meat on the floor for Harry, who promptly shifted over to make room for Gus beside him.

"She won't say it, but she'll miss him, too," Bedivere observed.

I looked at him over the rim of my mug as I took a sip and let the coffee swirl across my tongue. Goddess, that was good.

I made a mental note to thank Baba Yaga if—when—I had the chance, sipped again, and put the mug down. "And you?" I asked the shifter on the other side of the table. "Will we miss you as well?"

Surprise sparked in the gray eyes. "I hadn't thought that far," he said.

"I don't know what effect the Morrigan's powers will have on my longevity," I said, "but if I—if Morok—" I shrugged. "I'll keep the house running as long as I'm able to, and you'd be welcome to stay."

Bedivere stared at me for a long moment, then inclined his head. "Thank you," he replied. "I'll think—"

A mighty *whump* shook the house, rattling the dishes on the shelves and sending Harry skittering under the table by my feet. Halfway upright, I stared at Bedivere, who remained unchanged except for the resigned expression he wore as he stared past my shoulder toward the window.

Before I could turn to see for myself what was there, the door to the garden flew open and a triumphant Baba Yaga exclaimed, "We come back, and we have gods!"

CHAPTER 34

THIS WAS IT. THIS WAS THE MOMENT.

I stared at the Crones gathered at the foot of the stairs up to Baba Yaga's hut, which would take them all, Harry and gods and goddesses included, to the cavern. It would get them there all at once, the witch had said, instead of one of the goddesses or Bedivere having to make more than one trip. Bedivere, of course, had declined and left already, and I ...

I was going in a different direction.

Anne cleared her throat. "You'll be careful?" she asked. "No unnecessary chances?"

It seemed an odd request, given where I was heading and what I would be doing, but I nodded anyway. "You, too?" I asked, my question equally ridiculous.

Anne laughed, then wiped away a tear. "Yes," she said. And then she was hugging me, and I was hugging her, and everyone was hugging everyone, and I was giving Harry a last scratch under the chin, and Baba Yaga was urging them to hurry, and they all climbed up the stairs ...

And then the house on chicken legs was sagging under the extra weight, lifting itself up again, and sprinting into the woods. I watched it dodge trees until it was out of sight, and then I turned back to the only one of us who would remain behind and threw my arms around her granite waist, squeezing hard.

"I'll see you for dinner," I whispered even though we both knew it wasn't true. I very likely wouldn't be back in time for dinner either tonight or any night, but saying so would be too hard—too fraught with emotions that the gargoyle simply didn't do—and I wouldn't leave her like that. I couldn't. I cleared my throat.

"Pot pie?" I asked.

Keven's arms squeezed back gently, accepting my pretense and the compassion behind it. "Anything for you, milady," she replied, her voice gruff.

I clung for a moment more, then released her and stepped back. My gaze searched the open doorway behind her for a familiar splotch of orange, but unsurprisingly, Gus was nowhere to be seen. He disliked emotion as much as Keven did. It was no wonder he'd abandoned me in favor of her. Pulling my cloak—repaired one last time by Baba Yaga—around my shoulders, I headed for the woods and the ley that would take me to Odin's camp, bringing my focus to bear on what was coming.

What happened in the cavern and the world beyond it no longer belonged to me. I had done all I could. I'd brought together gods and Crones to do what I should have done but could not do, and now I would do the next best thing.

Not until I stepped into the ley did Edie say, *"Huh. I wonder why Odin's camp is so quiet today."*

DEAD.

It was quiet because they were all dead.

Valkyries, Thyra, and Viking butler lay strewn about the snow, splashes of crimson all around them, swords uselessly drawn and still clean. They hadn't had a chance. My head drooped, and I viewed the tableau with tired eyes. Fuck Morok, I thought dully. Fuck him a thousand ways to hell and back.

I hadn't liked Odin's cohort particularly—or at all—but they hadn't deserved this. And now Odin-Morok was gone, and I didn't know where to start looking for him, and—

My heart jolted, and my chin jerked up. Horror flooded me. I did know. I knew exactly.

"The cavern," Edie breathed. *"He's gone to the cavern."*

It took all of three minutes for me to follow. Three minutes, five changes of ley, and an entire lifetime. The last ley deposited me at the foot of the waterfall, and I staggered as I stepped out of it, slipping on the ice-slick stones. Memories flooded back as I stared into the curtain of water. Me and Natalie staying behind the others to say goodbye to Paul and Braden. Picking our way along the edge of the river and through the waterfall. The horned god.

I shuddered. Cernunnos had almost killed me that time, but I was more powerful this time. Much more powerful. I could do this. I had to do this.

The whicker of a horse caught my ear, and I looked across the river to where a massive black horse stood watching me from the other side. Odin's horse.

I had to do this *now*.

I took a deep breath, made sure I was connected to my magick, and plunged through the waterfall.

I traveled as quickly as I could. It was surprisingly warm inside the cavern, so there was no ice, but spray-slick algae still made the going treacherous. I passed the point where Cernunnos had first attacked me, then the spot where he'd come at me again. The sound of the falls faded to a dull background roar, and I could hear my own inhale and exhale, but nothing else. No horned god, no chant of magick being raised to open the door, no—

Something slammed into my legs at knee level, and I staggered backwards and fell to the floor. Immediately, the something landed on my chest and began wriggling in delight. I could see nothing more than a vague shape in the nearly dark cavern, but I'd know that wriggle anywhere.

"Harry!" I wrapped my arms around the little dragon and hugged. "What are you doing here? Where are the others?"

"Claire? Is that you? No wonder Harry took off like that," Nia said. "What in the world are you—"

I pushed the dragon off me and scrambled to my feet. "Odin," I interrupted. "Where is Odin?"

"I have no idea. I thought you were going to—" Nia stopped. "He wasn't at his camp."

"No. And no one alive was, either."

"Oh," they said, and then again, "*ohh*."

I flinched as a shadow moved among the other shadows, then sagged in relief. "Bedivere. Odin—"

"I heard. I'll have a look around." The shadow dissolved, and there was a whisper of fabric settling against stone, then the click of toenails receding into the distance, back the way I'd come. I turned back to Nia.

"Do you have the door open?" I asked. "Has anyone gone through yet?"

"We'd just opened it when Harry ran off," they replied. They caught my arm in the near-dark and tugged me along behind them. "This way. Some of the gods are going through first, and then us."

We'd turned a corner, Harry prancing ahead of us, and I could see a faint glow in the distance. The door. And still no sign of Odin. Or Cernunnos. Sensing my anxiety, Nia increased their pace. When we were almost there, Anne, Maureen, and Freya looked around at the sound of our approach. The others were already gone, and my heart gave a small, surprised squeeze. It was really happening.

"Done already?" Freya asked, her voice too heavy for sarcasm.

"His horse is outside," I replied tersely. "We need to speed things up."

By the light of the door, I saw her put her hand on her sword. "Or we could—"

"No." I stopped her from drawing her blade. "Go. He

belongs to me, remember? You have a job, Freya. You need to look after the Crones and Harry. You promised."

Freya stood, stiff and unyielding, her face a twisted mask of fury and hatred as she wrestled with desire for blood and the knowledge that she couldn't take down Morok anymore, no matter how much she wanted to. Not with the Crones holding onto the bulk of her powers. She still hadn't moved when Baba Yaga waddled over to us and patted the hand I was using to hold Freya's sword in place.

"I look after little one," she promised me, "and I help uzzers, too. Come, Crones. We go now. Freya bring baby wiss her."

She turned and ushered the remaining Crones before her, following the figures of two gods I didn't recognize toward the door. Mary started in their wake, then turned back to me. She crossed the few steps to take my free hand in hers.

"I will do everything I can to keep your Crones safe, Just-Claire," she promised. "For as long as they are with us."

And because that might well mean forever, I swallowed hard against the knot in my throat and blinked back my tears as I nodded. "Thank you," I whispered, "Just-Mary."

Mary Magdalene smiled, pressed my fingers one last time, and then turned and strode through the doorway. The light flared bright, her figure disappeared, and the light dimmed again. I glanced around the cavern. That was it except for—

Harry leaned against my leg and meowed.

Meowed?

I stared down at the dragon on the cavern floor—and the cat sitting beside him. Gus's yellow eyes blinked back at me. So that was why he hadn't come to say goodbye at the house.

I sighed and, unsurprised and still holding onto Freya's sword-clutching hand, leaned down to scoop him up. "I know," I said, burying my face in his warm fur. "I love Harry, too, but we can't go with him, my friend. Not this time."

I turned to the only remaining goddess and met the ice

blue gaze one last time. "You have to go, Freya. Now, before—"

"Leaving without me?" asked a deep, wretchedly familiar voice from the shadows behind me. "I'm wounded, I am. Deeply."

Shit.

My entire being went still. And then cold. And then—

"You *bastard*!" Freya hissed. "How dare you step into my Odin? How *dare* you?"

She shook off my hand and there was a hiss of metal against hardened leather, then a glint in the light from the door. Clutching Gus to my chest, I ducked and felt the whisper of a blade passing by my cheek. Odin-Morok waved a hand, and the sword flew from the goddess's hand across the cavern, landing with a clatter against the wall.

"Freya!" I growled. "*Focus*, damn it."

"Yes, Freya, focus," Odin-Morok taunted. "You have a Between to stop, remember? And I'm here to make sure you meet it face to face. All of you. Well, that, and head up the Council, obviously. I've waited years for that one. But we'll discuss that on the other side, shall we? Claire Emerson and I will see you there in a moment."

Freya's gaze flashed to me. Before I could open my mouth to warn her, Odin-Morok's hand came up between them, smashed into her chest, and sent her flying backward through the door.

"Claire, watch out!"

Edie's warning came a fraction too late. So did my spin away from Morok. He seized my arm, tore Gus from my grasp, and flung the cat away. Harry screeched and flew after his muzzer, and the dark god dragged me toward the Otherworld.

"Our turn, Claire Emerson," he said cheerfully. "Let's go play, shall we?"

"Joke's on you," I growled back, reaching inside my core for the power coiled and waiting there, "because I can't."

Morok scowled at me. "What do you mean, you can't?"

I scowled at me, too, because the power was there, all right, but it wasn't responding. And we'd reached the door, but that wasn't responding, either, and Morok's expression was turning darker by the second, and what the hell was wrong with my magick?

"I can't go through the door," I said. "I'm bound to Earth."

"Bound," said Edie. "That's it! He's binding your magick. You have to make him let go of you."

Binding—he could do that? A frisson of uncertainty ran through me. How was that possible? I had more power than I'd ever had when I faced him before, and he'd never been able to—

Shit, I thought again. He'd been prepared for this, the way I'd been prepared ... only better. Much, much better.

What the fuck was I supposed to do now?

Before I could gather my wits, a bellow of rage echoed through the chamber, a new figure launched itself at Morok, and the two of them slammed to the floor.

"Lucan, no!" snarled another voice. My startled brain recognized it as Bedivere's as the shifter morphed into wolf in midair and landed on top of figures rolling around on the cavern floor, and—

Lucan?

What the fuck was he doing here?

"He's your protector, my friend. He always will be," Edie said. *"Did you really expect him to stay away?"*

But I had no time to answer her. No time for reason, because with Morok's hold on me broken, the power that had been coiled inside me was unwinding through my veins at a speed that threatened to tear me apart if I didn't get a grip on it.

I was trying, but I was failing.

And then Lucan was flying across the chamber the way Gus had done, only he was landing far, far harder, and he wasn't getting up again, but Morok was—and the dark god had Bedivere's snarling wolf by the throat. Panic seized me. This wasn't how it was supposed to have gone. Everything was happening too fast. I couldn't think, and the power in me was writhing like a wild thing with no way out, and Lucan wasn't supposed to be here, and—

Morok swung around and smashed Bedivere against the cavern wall behind him. The crack of skull against rock was audible and sickening. Bedivere's single, sharp yelp echoed through the cavern, underscored by a hoarse, ravaged bellow from his fallen brother, and then his wolf went limp in Morok's grasp. The dark god seized the back of Bedivere's neck and twisted it for good measure, then flung the carcass into the far corner and turned on me.

"Enough," he snarled. "So many times you have gotten in my way, and I've had enough. No more games, you bitch. You can't come through the door with me? Fine. You die here."

He reached both hands toward me, but I ducked away, seized the power with every atom of focus I could muster, and turned it loose—on purpose. Shock flashed across Morok's face as white-hot Fire exploded against him, but he emerged from the flames unscathed. As powerful as I was, he was equally so. I needed more—

And that *more*, I suddenly remembered, was all around me.

Because Confluence.

A meeting of three rivers. A place that connected us to land, water, sky—and to the Otherworld itself. Power surrounded me in spades, and it was already responding to my call. My Fire swirled around me, through me, became me. The confluence of the remaining elements rose up from the Earth itself, wrapping around me, merging its power with mine. So much power. Uncontrolled and exhilarating, its fury filled me, and then that, too, became me—and I released it against Morok.

The first onslaught felled him to his knees. The second crushed in on him from above, below, front, back ... all sides. It was like watching the sphere close in on him all over again, except this time, *I* was the sphere. I could feel his skin giving way beneath my touch, his bones beginning to yield.

Then, for an instant, a heartbeat, my lack of control—no, my enjoyment of it—horrified me, and I faltered.

It was enough for Morok to recover. He shoved the magick away from him and lunged upward at me, and his hand closed around my throat the way it had Bedivere's. At his touch, my connection to the elements shattered. He pushed against me, driving me back until I could feel the door to the Otherworld at my back, hard and unyielding, refusing me entry. He thrust his face into mine, his eyes wide and wild as his fingers tightened—and then I saw it again.

Only this time, I recognized it for what it was.

Deep in his eyes, a crumbling around the edges of his pupils. His center. His soul. The same crumbling I had seen at the edges of Camlann as the Between had begun to devour it. The Between was no longer just coming for us, it was here. And I was about to die at its hands.

EVEN AS THE REALIZATION SANK IN, THE EDGES OF MY OWN vision began to dim. I clawed at Odin's hand, but Morok's magick had locked it onto me, and I couldn't pry his fingers away. He was too strong. He was more than a god now. He was the Between itself, and—

A snarl of rage echoed through the chamber, and from the corner of my eye, I saw a wolf leap from the shadows of the floor. Hope flickered in my muddled, fading brain. Bedivere?

But no—this wolf was bigger, rangier, unblemished. And Odin was turning toward it, and—

Lucan's wolf slammed into the god's chest, and Morok's fingers loosened, then released me as he fell backward, carried by Lucan's momentum and weight.

I toppled sideways, sucking air into my oxygen-starved lungs as flashes of memories overlaid the present. Then, it had been a crumbling skyscraper and Lucan's wolf slamming into Kate-Morok, the force carrying them both through the portal to the Camlann splinter; now, it was a cavern, and he carried Odin-Morok through a rapidly diminishing door into the Otherworld.

Both times he had disappeared with the god, both times he had been beyond my reach.

Both times, my magick had not been able to save him, and all I'd been able to do was to stare in helpless—

A flash of blue caught my eye, and I turned my head in time to see Harry take to the air, his leathery wings beating furiously and a look of pure determination in the jeweled eyes flickering in the fading light from the door. He flew straight at it. For an instant, the door faded completely, and I thought he would smash into the solid stone that remained, but at the last second, it flared open again. Harry was gone.

A plaintive yowl sounded, and before I could stop him, Gus leapt at the door, following his dragon baby.

"Gus, no!" I tried to yell, but the words emerged as a whispered croak from a throat that throbbed from Morok's hold on it.

The door flared again, as if to accept the cat, but suddenly, he flew sideways as if hit by a gust of wind, rolled across the floor, and landed against my feet. He scrambled upright, but the cavern plunged into darkness as the door vanished, taking its glow with it—along with Lucan, the Crones, and Harry.

They were gone. All of them. Gone, with no way to get them back.

Silence as absolute as the dark fell over the cavern, unbroken by even the sound of my breath, because I wasn't breathing. I couldn't breathe. I—

The door flared open again, and Morok stood framed in it.

Hatred rose in me, bitter on my tongue and ice-cold along my limbs as it pushed me to my feet and stretched my arms wide. Magick surged back to life beside it, tasting my rage, inhaling it, drinking from it, absorbing it like soil absorbed much-needed water. It grew again into the power that wasn't mine and threw itself against confines that I hadn't put in place but were just ... there. It wanted out, desperately. It wanted to wrap around Morok again and crush his very existence from him. It wanted—

Jesus fuck, what was *that*?

I stared at the blackness uncoiling from the god's eyes, reaching toward my side of the door, toward me. The power in my core snarled in return, and reflexively, I grounded myself in Earth and raised my hands. It wanted me to turn it loose? Good. Because fucking hell, I wanted it, too, just as I'd wanted all the rest of it.

The destroyed shades. The crispy mages. The ceiling I'd caused to collapse on the endlessly bickering goddesses who were to blame for the whole, fucking cosmic mess that was Morok.

I'd wanted it all, and now I wanted this. I wanted it with every fiber of my being, just as Edie had said.

The magick blasted outward from me, its full force directed at Morok, surrounding him and squeezing in on him as I again became the sphere. He took another step toward me, pushing back, but I didn't falter this time. I knew exactly what I—

Somewhere far away—at the mouth of the cavern,

perhaps—a crow cawed. Memory threw me back into another cavern at another time, when I'd been on the verge of dying after being bitten by a gnome, and the Morrigan had stood over me and pointed at a wooden cup on a table.

"*Drink,*" she had commanded, but I had refused, galled by the stench of the liquid within. She had pronounced me Crone then, and herself pleased.

"*That was the Cup of Power,*" she'd said. "*If you were tempted by it, I would have let the infection take you here and now. But you weren't.*"

The Between uncoiling from Morok's eyes was halfway to me, unimpeded by the magick holding the god himself at bay.

The distant crow cawed again, and another memory surfaced.

"*Power corrupts,*" Keven said. "*The Morrigan was afraid that if she remained with Morgana, they would become like Morok.*"

Oh, fuck. Realization was a cold deluge that made me gasp out loud. I may not have sipped from the Cup of Power that the Morrigan had offered me, and I may have learned to lock down my wants along the way to my magick, but that had been then, and this was now, and—

My magick wavered, Morok took another step through the door, and the Between spread wider, farther.

Now, dear goddess, I wanted this. I wanted the power to destroy, in part because I didn't know how to stop Morok without it, and in part because—

"*... if she remained with Morgana, they would become like Morok.*"

Another cold deluge descended over me, this time one of utter clarity. That was it. That was what I was feeling. I might not have had all of the Morrigan's power in me, but I had enough, combined with Morgana's magick, to corrupt me just as Morok's power had corrupted him. To make room in me for the Between, the way Morok had made room for it in him when he refused to give up Merlin's power.

Fucking hell. *That* was what I was up against. This wasn't

about Morok at all. It was about what had already devoured him from the inside out and what was coming for me through the doorway now. What wanted to come for Earth *through* me.

It was about power itself.

Suddenly, at last, I knew what I had to do. Knew how this would end.

Morgana and the Morrigan could not be allowed to continue to exist in me. Not together. I had to sever one of them from me. I had to do what the Morrigan had said I could not. And I had to do it in a way that would shut Morok out of this world forever.

As for the Between that had almost reached me ... well, I knew from the Weaver that I could not stop its relentless advance through the universe, but I could slow its taking of the Earth. And I could refuse to be its gateway. I dropped my hands to my sides.

Misgiving tore at me as I thought about the others that I would be sacrificing if I did this. The ones who would be trapped in a world with Morok and a Between they didn't know existed in him.

Lucan, my fierce and beloved protector until the very end.

I took a deep, centering breath.

The Crones who had willingly gone to do what I hadn't been able to myself.

Freya, who had learned at long last what it meant to be Crone herself.

I curled my hands into fists.

Harry, who had been so much braver than he should have had to be.

I set my jaw.

Jeanne waiting in Edie's house; Keven, who would return to stone atop a gatepost, guarding a house that would cease to exist and a pot pie that would never be eaten; Paul and Natalie and Braden, and all the milestones and love and joy that I would miss ...

I reached inside myself to my very core and the power that pulsed there.

Know, the Book of the Fifth Crone whispered to me gently. *Accept. Trust. Be.*

Know this is the answer.
Accept that you will die.
Trust that you will know how.
Be strong.

With a scream that would surely follow me into death, I tore the Morrigan's power away from myself and threw it at the door with all of my remaining strength.

A roar of fury filled the cavern, drowning out my own voice. Light flared across the doorway, and behind it, Morok lunged toward me. But it was too late. He was too late.

The Morrigan's power, freed from my physical confines, whirled and sparked with all the colors of the rainbow—all the colors of the ley lines that connected the entire world. It slammed into the light that was the door. Wove together with it. Meshed with it. Together they flared with a brilliance that seared my eyes, and then they went dark, and Morok's roar of fury—the Between's roar of fury through him—was cut off forever.

Along with my friends in the Otherworld.

I SURFACED IN THE DARK TO GENTLE HANDS LIFTING MY HEAD and shoulders and cradling them. For long seconds that might have been hours, I couldn't place where I was. Or when I was. Or really, if I was. Slowly, awareness returned, and I felt the hand stroking my hair back. Heard a voice calling a name.

My name.

"Claire? Claire, wake up," it insisted.

I frowned. Was that Jeanne? It couldn't be, because Jeanne wasn't here. She hadn't come with me to—

I inhaled a great lungful of air, choking on it as I surged upright into full consciousness. Life flooded back into me, bringing all of its events with it, and my heartbeat thundered in my ears.

Lucan. Harry. Morok. *The Between.*

Frantically, I patted myself down. I was still here and—I looked up from the filthy front of my robe at the cavern wall. A lantern sat on the floor next to me, its illumination enough for me to see that there was no door anymore. Had I stopped the Between in time? What if it was already inside me, the way it had been in Morok? Would I know? Would I feel it?

I tried to climb to my feet, but my head swam, and I sank back again.

"Easy," said the voice at my shoulder. "Give yourself a couple of minutes. You've been out for a while."

My head twisted around, and I stared at Jeanne, taking in the familiar brown eyes behind red-framed glasses and a plaid shirt peeking out from under a half-zipped parka. I blinked twice to be sure, but she remained.

"It *is* you," I croaked. "But how—?"

Jeanne grimaced. "You're not going to believe this, but—"

I followed the point of her hand toward my outstretched feet and the orange cat sitting beside them. "Gus? Gus came and got you?"

"Yes," Jeanne said. "And no."

I frowned. "I don't understand."

The orange cat sighed and—

The orange cat sighed?

"Houston," it said in a woman's voice that I hadn't heard outside my head in a long, long time, "we have a slight situation."

CHAPTER 35

WE BURIED BEDIVERE THREE MONTHS LATER, IN EARLY SPRING.

Jeanne stayed with Braden, and Paul and Natalie came with me to the cavern to collect the body of his wolf. The cold of winter still lingered in the depths of the earth far back from the waterfall, and he was blessedly intact when we picked him up and gently placed him on a blanket I'd brought from Edie's house.

We found the remains of Cernunnos near him.

"Odin?" Natalie asked, as we looked down at the tatters of moss-covered clothing and the gleam of horns lying between the cavern wall and a large boulder.

"Probably," I said. "Maybe Cernunnos saw Morok in him and tried to stop him."

"Do we want to …?"

"No." I shook my head. "He belongs here. Earth has already reabsorbed most of him."

We turned away together, and I cast a final look at the back of the cavern where the door to the Otherworld would never be again. Could never be, now that it had been sealed with the Morrigan's powers. A door behind which Lucan and the Crones and Harry might still fight on against the Between, or …

I suppressed a shiver at the *or*, because I would never know.

"Maman?" Natalie asked from the end of the tunnel leading out.

"Coming," I said. I cast a final-final look at the wall imbued with the Morrigan herself, and then followed Natalie out to join Paul, who had gone ahead of us with Bedivere's body.

I'd chosen 13 The Morrigan's Way as his final resting place, at the foot of the gatepost where a stone gargoyle would keep watch over him. It was a short drive there, and although the ground at the edge of the forest was still half-frozen, it didn't take long to dig a wolf-sized hole. Or to fill it.

"Do we want to mark it, somehow?" Paul asked, standing back when we were done.

"The gatepost is marker enough," I said. "Thank you for your help."

"It was nothing," he replied gruffly.

"Do you want a few minutes?" Natalie asked. "We can wait in the car."

"Actually, I think I'll walk home," I said, turning my face to the warmth of the early April sun. "It's a nice day, and I can use the exercise."

Once, a few short months and a lifetime ago, they both would have fussed about it being too far for me. Now, neither of them even blinked at the suggestion. Paul stripped off his gloves and gave me a hug, Natalie told me she'd leave a bottle of water for me at the side of the road, and a few minutes later, the sound of the car engine faded into the distance, and I was alone.

I stood for a moment just listening to the woods around me, remembering the first time I'd done the same. It had been September then, with the sound of cicadas and crickets filling the air and reds and golds beginning to claim the leaves. Now, the sounds were birds returning from their winter residences, and only the faintest flush of spring green colored the trees.

I looked up at the gargoyle crouched on the stone gatepost that no longer held a gate.

"You'll look after him for me, won't you?" I asked her. "He was a good man. Just like you were a good woman, Keven. Oh, I know you don't like to hear that, but it's true. You were the first of us, and you set the bar high. I haven't heard anything about Mages since Morok crossed over, so I don't expect that I'll have much call to use your magick anymore, but if I do, I promise—" I broke off and cleared my throat, then finished in a whisper, "I promise I'll live up to your trust."

I put my hand out to the gatepost, tracing my fingers over the place where a plaque had once proclaimed the address. It, too, was gone now, no longer needed to mark a path that led to a house that was bigger on the inside than it looked. A house that, like the gargoyle that had been set here to watch over it, no longer lived, now that the magick that had enlivened it had been bound into a seal across the Otherworld door.

"I miss you, my friend," I told the gargoyle, my voice catching again. "You and the house and the garden. I miss the kitchen, especially, I think. I was looking forward to that pot pie. But life is okay. I'm back at Edie's house, and Jeanne has moved in with me. She can't make a pastry to save her own life, but her broccoli and chicken casserole is amazing. The neighbors are a bit weird with us—well, with me—after everything that happened in town, but I'm keeping a low profile, and they're settling down. Ish."

I took my hand from the cold stone and tried to tuck them into the folds of my robe, then remembered and stuck them into my jeans pocket instead. "Oh, and I still have Gus, too, of course. He's just ... a little different now. It's a long story, so I'll save it for another day, if that's okay. Because I'd like to come back again. Just to say hello and see how you're doing, and—"

I froze as the crunch of a foot against gravel stopped my flow of nonsense. A throat cleared behind me, and caution flared in my core. Three months hadn't been nearly enough to dim my wariness—which might explain why my neighbors remained a little jumpy around me, when I thought about it. Well, that and the multiple visits from the police as they tried to figure out what had happened in Confluence that day and exactly what my part in it had been. But that was a whole other issue.

I gathered myself and called what was left of my magick —Morgana's magick—to my fingertips, just in case. As power went, it wasn't much anymore, not in comparison to what I'd once wielded, but it was ... comforting ... to still hold it. I turned toward the road.

A woman stood on the shoulder. She was stocky and sensibly dressed, from her lightweight navy jacket to jeans and sturdy sneakers, and the straps of a backpack were looped over her shoulders. With that and the broad-brimmed hat planted firmly on her head, she looked like a lost hiker. I began to let the magick slide away from my—

"Claire Emerson?" she asked, her voice brisk.

It was not a question I expected from a lost hiker, and my freshly minted smile faded into suspicion as I drew Morgana's magick back to me. I frowned. "Do I know you?"

"My name is Monica Barrett," she said, holding out a cloth bundle in one hand and folding back its layers with the other. "Sister Monica to most people, although I'm not really a nun anymore, and—" She thrust her handful of what looked like bits of black rock toward me.

"And I need your help to save the Weaver," she finished firmly.

Because of course she did.

Dear Reader,

When I began writing the Crone Wars, I thought there would be two or three books. And then there was a fourth. And now there is a fifth. And wait ... will there really be a sixth?!

Why, yes, dear reader. Yes, there will. But not just yet.

Because you know that Sister Monica Barrett you just met? It turns out she's important. Really, really important. She is SOMEONE, you see, and she'll be joining Claire in the final book of the Crone Wars, because her story is inextricably entwined with that of the Crones ... almost as if it's part of the Weaver's web. Oh wait ... it is!

But Sister Monica's story is also a story in its own right. An exciting story. A thrilling story. A story that made my happy little writer-brain go, "Oooh!" when its dots connected to the Crone Wars. And it needs to be told—nay, it begs to be told—before Sister Monica and Claire can save the Weaver together in book six.

So, as unorthodox as it might be to pause a series in order to write another, different trilogy ... that is exactly what I'm doing. Welcome to Web of Obsidian, book one of The Obsidian Sisterhood, releasing in October of 2024. I can't wait for you to read it.

I'll see you there!

Lydia

Acknowledgements

Sometimes writing can be a lonely pursuit ... and sometimes, you are blessed with an amazing support network to cheer you on through the entire process.

I'm one of the ones who is blessed, and this is my opportunity to say thank you to all of the people who help make my writing far less lonely and my books possible.

First, to my husband Pat, the rock in my life whose belief in me has never once faltered even when my own has; to Marie Bilodeau, my bestest writing friend who somehow seems to know exactly when to listen to me grumble and when to give me a swift (and much needed) kick in the pants; and to my friend and copy editor Laura Paquet, whose stellar work always, always makes the story better.

Thank you also to my cover designer, Deranged Doctor Design, for another knock-out cover; to my interior layout designer, Priya, for both her work and her patience with my perpetual lateness; to my proofreader Trish Long for all the many catches of missed words and misplaced punctuation; and to beta readers Ceri Smith, Pam Samson, Elaine Sweatman, and Kim McCaveney for their valued (and valuable!) feedback. This book exists because of you all.

And last but far from least, my fantastic Facebook community, who have cheered me on endlessly through thick, thin, and insane house renovations. The many Wonder Woman memes that you shared with me made me laugh and kept me going, my friends ... thank you.

ALSO BY

The Crone Wars

Becoming Crone

A Gathering of Crones

Game of Crones

Crone Unleashed

The Grigori Legacy

Sins of the Angels (Grigori Legacy book 1)

Sins of the Son (Grigori Legacy book 2)

Sins of the Lost (Grigori Legacy book 3)

Sins of the Warrior (Grigori Legacy book 4)

Other Books by Linda Poitevin

The Ever After Romance Collection

Gwynneth Ever After

Forever After

Forever Grace

Always and Forever

Abigail Always

Shadow of Doubt

About The Author

Lydia M. Hawke is a pseudonym used by me, Linda Poitevin, for my urban fantasy books. Together, we are the author of books that range from supernatural suspense thrillers to contemporary romances and romantic suspense.

Originally from beautiful British Columbia, I moved to Canada's capital region of Ottawa-Gatineau more than thirty years ago with the love of my life. Which means I've been married most of my life now, and I've spent most of it here. Wow. Anyway, when I'm not plotting the world's downfall or next great love story, I'm also a wife, mom, grandma, friend, walker of a Giant Dog, keeper of many cats, and an avid gardener and food preserver. My next great ambition in life (other than writing the next book, of course) is to have an urban chicken coop. Yes, seriously…because chickens.

You can find me hanging out on Facebook at facebook.com/LydiaMHawke, and on my website at LydiaHawkeBooks.com, where you can also join my newsletter for updates on new books (and a free story!)

I love to hear from readers and can be reached at lydia@lydiahawkebooks.com. And yes, I answer all my emails!

Printed in the USA
CPSIA information can be obtained
at www.ICGtesting.com
LVHW031951010424
776083LV00001B/176